MW00619349

DEBRIS & DETRITUS

THE LESSER GREEK GODS RUNNING AMOK

DEBRIS & DETRITUS

The Lesser Greek Gods Running Amok

Patricia Burroughs, Editor

With Foreword by Rhonda Eudaly

Story Spring Publishing, LLC
Pekin, Illinois

To all the lesser-knowns among us.

We all have a story to tell, and we're starting here.

TABLE OF CONTENTS

Foreward iii

The Night I Shot Johnny Valentine 1

That Sweetest Cup 15

Expense Claims Are Hell.. 19

Chaos, Inc. 53

HeartStones... 65

Small Gods.. 103

Queer Eye for the Dead Guy....................................... 121

Used Goods 137

Garbage In, Monsters Out 163

Shabby Chic 185

The Bovines of Bybanos... 207

Sweet Dirty Love 219

The Groom Wore Wings... 229

By Any Other Name... 255

Realms 273

"Let's put on a show!" 289

About the Authors..291

About the Editor..300

About the Cover 301

About Story Spring Publishing 303

FOREWORD
RHONDA EUDALY

Once upon a time, a relatively new writer supplemented her income by working in "The Family Business" of building broadcast radio transmitters with her father. One day, this writer worked in a remote location with her father and his friend and colleague, Mike, both of whom were Old School Radio Guys. The unlikely trio dealt with the tedious task of cutting and cleaning copper pipe . . .

Not only was this task tedious, it was also hot and dirty. We were exhausted. As we were cleaning this copper pipe, Mike boomed out—in his trained, Old School Radio Voice—"Debris and Detritus!" I popped off, not missing a beat, "The lesser known of the Greek gods!" Hilarity ensued—booming laughter, crying, realizing we were punch drunk from being exhausted . . . but in that moment, it was *the most hilarious thing EVER!* And it triggered a plot bunny . . .

My friend and now collaborator, Julia Mandala, was putting together an anthology about Hell. Debris and Detritus wanted to be written. A story burst forth in all its random craziness, but instead of a silly *Home Improvement* vibe, Debris and Detritus went a more alternative route. The story practically wrote itself; sadly, it refused to title itself, and for the longest time, I was stuck with a title I hated.

Unfortunately, the story did not place in the anthology, because darn it, just as mine was about to be put in . . . Mike Resnick sent in a story. (That's my story, and I'm sticking to it!) Nor did it sell with the seriously crappy title—so fast forward to a ConDFW many moons ago, where I'm telling this story to Aaron Allston. He graciously renames my story for me. It went from "Hell's Housekeepers" (see?) to "Queer Eye for the Dead Guy."

Selling the story still took a while. Thank goodness for the wondrous people at Four Star Stories. They gave the piece a home.

Now, fast forward *again* to yet another ConDFW, where I told this story (*again*) as a warm-up to a panel. A lovely woman in the audience decided it was a fabulous idea for Debris and Detritus to have all their stories told and it should be a collection and that collection should revolve around my story. Then she made it happen with the most amazing gathering of writers.

This group of writers from all walks of life—and genres—came together from across the country and across the pond to make you laugh, to make you cry, to creep you out, or warm your heart. There are writers I've known for years that I've never shared a table of contents with as well as those I've worked with before. But most are complete strangers who saw something in this freaky idea and ran with it. It's a collection of mostly women writers, which I find amazing—but as I've heard Ice-T say of *Law and Order: SVU* writers, "Women writers write the sickest stuff." You can take that however you want.

I am astonished and amazed by the fact that this happened—surreal is the term I've been using. Sadly, neither Mike nor Aaron is with us any longer to see what a couple of random thoughts have wrought, because I totally owed them drinks for this. So enjoy the resulting stories, and thank you for coming along for the ride. Hopefully we will make you laugh, cry, check under your bed, and maybe even sleep with the lights on.

When you're done, raise a glass to all the lesser-knowns among us. We all have a story to tell, and we're starting here.

RHONDA EUDALY

The Night I Shot Johnny Valentine

Max Adams

THE NIGHT I SHOT Johnny Valentine, I was not expecting to shoot someone. Johnny Valentine was not expecting to get shot either, if his expression was any indication.

I would have shot Johnny for his name alone. It's a really annoying name. But I have been trying to curb my murderous ways. This is not easy if you are the bastard daughter of a pack of vengeful Olympian gods crossed with a vengeful tribe of warrior Spartans. My twin sister, DT, gets very annoyed when I say this. DT likes to pretend she's the nice demi-god in the family. She's really not. She doesn't just shoot people. She evaporates people from time to time. And this was DT's fault, anyway, for courting a hoarder.

DT loves hoarders. She says their homes are tributes to us, and she visits them all the time. I told her the other day I saw a woman on Sixth Street drop a full beer, and I did not assume that was an act of worship. But did she listen? No. Thousands of years, and DT is still petulant and childlike—

1

another personality trait I chalk up to our unfortunate ancestry that she does not find amusing. (My sister has no sense of humor.) Anyway—

Johnny Valentine's mother was a hoarder, and DT would go traipsing over to Mother Valentine's regularly to check in on her. DT dragged me along once. The Valentine abode is a small, square house on a thin little street off North Lamar in Austin. Its claim to fame outside is two broken-down, two-door maroon Chevys in the overgrown drive (who gets two maroon cars?) and very old, yellow, peeling paint. Its claim to fame inside is newspapers from around the entire world in stacks that are sometimes five and seven feet high. It's like the Tardis. Outside it looks tiny, but inside, it can hold the world's entire history of newspapers. (Shut up, demi-goddesses can like *Doctor Who*.) Old, yellowed, newspaper towers with thin paths between them and the occasional mail order ceramic aquatic figurine sitting atop those stacks to hold them steady.

It kind of is a tribute, when you really take it in. I'm just not fond of ceramic frogs.

During DT's last foray, though, ghastly news! Mother Valentine had died in slippers and a tatty pink terry cloth robe, sitting in the only clear spot in the living room—a small space among the newspaper stacks, featuring a Naugahyde recliner and ancient cathode-tube television set. And Sister Valentine—oh yes, there was a daughter—was on the scene cleaning house.

DT was so upset, she materialized and knocked two pillars of 1970s New York Times stacks and one green ceramic frog to the ground. So, natch, Johnny Valentine saw DT and went all Supernatural on our asses. He trailed her home to this mansion we have been staying in that is in probate or some such while angry children fight over the estate, and Johnny Valentine broke through a boarded-over window, whipped out a shotgun and shot me—not DT, oh no, that would have been justice—me! With two pounds of rock salt.

Okay maybe it was not two pounds. But! Demi-goddess or no, do you have any idea what two shotgun blasts of rock salt do to a girl's hair? And. Her. Shoes?

Which is when I pulled a natty little derringer that I assume belonged to Emory Quail, our deceased mansion benefactor, out of an antique oak desk drawer in what must once have been a library and shot Johnny Valentine back. Right in the ass—since by that point Johnny was figuring out he was not the hero of a Supernatural TV episode, I was not a ghost who would dissipate at the first sign of rock salt, and that he was in trouble.

(I'm surprised that derringer fired; it was terribly old, and I did not even know if it was loaded, but it was loaded, I was enraged, and fire it did.)

(Also, people, can we have a small conference on rock salt here? If you are going to attack the bastard demi-god daughter of a war god with rock salt, don't make it road salt. Go out and get something nice, maybe kosher sea salt or a nice bath salt. Seriously, road salt? That is not respect.)

Johnny was a strapping young computer nerd—which is to say too old to live with his mother, overweight, very tall and awkward, and tragically attired in a hoodie, ill-fitting jeans, and a T-shirt advertising an anime character—so the bullet didn't really slow him down. Johnny had a lot of padding in his left butt cheek. But when I picked up the 200-pound antique oak desk and smacked him with that, he went down.

Now here I was, sitting on the third-story roof looking out over the oaks surrounding the house and at the distant downtown buildings of Austin as the sun was setting. Those buildings are all glass-faced and really gleam when the sun is setting. Also, Austin trees never grow really tall. Something about the water table and some sort of stone underground table stopping the roots from growing. Those oaks just grow up to the roof, and then they stop. Sometimes I think these Austin oaks are like demi-gods. We never quite go up to Olympus. We go only so high and then we stop. But I digress . . .

There I was, smoking and sitting on the broken slate-tiled roof. And there Johnny was, downstairs, strapped to a lone surviving antique desk chair in a room filled with empty mahogany shelves that at one time may have contained books but now just held cobwebs and memories of books—probably sold off during hard times or some war—with a derringer bullet in his left butt cheek and shouting about some ancient tree (clearly not an Austin oak) he was going to get a limb from to stab me with.

Men!

I'm terribly fond of Austin. It is a city full of spoiled college students who have never learned to pick up after themselves and who like to drink a lot. Every Sunday morning, the city is full of discarded party streamers and plastic drink cups and forgotten pieces of clothing and footwear that college students manage to lose on Friday and Saturday nights. I always wonder how the person who lost one shoe got home wearing only one shoe when I see some Converse sneaker lying in the road. But I love it. "Now that is tribute," I will say to DT. And DT will say, "Oh Bris, you just will never understand."

(DT thinks she is smarter than me because she was born 12 minutes earlier. She might be right; she is the one who dematerialized when Johnny Valentine came crashing through that boarded-up window so SHE did not get her hair filled with rock salt. I'm not going to tell her that, though. She's already too smug.)

So I'm sitting on the roof mourning my designer shoes and picking rock salt out of my hair and hacking Johnny Valentine's iPhone when DT rematerializes on the roof next to me, and for once she thought something was funny. Bastard! But finally she stopped laughing—at my hair! And we sat there on old broken slate roof tiles staring out over the old oaks' tops at the setting sun's light gleaming on Austin downtown buildings—thinking murderous thoughts about Johnny Valentine.

DT, of course, thought we should just vaporize Johnny Valentine. That's actually what she did to old Emory Quail, the manse's former resident, who was a lovely woman if you did not mind her shouting, cursing, spitting, refusing to put in her false teeth and—

Throwing any objects she was not too frail to lift.

Emory was too frail to lift most objects when we met her, being ninety or so, with gnarled hands and a cane to walk with that she leaned so heavily on sometimes I thought she would break it. And that is leaning hard since Emory could not have weighed more than eighty pounds.

Emory never hurled anything bigger than a very thin paperback book. A romance novel, if I remember correctly, which seemed very out of character for Emory. I admired Emory for the effort, though, and wondered just what sort of objects she threw in her youth. But—

The house was perfect, practically boarded up already, and stuffed with so much debris and detritus counting back centuries and generations even I was ready to admit it really was a tribute. There was an entire bedroom filled just with old antique mirrors stacked one against the other. Tall, upright mirrors with heavy ornate wood and metal frames, back to back against walls, and furniture filling the whole room. A music room with an upright piano in it that could only be reached if you wove between stacks of boxes and antique wooden furniture, sometimes needing to turn sideways just to squeeze through to reach the piano. It made you wonder why the library was the room that was empty. But still.

It was—perfect.

DT's logic, murdering Emory Quail, was if Emory Quail went missing, it would be years before anyone could even claim she was dead so we would have the house to ourselves. It's valid logic, and we'd been there almost seven years before the Quail clan finally got a death certificate and started fighting over the property itself. And then a few more years while the Quail clan relatives were battling things out in court. It looked like there would be years to go.

Till Johnny Valentine kicked in a boarded-up window to attack me with a shotgun filled with rock salt. Rock salt! For feck's sake!

DT was horribly disappointed in me for shooting Johnny in the ass instead of some more calculated and vulnerable anatomical kill zone.

I, of course, pointed out, and very logically I think by the way, that it's not easy aiming and firing a gun on the spur when you have a face full of rock salt.

Meanwhile, downstairs, it sounded like Johnny was getting winded. The shouting was gearing down. Finally! There were no close neighbors to hear him, but all that shouting was stressful and annoying.

"So," said DT, "What are we going to do with him?" Giving me that dark look that means "You really should have aimed better, and then we would not have this inconvenience."

You cannot exactly call the police about an intruder you just shot in the ass when you are a several thousand years old demi-goddess squatting in the failing-down manse of an aging spinster heiress your twin sister vaporized because the woman just wouldn't share. Twenty-three bedrooms, and Emory Quail wouldn't even negotiate. One altar and the third floor. That's all we asked! She couldn't even walk up the stairs to the third floor! I call that selfish.

Also, we couldn't exactly spring Johnny Valentine. He would blab, and he did have a bullet in his ass. That's called "proof." Authorities would investigate. Bloggers would blog. Most people would think Johnny was crazy, but if he didn't come back, some zealot would actually believe him and come looking. And what if it was a religious zealot? They are the worst! There would be chanting and incense and people throwing holy water about and maybe even more rock salt—

I'd probably have to shoot someone again!

Just thinking about it was exhausting.

We could, of course, just kill him. That's what DT wanted to do. Though I'm really trying to stop doing that. Seriously. I took up smoking in the first place just to calm my nerves and try to NOT kill people. But I had been perusing Johnny's iPhone, and Johnny kept an online journal of some kind and had posted about us and his "mission" to go "ghost bust." Plus, he apparently hung out with other computer ghost-hunting zealots in online forums who would know where he disappeared, and then they would come about waving rock salt and ancient tree limbs, too, and the madness would. Just. Never. Stop.

Ahhh!

This is the problem with modern times. In the old days, a misfit like Johnny Valentine would just live in his mother's back bedroom and be eschewed by his community. Now there is the internet, and village idiots have friends. What a disaster.

"We have to move." I didn't like saying it, but someone had to. So, I did.

Austin is a city where someone whose clothing is a little off can really blend. A lot of people in Austin are touched when it comes to fashion. This was convenient for us because DT is a little touched when it comes to fashion, too. DT has just never quite recovered from the loss of the toga era and tends to waif about in long flowing garments looking a bit too Helen of Troy. But that does not stand out when a pale spindly man on the corner with an arresting white thicket of chest hair wearing nothing but a green sequin Speedo and stars and stripes top hat is hopping about.

I can't blame DT for her toga fixation. When our mother turned up knocked up, our war lord grandfather married her off quick to another war lord, and we were born into war lord royalty and treated like the princesses we were—right up until some of our "oops, someone has been making it with a god" traits appeared. Little things. Like lifting too heavy furniture and, um, vaporizing the hired help. (This is a very bad habit DT has had for a very long time, this vaporizing thing.) Then "Dad" knew he had been had, and we were not daughters of his loins, and he was . . . let's say a mite vexed. So, there was a war.

(I told you my family members were excitable and murderous, right?)

Still, we *were* demi-gods, and we did get a temple for a while, and handmaidens, and that was fun. But all things must end, and the temple was burned. I'm pretty sure the war god's full time goddessy wife instigated that. So jealous! So we traveled. But DT still clings to happier times. You know, human sacrifices, handmaidens, flowing robes. She's never snapped back from the burning of the temple.

I, on the other hand, embrace new fashion. I was wearing a cute little number I picked up online from Forever 21 when the rock salt debacle occurred. And. Those. Shoes. Were. Prada!

But it still had to be said.

"We have to move."

"I'm not doing Portland again."

DT was right. Portland was terrible. Togas and Birkenstocks? Never again.

"Greece?"

"Fire and refugees. No."

We sat and thought. Johnny was getting his second wind and starting to yell downstairs again. Nerve-wracking!

"Are you sure I shouldn't vaporize him?" (DT loves to vaporize people. It's a character flaw.)

"No."

I pulled out my smokes, lit another one to quell vaporizing fantasies, and perused Johnny's iPhone some more. Who on earth has pizza on speed dial? Also, he had managed to snap a couple shots of DT in her flowing gowns looking all Medusa and upset and hurling yellowed New York Times and green ceramic frogs about. And uploaded it to some conspiracy ghost hunters nut site. Shit.

I fried the website and photos but had to put the phone down when I found a locked file full of really unfortunate nude photos of Johnny. Sweet Medusa, my eyes!

DT brightened? "San Francisco?"

"No."

DT is crazy for San Francisco, and it is easy to blend in San Francisco, but San Francisco is too packed with humans. Buildings are side by side with only a foot between them. You cannot keep some closet nudie ghost buster strapped to a chair in a house with neighbors one foot away, hearing him shout about mauling you with a Norwegian tree.

"We could do an Irish castle again."

"No, we can't. Too many tourists. And they are priest-happy."

And then I had it. "New Orleans. We'll do a plantation again."

"Yes!" DT started to glow. DT loves New Orleans. So do I. Talk about party streamers and plastic drink cups. Yay! Also, it's not that hard to find a big old packed plantation or manor boarded up in NOLA, set away from the neighbors.

They don't really hunt ghosts in New Orleans either. They put ghosts on the tourist circuit. When we lived there before, DT used to just for fun pop over to some house on the ghost tour and appear to tourists for sport and frolic. I told her the toga didn't really work and she should try a hoop skirt, but she just said they'd think it was a night gown. It kept her happy. And away from places like the Valentines'.

New Orleans it was.

We still had to do something with Johnny Valentine,

who was still caterwauling downstairs.

"He really won't negotiate?" DT was being very civil now we were headed to NOLA. (DT used to totally kick in the womb, she was not a good womb mate at all, and we don't really like each other. But we are linked by blood and history, and DT can be very civil when she is happy—or is being devious.)

"He really won't. I tried." I really did too. But all that talk of stabbing me with the branch of some archaic tree put me off negotiations, and I just gave up on him.

"We could just leave him here."

"Well, that seems crueler than vaporizing him. What if he dies of dehydration?" (Of course, I was thinking he sort of deserved it.)

DT is really fast. Once she makes up her mind, it's hard to catch her. One second she was there. The next she wasn't. And in that instant, Johnny Valentine's fate was sealed.

I sat on the roof, looking out over the city that for a while had been home. Johnny's yelling stopped.

New Orleans is good. New Orleans is full of hoarders. And ghost tours. DT would be happy. And street debris. So would I. For a while.

* * *

ABOUT THE STORY

I do not get to write short fiction too often these days. It was a real joy writing "The Night I Shot Johnny Valentine." I hope you enjoy time with Bris and DT as much as I did.

MAX ADAMS

That Sweetest Cup

Michelle Muenzler

MORTALS OFTEN MISTAKE ME for my brother—hungry times have worn both our frames to the bone, like sun-scoured bits of driftwood. It does not help that we wear our mistakes the same. Or our needs.

Yet some still have eye enough to tell the difference between us.

"You're not Detritus," the girl says.

Ragged as a crow, she pecks at the tossed-aside heel of a baguette from the Vietnamese deli down the street. She's built a crude shrine of cardboard boxes and greasy sneakers in the alley's recesses and perfumed it with discarded packets of fish sauce and the weeks-old sweat of her labor.

"No," I say, savoring the scent of her offering, "I am Debris." Less is more when speaking with mortals. Their kind has little respect for chatty deities.

Her beady eyes pick me apart while she ponders my usefulness. "Hmm, well I suppose you'll do. Not much difference between the two of you anyway, far as I can tell."

My cheek twitches in annoyance. Once, everyone knew

the difference between us, but now . . .

Mortals can be such fools.

"I want my stuff," she says. The stale baguette crumples in her fist, spilling crumbs across her knees. "All the crap my parents threw away when they kicked me out was *my* crap. A part of me. They had no right."

Oh, how my brother would have loved this girl, had he bothered to answer her call. He is a flighty soul, though, too much the son of the river that birthed us.

"And you wish me to retrieve them for you?"

"Of course," she says. "Can you do it?"

"Yes."

"*Will* you do it?"

I smile knowingly. "Yes."

This poor lost girl—I understand her far too well. We were born, my brother and I, of a sea nymph's trickery. Of the ejaculate of Ares thrust unsuspecting into the still waters of Lethe, the action forgotten as soon as it was begun. Discarded by our own parents. Left unclaimed on that tepid shore with only stones to comfort us.

My brother embraces the simpler aspects of our adrift nature. He collects the easy discards—potshards dredged from old shipwrecks, plastic bottles floating unwanted in the southern currents—and creates beautiful art. Sculptures so haunting in their loss as to make the Erinyes weep.

It is unfortunate it was not my brother the girl drew here with her need.

He would have served her better.

* * *

When I deliver the first bits of flotsam from her previous life, the girl is pleased. She praises my ability, burns discarded fast food wrappers in my honor. It is a glorious and heady feeling to be worshiped once more. To be wanted. I grow fat on her offerings.

It isn't until the ring she becomes suspicious.

"Why's there blood on it?" she asks. She has a room now, a small efficiency apartment paid for by the careful hocking of her more valuable belongings.

The ring in question is a bit of silver wire twisted into the shape of an Ouroboros. Her mother had intended to toss it out, but it slipped free from the trash bag under the rough handling of the garbage collectors and settled comfortably in the curb's cracks to await a new owner. If I were my brother, I'd lie to the girl—words are as easily thrown away as children, after all. But desire, that fatted bleating lamb, sings too loudly in my veins.

"The ring was claimed," I say, "and so for you, I made it lost again." It is my nature, after all. You cannot have debris without destruction.

Oh, how her face twists! How her chest heaves!

And how unexpected the gossamer threads of innocence spilling from the newborn cracks in her self-righteous shell.

The scent of that particular loss blooms headier than any ambrosial draught; it intoxicates in a manner matched only by Dionysius' debauchery of old. Sweetly, ever so sweetly, I pool its fragrant nectar in my palms and drink until my teeth ache and my stomach's full to burst, and even then I do not stop.

Let my brother have his art; let him have his trash and lonely hours combing a thoughtless sea.

This mortal dreg belongs to me.

* * *

About the Story

I have a fondness for the lost, for the broken dreams of old gods. In Debris and Detritus, I found two twins, seemingly alike until the layers are peeled back, until their very names are unraveled to their core essence. And that is where this story emerged, a tale of one twin in particular being true to his nature in a world that seems to have little use for gods made flesh and much less understanding of the damage in thinking them tame servants for mortal whims.

Michelle Muenzler

Expense Claims Are Hell

Antioch Grey

Susan liked Mondays.

Weekends were busy, filled with exorcisms, banishings, removing curses, and general works of goodness. Monday was the day that the forces of darkness took the day off, slept in, and planned for the week ahead. Even werewolves stayed at home if a full moon fell on a Monday, catching up on whatever it was they did when they weren't out hunting rabbits or people.

The added fillip was thinking about all those people who went to work on a Monday to battle their own forces of darkness—the boss, the commute, the annoying colleagues, and all the aggravation of a nine-to-five office job.

Susan had none of that. She had waking up late, a sturdy breakfast, and staying in her pyjamas until lunchtime, and the smug sensation of being ever-so-slightly a force of darkness herself. It was only ever-so-slightly though, so she could wear sensible flannel pyjamas, unlike true evil, which tended to wear slinky black negligees—all the better for entrapping men and stealing their souls.

19

Stealing something anyway, something that would pass for a soul in today's crass world.

Unfortunately, it wasn't the forces of darkness that she had to contend with that Monday.

Her phone gave that constipated chirp that signalled that a message had arrived asking her to deal with something nasty.

She punched the pillow.

"What?" she said.

"You have one message," the phone replied.

"I know that. Tell me what it says."

The phone recited a post code for the location, a general code for the Local Difficulty, and then made a spluttering noise. Susan plucked the phone from the bedside cabinet and peered at the message through half-closed eyes.

There was a specialised emoticon at the end of the message to show that it was authentic and had been sent by one of her bosses. It looked like an emoticon for constipation, which brought to mind her boss's face when reviewing the expenses claims.

"Bugger," she said.

Adding, after concentrated further thought, "Double bugger. There's only one set of gits who don't keep to the Monday truce."

The post code was at the ends of the earth, or at least the Northern Line. The Tube was hot, overcrowded, and delayed due to overrunning engineering works. She wondered idly what that announcement was covering up and which one of her colleagues had been sent out to deal with whatever it was that had blocked the line.

She made a surreptitious offering to the Dark Gods of the Railways, and the Tube train passed through safely.

The post code led her to a garden.

It was a big garden, attached to a fine house that had been there before the city swallowed it up. It ran to acres of woodland, sculpted topiary, and long borders, but it fell well short of the usual Wild Places that attracted the strange and unearthly. It was also open to the public three days a week and every other weekend.

A man was waiting for her by the gate with the anxious look of a person who had seen too much and was looking for someone to take over responsibility for dealing with whatever it was.

"I'm Susan," she said. "I believe you have been expecting me."

"Adrian," he said. He held out his hand uncertainly to be shaken, imposing a sense of order on things by following the rote politenesses demanded of two Brits meeting on business.

"So, what's the problem?" she said.

Adrian's unease deepened. "I don't know what they told you . . ."

"Not a lot—they don't like to give us any preconceptions."

"We have some fine statues here, brought back from Greece by one of the family six generations ago when they did the Grand Tour."

Susan nodded.

"They've started talking."

Adrian had the look of a man who expected to be disbelieved, because he didn't believe it himself. Susan didn't tell him that talking statues was low down on the pecking list of strange things she had dealt with because there was a fine line between instilling confidence in someone and completely rearranging their world view.

In her experience, people wanted to think that their problem was an aberration and that the world generally made sense. This was obviously nonsense and not true, but Susan understood the need to cling to comforting illusions.

It was, after all, why she still completed her expenses claims.

She put on her best expression calculated to soothe the general public—a little stern, a lot competent, and a tiny soupçon of self-deprecating humour.

"Ok. So, I assume you're familiar with the history of the place—is there any suggestion of human sacrifice, or any sort of ritual cult activity?"

Adrian's expression brightened. It wasn't just that someone believed him, but someone was going to take the problem off his hands. "The only thing that has been sacrificed in this vicinity is a couple of cans of Special Brew, or a packet of crisps and—very possibly—someone's virginity in some cheap bunk-up against a tree," he said. "We do get teenagers breaking into the garden after hours for that kind of thing, but there's never been anything more exotic than that."

"Right. Well you had better show me the statues, and I

will see what I can do."

Adrian opened the gate and stood back politely to allow her to pass through first.

It was probably politeness, but she still paused to check that the gate was a simple door and not a portal and that there was nothing hungry lurking behind it. She stepped through smartly and then shifted to the side, away from Adrian, just in case he had been possessed and was waiting for her to turn her back so that he could pounce on her from behind.

No portals. Nothing lurking. No stunning blow from behind. So far, so good.

Adrian moved around her and then led the way down a narrow garden path flanked by meadow grass and the sort of flowers that farmers called weeds but which trendy gardeners loved to put in long borders.

It was pretty, she thought. It would be a shame if something happened to it.

The path wound its way down through the meadow to a gap in a serpentine green hedge and then into a lawned area surrounded by elegant white statues in various states of undress. They were a little worn, but enough detail remained to identify them from their attributes: Athena with her owl, Hera and a peacock, Hermes and his winged sandals, and a big burly chap with lots of facial hair and a thunderbolt who could only be Zeus.

"Which ones have started talking, then?" she asked.

Adrian pointed to the far end of the lawn where two large lumps of stone were squatting in front of a statue of

Demeter.

Susan stared at Demeter. "She's not talking now . . . "

"Not her," Adrian said, interrupting her.

Susan looked at the statue again. "Oh."

Whatever the lumps were, she'd never seen anything like them before. Mind you, in this job, you didn't tend to get much repeat business, apart from the vampires, and that truce seemed to be holding for now.

She had never heard that trolls were real, but maybe they were . . .

* * *

It was an interesting question whether she would be better off walking up to the . . . things, or try and flank them. If they had poor periphery vision, she might be able to sneak up on them, but was that wise with something Magical? That tended to result in hexes first and questions later, and there was always a chance that this could be resolved by negotiation.

Or threats. And you had to be facing an entity to deliver threats, so it was the full-frontal approach . . .

Susan coughed, politely announcing her presence to the entities. If there was any reaction, she couldn't tell.

She moved forward slowly, keeping a weather eye on the blobs. There were no sudden moves; there were no moves at all. At fifteen feet she stopped and waited. If they didn't move now, they really were just lumps of rocks, and she could go home and have the rest of her Monday off.

"'Ello," said a lump.

"Yeah, 'ello," said the other lump.

"Good morning," Susan replied. "You seem new round here."

"I suppose we are," said the first lump.

"New to here anyway, but not really new overall," said the second lump.

"So you're old?"

"More immortal," said the first lump. "You know how it goes."

Susan had the sinking feeling that she did. "So, what brings you to these parts?"

The lumps would have shuffled their feet in embarrassment if they'd had feet.

"Who did you cross?" Susan said, with a sigh.

"Not cross," protested the first lump.

"If certain gods were more reasonable and more appreciative when others were trying to help them, then this would never have happened," said the second lump.

"You expected gods to be reasonable," Susan said. "It's really not in the job description."

"I'd object to that remark, being a god," said the first lump. "But, for once, I feel like siding with a mortal."

The second lump shrugged. "I agree. She has a point."

"What Pantheon are you from?" Susan asked.

The two lumps conferred. "I don't really understand the question," said the first lump. "There is really only one set of gods."

"Not really," Susan said, wondering whether it was wise to introduce her new acquaintances to comparative theology. "Rather more than one, to be accurate."

"If you mean those Eastern gods, well, they're just different aspects of us," the first lump continued.

"Yeah, we're all drawing from the same well, except our well is nicer, with columns and lots of marble. And sunken baths."

"Greek, then," Susan said. She let the matter of other pantheons drop. The Greek gods tended to be sniffy about the Roman gods as cheap copies of themselves, viewed the Eastern gods as primal urges which they had sublimated and improved on, the Norse gods were just barbarians, and anyone else were Johnny-come-lately upstarts. Just like any other god, they viewed their Pantheon as the one true Pantheon, and the others as . . . well, inconvenient.

Susan had often wondered whether the gods had the neighbours round in heaven where they would gather round the heavenly wine and nibbles and complain about her at number 26 who was no better than she ought to be and how the snake gods were lowering the tone, what with not even bothering with clothes or limbs.

She was in no hurry to volunteer to experience this. Firstly, she would probably have to be dead, and secondly, she had the feeling she would end up as cup bearer or whatever and serving the nibbles. She'd been a part-time waitress, once, and she had no interest in repeating the experience with a clientele who wouldn't dream of tipping.

Gods did like to be the centre of attention. And talking, lots and lots of talking. It was their Achilles' heel.

Susan congratulated herself on the culturally appropriate metaphor. "So, what are two fine Greek gods doing hanging around in a garden in north London?"

"Looking for a way home," said lump one. "But she's not talking."

"Er, Demeter?"

"Yeah. We thought she might put in a good word for us."

"With whom?"

Lump one replied, "The son-in-law."

"Hades?"

"That's the one.

"I hate gods," said Susan. "I really do."

"You and me both," said Lump One. "And I am one."

Susan wished there was a book of etiquette to deal with situations like meeting strange (non-hostile) gods for the first time. She knew what to do when the god was trying to rain down hellfire or sacrifice some followers to open an eldritch portal, but not what to do when the god was shambling around looking a bit lost.

In the end, there was only one thing to do, the thing that any Brit did when faced with an awkward situation that had no precedent.

"Do you want a cup of tea?" she asked.

"What's tea?" replied Lump One.

"Yes," said Lump Two and poked his mate in the ribs. "Whatever it is, we want it."

There was a little cafeteria in the grounds of the house to service the day trippers' need for sustenance and tea, and Adrian had the key to the nearest thing to Heaven that could be found this side of the aetheric boundary.

"I'm not sure we should be doing this," he said, turning the key in the lock. "I'm only supposed to use it for the loo."

"If you want to disappoint two gods . . . " Susan said. "But I warn you, it tends to lead to seven years' bad luck."

"Only seven weeks," Lump One said. "We're only minor gods, though I say it as shouldn't."

"Still nasty though," Lump Two added, just in case anyone got any ideas that a short smiting stopped short of being a full smiting.

Adrian pushed the door open, conceding the point, and allowed Susan and her two followers to shuffle into the small space round the back of the café where the kettle and tea things stood on the side of a long stainless steel counter.

"So, what's this tea then?" Lump One said.

"It's a drink," Susan answered, filling the kettle. "It's hot, it's soothing, and it's good for drinking in all sorts of crises."

"Is this a crisis?" Lump One asked.

"There's no blood," Lump Two replied. "Usually there's blood in a crisis. And limbs. Limbs that are not usually attached to bodies. That's an infallible sign."

"Or the sacrificial fires going out," Lump One said. "You don't see a lot of that these days."

"There's a definite lack of sacrificial fires to go out," Lump Two said. "It's a disgrace."

Susan poured the hot water into a novelty teapot in the shape of a London bus and swirled it round to brew properly.

"Milk?" she said to Adrian, who nodded yes. He kept looking at the two self-described deities with something halfway between horror and admiration. Like someone who had a live snake by the tail and was wondering whether it would be better to try and get a better grip closer to the head or just throw it away and hope he could run faster than an angry snake.

Susan knew how that felt, though her job was mostly predicated on getting a better grip both literally and metaphorically.

"So," she said airily, pushing a mug of dark tea towards the two Lumps. "What are your names?"

Lump One and Lump Two exchanged wary looks.

"I can't make an offering of a biscuit without knowing what gods to call on," Susan said, trying to pass off the issue of the Knowing of Names as something minor she was mentioning in passing, just as a courtesy really, and with no intention of using a Name to banish an entity back to whence they came.

"You can call me Detritus," said Lump One.

"Debris," said Lump Two.

"You don't need our real names," Detritus said with a look that spoke of smiting if someone was foolish enough to press the point.

"No worries," Susan said mildly. "I offer you, Detritus, a chocolate hobnob as an offering to secure your good will. I offer you, Debris, a Jaffa cake as an offering to secure your good will. May you both look kindly on me and mine."

"We accept your offerings," both Lumps said, then

snaffled their biscuits.

Susan didn't feel the cold fingers of fate running down her back, which just goes to show you how little fate knows about anything.

The lumps peered at their tea suspiciously then took a cautious sip apiece, followed by a nibble of a Jaffa cake.

"That's nice," said Debris.

"Relaxing," said Detritus. "I feel all calm and ready to take on any task."

"Yes," said Debris. "So if you'll just offer up your prayer request, we'll sort that out before we head back."

"If we can work out how to head back," added Detritus. "But answering prayers first."

Susan had the feeling she'd made a huge misstep. "I don't have a prayer that needs answering," she said. "I've made a propitiary offering as a matter of good manners but that's all. I don't need a favour."

"We have to reciprocate your offering," Debris said.

"Not have to, really, but we want to. We're not like those stuck-up posh gods you know—we keep our word," Detritus said.

"Bugger," said Susan, and no more heartfelt prayer had ever been uttered by her.

* * *

It is embarrassing, at her level of experience, to acquire two shambling gods determined to grant her a wish, or a prayer at least.

"You need to ask us for something," Debris said.

"Something unrelated to home décor," Detritus added

quickly, but wouldn't be drawn on why.

"Is there someone you want smiting?" Debris said. "We could manage a small smite."

"A smite-ette," Detritus said.

"Lots of people," Susan said darkly. The bloke who had sat next to her on the train journey here and put his feet on the seat opposite, he was in need of a good smiting. And the mechanic who'd serviced her car, who she was sure had charged her extra for being female. And the chap who administered her expenses claims, and who wanted receipts for everything, and had no sympathy for anyone who didn't manage to have a countersigned fee note in triplicate simply because they were being set fire to at the time.

But if you started down that road, there was no stopping until you turned into a Dark Practitioner and started wringing the necks of chickens at midnight and cursing your enemies.

"But no one in particular," she added, letting that particular dream of vengeance pass quietly away.

"Some crops that need to be encouraged?" Debris asked. "Technically, we ought not to do something like that as it's not strictly our line of work, but that was a very nice biscuit."

"Very nice," said Detritus.

Susan shook her head.

Susan had no crops. Susan had a small courtyard garden surrounded by pots of fake plants that looked pretty all year round and needed neither watering nor weeding but which confused the local snails no end.

"A swain you wish to seduce?" Debris suggested.

"Got one, thanks," Susan replied. Or as near as she was going to get to one in her line of work. Her shabby little necromancer had tidied himself up, bought a suit, had a haircut, and had bought her a present. Admittedly, *Demons and How to Thwart Them* wasn't the most romantic gift, but it was useful, and it was the thought that counted. It wasn't as if she needed to do anything more complicated than buy him a pint and show him her bra to seduce him. The higher arts of champagne and lingerie were not necessary.

"Perhaps we could think about it later," Susan said. "Once we've worked out how to get you home."

They looked at each other. "Well," said Debris.

"Let's not rush into anything," added Detritus.

"I mean, I'm sure they're missing us, but perhaps they should be given more of a chance to miss us, if you see what I mean," Debris said.

"Absence makes the heart grow fonder," said Detritus.

"Out of sight, out of mind," offered Susan, more in hope than anger, but they were not to be moved.

"So, as our worshipper, you need to find us a temple to inhabit," Debris said. "Somewhere we can lay our godly heads."

Susan did not believe in taking her work home.

She reached into her pocket, took out her phone, and sent a text message – *Need somewhere to keep two gods out of trouble for a while. Any suggestions?*

She didn't have long to wait for a response.

Warehouse in the Old Kent Road. I'll meet you there.

"Right," she said. "You'd better come with me. I've found you a temple."

It was fortunate that the Great British Commuter took everything in their stride, tucked up in their own worlds, protected by headphones and smartphones from the harsh realities of existence. Susan did not fancy explaining to others whilst she had two rocks lumbering after her, even if they were lumbering rocks with tickets.

They had to change twice, and then take a bus, to reach their destination: a gloomy building tucked down a grubby side street that looked like it had not been cleaned since the Victorian era. It was just the sort of place that a necromancer would choose to conduct their experiments— short on visitors and so far away from the passing traffic that screams would not be heard.

It was perfect for storing gods.

"Hello luv." Stephen's head appeared from the shadows, almost disembodied in the dark depths of the doorway that could dimly be seen to one side of the alley. "Will this do?"

"It's just what I need," Susan replied.

There was an awkward pause whilst they worked out whether there would be kissing, and if so, where, until Susan took the lead and dropped a short, sweet kiss on his mouth. Stephen turned a shade pinker and ducked his head, his hair falling round his face.

"Ooh," said Debris. "Is this your swain?"

"Yes," said Susan, surprising Stephen into a quick grin.

"I've never been a swain before," Stephen said. "Will I have to recite poetry, and wear straw behind my ear?"

"Poetry is always nice," Detritus said. "It'll win any woman's heart."

"If you could see your way clear to a nice offering, we could make sure that Susan here stays yours for ever, or at least until someone else makes a better offer to us," Debris said.

"And she's no Helen, so you should be safe there," Detritus continued. "Not many will be falling over themselves to make a better offer. No offence."

"Plenty taken," Susan said.

"I'm a necromancer," Stephen said. "I might need help with romance, but I'm a dab hand at death. I can take care of any rivals myself, thank you very much. I know a couple of very hungry demons, and some very nasty spell traps."

Susan grinned. That was her kind of man.

"This is Debris and Detritus. Don't offer them any tea, don't offer them any food; in fact, don't offer them anything at all without agreeing a price up front."

"Right oh," Stephen said. "I invite you to take shelter under my roof, and ask only that you leave the place in the condition you find it in and never breathe a word as to what you find here."

"Fair enough," said Detritus.

"Done," said Debris.

The three of them crossed the threshold, Susan first, and then the two gods bringing up the rear. Inside, the warehouse was bright and airy, and largely empty. There was an ornate carved bed at one end, a long line of bookcases along the far wall filled with the sort of books that amateurs should not be allowed within ten feet of, and a large Persian rug in deep shades of red.

"Kitchen and bathroom through there," Stephen said, pointing at a couple of doors.

"I thought this was a warehouse," Susan said.

"So did the Council," he replied. "It's no good having a secret lair that someone can find by looking you up on the voting registry, is it?"

"This is your lair? It's lovely." Susan moved deeper into the building, her fingers twitching towards the books. "Are you sure you're happy to take this pair in?"

"They can't get up to much in here. It's the centre of a large protective circle that damps down most magical activity apart from mine." Stephen waved a hand in the direction of the floor. "It's built in, unscuffable and unmovable."

"We're not magical," said Debris.

"We're gods," said Detritus.

"Whatever you say." Susan didn't want to get involved in complex theological arguments, particularly with gods who tended to sulk if you disagreed with them and start smiting. She wanted to pack them off to heaven, have a nice alcoholic beverage of her choice, and sweet talk her swain into letting her read some of his books.

"You really need a sofa in here," she said, thinking of the books.

"I second that," Debris said.

"In a nice taupe," Detritus added. "Perhaps with a red stripe."

"Red makes me think of blood." Stephen's eye twitched. "And taupe makes me think of cold, dead flesh."

Debris and Detritus looked at Stephen, with the long hard look of gods trying to work out whether a worshipper was several thuribles short of a censing.

"Right," said Detritus.

"Ooookay," said Debris.

"Black goes with everything," said Susan. "And doesn't show the dirt or the bloodstains."

It was Susan's turn for being stared at hard.

"I'm not sure you're the right class of worshipper we are looking for," Debris said.

"No," said Detritus.

Susan shrugged. "You'll be the first gods I've met who were fussy about blood."

"We don't mind people making offerings. That's right and proper," said Debris.

"But not on the soft furnishings," said Detritus, and shuddered.

"In my line of work, you tend not to be that fussy about that sort of thing." Susan shook her head sadly. "It tends to get messy. If it's not the blood, it's the unguents, the herbs, and the salt you track in from the circles . . . "

Stephen grunted in agreement, and the two gods exchanged long looks, silently communicating their disappointment with the modern world and its inhabitants.

"Do you have some tea?" Susan asked. "Not for them—that's what started all this. But I'm gasping."

Stephen opened the door to the left to reveal a neat but

snug kitchen, well equipped with all the equipment a budding chef would need and which would also usefully double up as a necromancer's tools of the trade.

She hoped he cleaned his tools between uses.

"Earl Grey, or something more robust?" he asked.

She followed him into the kitchen, pressed up against him so she could feel the heat of his body and catch the scent of herbs in his hair. Stephen wasn't objecting to her closeness.

"Earl Grey will be fine," she replied. "Have you any ideas about how to get rid of our guests? They say they can't go home until they've answered my prayers and I don't have any that need answering, unless you count the trains running on time, and I don't think they're powerful enough to sort that out . . . "

Stephen snorted with laughter. "I don't think anyone is."

"And they can't go home, even if they wanted to," Susan continued. "Apparently, they don't know how."

Stephen filled the kettle, and set it to boil. "Standard dismissal charm work, level one, with a couple of extra ounces of salt should see them off. But not until you've had your prayers answered. Of course, you could always argue that they're too late, they were already answered when you met me."

"You're cute," she said, and nudged him with her hip to ease the sting of her words. "But not that cute."

"I'll settle for cute," he said.

"And I really am grateful for your help with these two," she added. "Can you imagine what havoc they would cause on a job?"

As it turned out, they didn't have to imagine.

Susan got another text, another job, another trip across town, and two bulky shadows who refused to be left behind.

"What if you need us?" Debris said.

"You'd look very silly getting yourself killed when we could have saved you by answering a prayer," Detritus said.

So, in the end, Susan took Debris and Detritus along with her and couldn't prevent Stephen from following along behind. Not without a strong hex, and hexing is no basis on which to form a relationship; certainly not in the first few months, anyway.

"All right, but we're going by taxi this time," she said.

Her employers had an account with a taxi firm. It was supposed to be for emergencies, because even they had to admit that you couldn't take a tentacle monster on a bus, even in the shabby parts of town.

Debris and Detritus took some persuading to get in the back of the car, eventually taking the long seat at the back, leaving the two smaller facing seats to Stephen and Susan.

"I could get used to this," Stephen said. "I usually get a bus, not a taxi."

"The London commuter is a patient unquestioning beast, but there are limits," Susan said. "I just dread to think how long it will take me to get my expenses back."

"We could help with that," said Detritus.

"Best not," Susan said. "I can't imagine what the finance department would make of divine intervention, but it would probably lead to additional forms to be filed in triplicate and probably docking my pay to boot. Gits."

"If you're sure," said Debris.

"Very," Susan said firmly.

They made the half-mile trip across London in the rush hour in forty minutes, which seemed suspiciously fast, but both the gods denied divine intervention.

"Probably just Luck," said Debris. "She's always been very helpful to us. I think she likes Detritus."

Detritus blushed.

"You don't owe her any prayers though," Debris added. "She's funny about that sort of thing. Whenever you call on her, she goes away."

"If only," Susan murmured.

The taxi drew up outside a typical Edwardian-style north London villa, red brick with white and black bricks picking out a geometric pattern above and below the bay windows surmounted with pitched roofs. A man was standing outside, looking up and down the road with an expression that hovered between worry and hope.

"I believe you're expecting me," Susan said, holding out her hand in greeting. "I'm Susan."

"I'm Nigel. I was told it was just you," he said, peering at her companions with suspicion.

"They're trainees," she said. "They're accompanying me on a learning experience. Gives them a taste of field work in a supervised and safe environment and gives me someone to help carry any equipment."

"Oh," Nigel said, his brow clearing. "That makes sense, I

suppose. I suppose you'd like to come inside?"

"I don't think we want to attract any more attention than we have to," Susan said.

"No." Nigel looked down the road again, checking for twitching net curtains and worrying about the effect of this on house prices. He gestured for them to go through the front door ahead of him. The entrance hall had the original flooring tiles, or good reproductions, and tasteful cream walls with cornices and a ceiling rose round the light fitting. "Would you like some tea?"

"Not for the apprentices," Susan said quickly. "And not for me, either. I'd like to get started straight away."

Denied the usual courtesies, Nigel floundered for an instant, unsure how to handle the arrival of paranormal specialists in his home. "Right. It's upstairs."

"What is?" asked Stephen.

"The ghost," Nigel said uncertainly.

"Trainee," Susan mouthed, and shook her head despairingly at the difficulties of educating young people today. "Upstairs you say?"

Nigel nodded. "Do you want me to show you?"

"That's all right. We can find our own way," Susan replied. "It's safer if you stay down here."

Nigel didn't argue.

Susan headed up the stairs in the lead, with Stephen close behind, and Debris and Detritus bringing up the rear with a noisy clatter.

The ghost was easy to find. There was a large damp patch in the middle of the hallway with a faint smell of the afterlife, mainly mould with a sharp tang of pain, and above it floated an ethereal figure wringing their hands and weeping.

"She's new, is she?" Susan shouted down the stairs.

"Yes," Nigel shouted back. "We've lived here twenty years, and this is the first time we've ever seen her."

"Are you sure you don't want us to help her move on to a better world," Debris said.

"Or anywhere else really," Detritus added. "I'm not sure we could get her into heaven, not looking like that. Her hair is a dreadful mess."

"Er, I'm not sure that . . . " Stephen began, only to be cut off by Susan opening of negotiations with the errant magical being.

"Right." Susan fixed the apparition with a hard stare. "So, why are you haunting this house?"

The pale woman made no reply, but just moved her lips in a soundless moan.

"I can see you're going to be difficult," Susan said. "That's all right, I've got all day."

"Perhaps we can help?" Debris offered.

"Though I'm not sure we've got any dominion over ghosts. They're not our bailiwick, as it were," said Detritus. "Always happy to give it a go, if you'd like."

Debris stepped forward to look more closely at the ghost, stepped in the slime puddle, and lost his footing. He put a hand out to steady himself to no avail, crashed to the floor, putting his arm through the wall to make a large hole. "Oops," he said.

"No, thanks," Susan replied, not taking her eyes off the ghost. It appeared to be smirking, and that wasn't a good sign. It would be vomiting ectoplasm next . . .

"What's happening?" Nigel shouted.

"Just some preliminary work," Susan replied. "There may be some slight scuffing of the paintwork, but we will take care of any damage tomorrow."

Detritus helped Debris to his feet, dusting him down and ostentatiously checking for injuries. He murmured something to his companion, but it was all Greek to Susan, largely because it was Greek.

"I was just testing her reflexes," Debris said.

"Yeah," said Detritus. "She seems a bit slow."

The entity snarled silently and poked a bony finger at Detritus, who stepped back, bumping into Stephen and treading on his toes.

Stephen bit back a swearword and pushed Detritus forward again.

"If we could all keep still for a moment?" Susan narrowed her eyes, assessing the haunting more carefully. Ah, there it was—the shimmering mark on the forehead, a sign to all who could read it that this was a supernatural entity of quite a different kind.

"Perhaps you'd like to explain why you're passing yourself off as a ghost?" she said.

The figure drew itself up to a full seven feet, its head curling round to peer down at their little group, then stretched out long, clawed hands towards them, fingers passing through Susan's body with a cold burn. Its mouth opened in a silent scream.

"Seen it all before," Susan said. "And better."

"Oh, be fair," said Stephen. "The bad breath is quite impressive. It could melt paint at forty paces."

"You never met the demon of Pinner." Susan shrugged. "Now that was bad breath. It took the paint off the skirting boards and melted the carpet. It was acrylic, being Pinner, but it was still impressive."

The demon glared at them.

"Now, are we going to do this the hard way or the very hard way?" Susan asked. "And when I say hard way, I mean hard for you. I've had a bad start to the day, I'm dying for a cup of tea, and I'm not in the mood to be messed around by minor demons dripping all over the hallway floor. So you can bugger off back to wherever you came from and leave this family alone and save me the effort of a full exorcism, or I can *make* you. Which is it?"

The demon waved its hands in the air, as if it were pleading for mercy.

"Two choices," said Susan. "Count of ten."

The demon shifted and swirled in an agony of indecision.

"Ten, nine, eight . . . " Susan marked the count off on her fingers, before she could reach seven, the pale figure shifted, shrank in on itself, and then finally disappeared.

"That went well," Stephen said.

"If you can trust it not to come back as soon as my back is turned," Susan replied. "I'll get the clean-up team to check up tomorrow, and sort out the watery mess while they are at it, and the hole in the wall. The technical geeks would love to get their hands on some samples to run tests on."

Debris and Detritus said nothing but shambled after Susan and Stephen as they descended the stairs.

A nervous homeowner was waiting for them. "That sounded . . . noisy."

"I'm sorry," Susan said. "It wasn't our best work, I admit. The stain on the carpet was already there, but the hole in the wall is new."

Nigel spluttered. "That's not good enough."

"You are free of a ghost," Susan returned coolly, "which was actually a demon, so it could have decided to eat you when it got bored, so a hole in the wall is a small price to pay. However, some of my colleagues will be round in the morning to help with the tidy up."

Susan paused. Nigel said nothing.

"There's no need to say thank you," she said. "Come on, you lot. Let's get out of here."

They were followed out to the kerb by the sound of Nigel muttering something unflattering about trainees under his breath. Clearly, he didn't want to risk the return of either the ghost or Debris and Detritus.

"Shall we smite him?" Debris said.

"Don't tempt me," Susan replied.

"Not our job," Detritus said. "We're not bad gods, tempting people from the path of good. We leave that to others."

"Zeus," Debris said, very quietly.

"Aphrodite," Detritus said just as quietly.

"All of them, really," said Debris.

"They're just looking for an excuse for a smiting," Detritus said.

"They're no fun," Debris concluded.

It was a sombre group that headed back to the warehouse in another taxi summoned by Susan. She didn't want gods hanging round any longer than necessary, but they were harmless and good natured, if clumsy, and she had some sympathy for their position. Gods were bastards, and the problem with Debris and Detritus was that they weren't bastardly enough.

And she didn't have time to teach them how to be gits before she sent them home.

"Tea?" Stephen asked as soon as they were through the front door.

"Thanks," said Susan.

"Yeah," said Debris.

"If we could," said Detritus.

Stephen looked at Susan, then shrugged. "Ok, tea and biscuits all round, and you can owe me a favour."

"It'll have to be a small one," Debris said.

"We're not much good," Detritus added.

"Nonsense," Stephen replied. "You're just not suited to the rough and tumble of demon smiting. It's only to be expected—you're only trained to smite humans."

"You're just being kind," Debris said.

"Yeah," said Detritus.

They collapsed into a small heap of godly misery on the

broad sofa, and watched whilst Stephen and Susan made the tea and put biscuits out on a plate for them all to share. The two of them eyed the offerings, then snaffled the Jaffa cakes.

"We will hear your prayers," Debris said, his voice muffled by crumbs.

"Mmmph," added Detritus.

"The bookcases," said Stephen.

Everyone turned to look at them.

"I need more room for books," he said. "And I can't put up more in here without disturbing the dark magic flows. So, I was wondering whether you could, in answer to my urgent entreaty, knock through into the next universe so I can put up some extra shelves."

"Yeah," said Debris.

"Easy," said Detritus.

There was a strange sense of the world pressing down on them hard, and then it eased off, and there was a dark gap between two of the bookcases about a book's depth across, but stretching off into a dark, fathomless void.

"Cool," said Stephen.

"Very cool," said Susan.

Debris and Detritus perked up a bit at that.

"Maybe the other gods are missing you by now," Stephen said.

"Maybe," said Debris.

"We still can't go back until we've answered your prayers," said Detritus.

"You'll just have to come up with a prayer for them to

satisfy," Stephen said. "Salting them just won't work otherwise."

"I can't accept any favours from a supernatural entity. It's against the rules—you never know when if you'll end up in their debt if the favour is bigger than your payment, and, frankly, the forms you have to complete to record it go on for pages and pages." Susan shook her head at the heavy burden of bureaucracy she had to carry whilst saving the world.

Stephen nodded. "It's why I prefer to freelance. No one audits my expenses, no one second-guesses what I've done, and my Friday nights are my own."

Susan flinched at the mention of expenses. "Do not bring audits into it."

"I could always have a word with Hades," Stephen said. "He does fall within my purview as necromancer, even if I've retired. A bit retired anyway."

Debris sighed. "He's not very fond of us."

"Not fond at all," Detritus said.

"So you want some leverage to bring to bear on him," Stephen said.

"Well, now I may be able to help there." Susan grinned the grin of someone with a good idea and a big enough lever to move a god.

* * *

The process for summoning Hades for, as Stephen put it, a friendly chat was quite simple. There was no blood involved, no chickens, no Latin incantations, and the circle was already drawn and built into the floor, which saved a lot of time.

Hades was summoned using Greek, of course.

He was shorter than Susan expected, and very hairy. He wasn't the most godly god she had ever seen and definitely warranted the lower case nomenclature.

"Evening, Hades," said Stephen. "Nice to see you—how's things keeping?"

"Well enough," replied Hades. "And why do you summon me, mere mortal? And how are things going with your young lady? Have you fed her some pomegranate seeds yet?"

"Early stages," Stephen said, with a sideways glance at Susan. "Plenty of time for the pomegranate later, I always say."

"Meet the mother first," Hades said. "That's my advice. Always meet the mother before you start sharing fruit with a desirable maiden. I'd have had a lot less grief in my life . . . "

Debris coughed. "Hello."

"Hi," said Detritus.

"What are those two doing here?" Hades asked, and there was a hint of thunder and smiting in his voice.

"They need to go home," Susan said.

"No," said Hades.

Debris and Detritus tried to look appealing, and failed.

"I am not giving them house room," Hades said. "Heaven isn't big enough for the both of us."

"I'm sure we can to some arrangement." Stephen waved his hands in an encouraging manner. "A favour for a favour—Susan here is very persuasive. She can persuade the tits off a demon. She could persuade Persephone to stay in Hell with you for a bit longer this year, or at least persuade her mother to allow it. It's not as if anyone would mind spring being a bit shorter this year. What with global warming and all, hardly anyone would notice."

"My wife and I are perfectly happy with the arrangements as they are." Hades frowned. "If you spend too much time together, the magic fades."

Stephen snorted in disbelief, which he turned into a cough.

"That's a shame," said Susan. "However, I am going to have to ask you to rethink."

Hades gave Susan a look that would have made any ancient Greek reconsider their immediate future, and their ultimate destination after death.

Susan just glared back.

"I would like to introduce you to Thomas," she said.

A small, goblin-like creature stepped forward in the circle, very careful not to cross its protections. "Hello," Thomas said.

"Thomas is, despite appearances, entirely human. He is our financial officer, and reviews all our expense claims," Susan continued.

Hades raised an eyebrow, looking supremely bored and unconcerned. "And?"

"And what Thomas is good at, more than anything, is not adding up or taking away, it's doubt," Susan said.

Hades straightened up, standing taller and stronger outside the circle. "Doubt?" he said.

"Doubt. He reads books about atheism at bedtime, he considers the scientific method, and above all, he double-checks and cross-checks all our expenses claims. Thomas, if Thomas had a nickname, would be Thomas the Doubter." Susan grinned, her mouth showing her teeth. "Can you guess why?"

"And what has this to do with me?" Hades asked, raising his nose and sniffing.

"Now that Thomas has met you, he will think about you all the time," Stephen said.

"Only, it's not that he'll be thinking about you precisely," Susan said. "It's more the doubting."

Hades flicked an uneasy glance at Thomas. "He's seen me. Surely he'll believe the evidence of his own eyes."

"I've seen Susan's expense claims in the flesh as it were," Thomas said drily. "I don't believe in them either."

"You see, he doubts everything." Susan gestured at Thomas. "He doubts the sky is blue . . . "

"Actually, that's an optical illusion," Thomas said.

"He doubts the grass is green."

"It depends what you mean by green."

"He doubts whether the moon is in the sky," Susan said.

"It's certainly not visible at the moment, so where is your evidence?" Thomas replied.

"Thomas doubts. He quibbles. He worries away at things until he proves they are true, or untrue." Susan's smile was the smile of a lion that had seen something tasty in the distance and was trying to look innocent and friendly as it came closer.

Thomas' smile was all sharp angles and abacuses, and Excel spreadsheets cross-checking to zero.

It wasn't clear which smile was the one that tipped the balance, but Hades said, "Oh very well," with very bad grace, and the deal was struck.

Debris and Detritus would be going home.

And good as that news was, the best part was that Thomas wouldn't be able to claim expenses for his venture into field work: he couldn't approve his own claims.

Susan smirked.

It was almost as if someone had answered her prayers.

* * *

About the Story

You may feel that there is a note of bitterness about expense claims. There is. If I told you about my last round of expenses, you wouldn't believe me. Slaying demons and bullying gods is far easier than persuading my employers to pay me money that they actually owe me.

Doubting Thomas is real, if a little less like a goblin.

Antioch Grey

CHAOS, INC.

CLAIRE M. JOHNSON

"YOU MUST DO SOMETHING, Father," Ares begged.

Shouts in support of Ares' plea filled the temple, the clamor insistent and so loud that Zeus was tempted to cover his ears. He didn't. That wasn't very kingly. Instead, he glared at his two miscreants, Debris and Detritus, who sat in opposite corners of the room; each of their chairs was surrounded by a cage of lightning bolts to keep them in place. Anything short of lightning bolts and they'd wriggle free. There wasn't a knot or a lock that they couldn't unravel or pick. It was rather amazing, assuming you weren't try to pen them in. Which he was. Hence the lightning bolts.

Their temporary incarceration didn't stop them from using slingshots to pelt each other and those around them with fruits and vegetables. An extremely well-directed tomato splattered against the robes of Poseidon. He was not amused. Before Zeus could do anything, Poseidon aimed his trident, first in one direction and then in another, and a wave of water doused the two hooligans. Neither niece nor nephew was his favorite. Come to think of it, they weren't anyone's favorite, with the exception of their mother, Hera, who was blowing kisses at them.

Zeus wished he could say that the two hellions were the gods exacting their revenge on him for his infidelities, but since he was king of the gods, he really couldn't blame himself. These two were the result of a passion-filled night that had smelled of fresh rain and roses, an orgy of two, a physical mating that was both lust and love, all in a massive effort to placate Hera after she'd discovered a particularly delicious affair he'd been having with a mortal.

Mortal women were so much easier; it was hard to resist them. Goddesses were the definition of high maintenance. Mortals, however. Ahhhh. No tremendous power that could be wielded against him. They weren't capable of leveling curses at him that meant anything other than words uttered in rage. And he could forget for a bit—an evening or an afternoon—that he was a god. He could take simple pleasure in another. Hera could never understand that joy in not being a god; not that he didn't want to be a god, but sometimes . . .

Hera's tantrums were legendary and none more so than when faced with his womanizing with mortals. It was bad enough when he was caught sneaking off with a goddess or nymph or a Titaness. She didn't appreciate it—to put it mildly—but consorting with mortals sent her through the clouds.

He'd never understand women. Never. Take, for example, her reaction to the birth of Heracles, the result of that truly wonderful night he'd had with Alcmene. He had to admit his conduct there had been shameful, impersonating her husband, the king of Thebes, while Amphitryon was away. But what is one to do when faced with such beauty, such wisdom? And she was tall. Always god catnip. No, Hera was not happy with him and tortured poor Heracles for years. Look at that twelve labors business. And then, *then*, after all that, she happily married him off to Hebe! At that point, Zeus threw up his hands in total confusion.

Their fights were the stuff of legends, but they usually made up fairly quickly. Well, there was that rebellion she instigated against him. He was not pleased in the least, and their relations were decidedly frosty for quite a while. But eventually, they'd mended their fences—until she'd discovered him canoodling yet again with yet another mortal. She was implacable in the face of his mortal dalliances. In order to appease her, he'd wooed her with lightning shows and rainbows. He'd sweet-talked his sister Demeter into ensuring the most magnificent harvest that year so that the mother of all would see fat, happy babies suckling on the breasts of fat, happy mothers. And then, of course, there was the lovemaking. The kisses slow and languid that said he was savoring her and cherishing her and that he did both desire and love her so much.

Which was true.

It was unfortunate that he also desired and loved a great many other women as well.

And as if to mock him, to throw all that passion in his

face, she'd birthed the twins. They were hellions from the day they were born. Twin monsters of mischief. Chaos followed them wherever they went. And if it didn't, they created it.

He felt a hand over his, the nails of that hand digging into his just slightly.

"Aren't they marvelous, my love?" she cooed in his ear.

"Not the word I would use at the moment," he replied. Currently, they were hanging upside-down by their knees from lightning bolts. Relieved of their slingshots, they were now spitting at each other, little bits of dirt flying across the room. Their cheeks were rosy and full from their exertions, if covered in splotches of mud. Was that a shriveled-up orange rind peeking out from behind a black curl of Detritus's hair?

Despite being perpetually filthy, the back of every knee, the crooks of their elbows, and between their toes crusted with grime—let's not even discuss the state of their ears— they *were* beautiful. Even sopping wet, obsidian-colored curls tumbled around their faces. Through some strange alchemy, they'd remained young children forever. Long- limbed and as agile as a pair of cats, they were almost impossible to tell apart but for the color of their eyes. Debris was blue-eyed, a color so true to sky that you held your breath for a second at the sheer beauty of them. Until he stomped on your toes and dragged a dirty palm across your robes. Detritus, known as the green-eyed monster, had eyes equally arresting. Her eyes were the color of emeralds, clover, and grass after a rainstorm.

Debris stuck his tongue out at his father as he tried to scramble between the bars of lightning. Zeus sighed. He couldn't keep them caged forever.

He crooked a finger at Hypnos and pointed at the twins. "Hypnos, if you please . . . "

Hypnos blinked twice, and the twins fell asleep. The sound of a hundred sighs of relief echoed through the chamber.

The six daughters of Themis, the goddess of eternal order, sat quietly on their thrones. If anyone could bring some sanity to this situation, it was them: Eirene (the personification of peace, and, boy, could they use some peace right now), Eunomia (the personification of law and order), Dike (personification of justice), Clotho (the Fate who was responsible for spinning the thread of life), Lachesis (the Fate who was responsible for measuring the thread of life), and Atropos (the Fate who was responsible for cutting the thread of life). Hopefully, there was to be no thread cutting; he loved these two, even as they drove him bat-shit insane. Asleep with their hands under their cheeks and the soft smile of slumber stretching from cheek to cheek, it was hard to imagine their unholy ability to create utter chaos in their wake. It was not a formal session—how could one formally invoke a punishment on a pair of seven-year-olds?—but Zeus hoped the daughters' wisdom would prove invaluable here. Heaven knows something had to be done. The entire heavens were in near revolt.

"They are monsters. Leaving destruction in their wake wherever they go," thundered Ares, which was a bit rich considering he was the god of War.

"Pot, kettle," hissed Demeter, who despised Ares. The first thing soldiers did in war was to burn the fields, destroying the harvest.

"Point," murmured Zeus, hoping that this wasn't going to devolve into a gigantic gripe session.

"Humanity cannot love in chaos, Father," implored Aphrodite. "A little chaos in love? That can add to passion. But not on the order that those two wreak." Even furious, her beauty was something to behold.

"Dionysus?" Zeus asked.

Dionysus toasted the crowd and then tipped his goblet over to reveal it was empty.

"Fucked up last year's harvest. Stomped their way through the vineyards, grabbing bunches of grapes to feed to the birds. Little bastards. If I get my hands on them—" A hiss from Hera and he stopped talking.

Zeus knew better than to ask Poseidon's opinion. The twins were limited in what they could do to the sea, but Poseidon would use every opportunity to undermine Zeus's authority. If he didn't find somewhere to park his little hooligans where their gift for chaos wasn't a factor, then Poseidon would incite another rebellion. The only reason he hadn't profited from the current political maelstrom was that Hera would do anything to defend the twins. She was a powerful enemy, as Zeus could attest.

Zeus looked in Hades' direction. Surely, his other brother . . .

"Absolutely not. The dead deserve some peace."

Zeus was so frustrated that little lightning bolts began emanating from his ears. This only happened when he was super-stressed. What could he do with them? Although they hadn't aged physically, mentally, their tricks and pranks and ability to sow disorder, confusion, pandemonium, and bedlam in their wake had increased in sophistication. And he had no doubt that their power would only grow as the years passed.

Interestingly, a little chaos in this world was beneficial. It demanded that people look to their better selves. To rise out of chaos was a powerful inducement for peace. But this? With these two, it was anarchy all the time: the harvest was destroyed, love thwarted, the hunter never catching the hunt, beauty denied, the slovenly triumphant. It would spiral down into madness if he didn't stop them.

He turned to the daughters of Themis. Falling on his knees, he beseeched them for guidance. "Please, my wise nieces, with all the wisdom that you possess, what should I do?"

They huddled together, six gray heads bowed toward each other, their voices so low that the sound couldn't even be described as a whisper.

Minutes and hours went by. Zeus stayed on his knees, waiting for their decision, knowing that he must be bound by it, given his plea.

Finally, they stood up. He always marveled at how their hair showed the burden of their tasks, but their faces were as unlined as if they were still girls.

"Rise, my uncle and father," they spoke in unison. "We

have come to a solution to your dilemma."

Zeus stood up and stifled a groan. His knees were killing him.

Bringing himself up to his full height, he beckoned Hera to stand next to him. She must abide by their decision as well. Tears streamed down her cheeks.

"Debris and Detritus must be exiled to someplace where their mischief will not be disruptive and destructive. Someplace where no one will even know they are there."

"There is not such a place on this Earth," cried Hera.

"There is," they sing-songed. "The U.S. Congress."

* * *

Gods save him, Zeus said to himself. Would she *never* stop weeping? The twins had been in exile for two weeks, and except for the occasional nap now and then, Hera had been crying the entire time. The fields were flooded and the harvest threatened. Demeter wasn't speaking to him, and Poseidon was grumpy, as the rain was playing havoc with the seas. Boats were torn from their moorings, and beaches were being washed away. Zeus could hear him muttering things like, "Damn fool woman." That was his bailiwick, and he was a possessive sort of god.

Fortunately, his mutterings were just out of earshot. Poseidon wouldn't openly tell Hera to stop her infernal caterwauling—because he might be irritated, but he wasn't stupid, and Hera's weeping might be annoying, but her temper was terrifying.

If Zeus had thought that the twins in exile would restore harmony amongst them, he was mistaken. Without the twins to distract them with their high jinks, the other gods began to turn on one another. After two days of bliss, the petty jealousies and spats that were always in the background came to the fore. Who got the better power? Who was prettier? Who was wiser? That these issues were even under debate was ridiculous. Not even the daughters of Themis had any words of wisdom. They threw up their hands and announced that they were taking a three-week vacation to a place called the Bahamas.

"Don't call us, we'll call you," they said in unison and disappeared. Great. Just when he needed them most.

And then there was Hera. As exasperating as her grief was, it was a reminder of how strong the bond was between mother and child. Or mother and hellions. Whatevs. He went over to her and put his arm around her shoulder. She rested her head against his shoulder. He dried her tears with the sleeve of his robe.

"It's not better without them," she whispered, her voice hoarse. This he had to admit. "Please bring them back. Please."

A bunch of grapes went sailing over his head. Food fights now occurred several times a day.

"I'll check on them," he promised. "And if things aren't okay, I'll bring them back." That was vague enough. "Okay" could encompass quite a bit of territory.

"Thank you," she said. She bracketed his cheeks in her two hands and gave him a kiss. It wasn't a sexual kiss but more the type of kiss a man and a woman who have been through much together give to each other. It was an acknowledgment of history, both good and bad, and love.

* * *

Zeus wasn't sure what to expect when he swooped in to observe the U.S. Congress. He avoided that part of the world. Too busy. Too much smog. Too many cars. He hated cars. Although he was loath to admit it, some things were out of his control, and carbon dioxide was one of them. These mortals would rue their foolishness. All the warnings by Poseidon and Demeter were being ignored. Some days, mortals were really dumb.

The twins were sitting in a corner, their arms wrapped around their legs, their faces woeful. Had he ever seen them unhappy? No, he had not! Zounds, what was going on here? When they saw him, they rushed up to him and gave his legs a heartfelt hug. This was also unheard of. Unbridled affection? He ran a hand through their curly mops. The world might be coming to an end. Their hair was clean. He stood back. So were their robes!

He knelt down to face them. "Whatever in the seven hells of Hades is going on here?"

Debris gestured toward the mortals fighting and screaming at one another. Detritus rolled her eyes in scorn.

"It's utter chaos," she said. "We can't do anything that is even remotely disruptive that they don't manage to do on a daily basis.'

"Hourly basis," Debris muttered.

Detritus nodded in agreement.

"Take us home. We hate it here," they said in unison. "Please, Papa."

They hadn't called him that in years. It was probably deliberate, but even so, it worked. He grabbed their hands and took one last look. The anger, vitriol, mendacity, and greed in this chamber was appalling. He could smell the lies, the ignorance, and the ambition. What an unholy stench. He couldn't leave his children here.

* * *

No one was happy to see them except for Hera, but no one protested either. All faces were resigned; this was the twins' home. It was far preferable to vent their frustrations against the two than turn on each other. As they discovered much to their chagrin.

As Zeus watched his wife gather her children into her arms, her face glowing with happiness, he couldn't help but feel that he'd done the right thing. A little fun was all right. Manageable. Perhaps even desirable. Some of these gods were so glum. So serious. A wee prank now and then? What was the harm? And maybe their brief sojourn had, somehow, matured them. Given them some perspective on how destructive chaos can be.

As Detritus pulled away from her mother, she flicked a booger into Debris' hair.

Maybe not.

* * *

About the Story

I've always told myself that I couldn't write short stories. That I needed too much backstory, too much dialogue to provide the handle that I need to develop a "voice" for a story. When I read a story or a novel, voice trumps everything. I can read what is essentially a mediocre book, but if it has a killer voice, then I'm willing to look over myriad sins. This was a personal test. Can I do this? I have to admit there were a number of fits and starts and a sense of looming failure. Most authors I know have faced writer's block at some point in their career, and its genesis is a fear of criticism and failure. Of course, if you don't write it, then you don't fail. But if you don't write it, then there is nothing to edit, fix, stretch, mold, massage, or craft. *Cracks knuckles.* Write one sentence. Just one. Then write a second one. Two sentences. Then . . .

CLAIRE M. JOHNSON

HeartStones

Robin D. Owens

Planet Celta, Druida City, 424 Years After Colonization, Winter
SOMETHING—SOME SOUND, SOME *pain* kicked him into consciousness. The splintering hurt rippled through the door, sharpened as it hit the metal hinges, then dulled a bit as it traveled through his walls and floors, then eventually dissipated through his whole three-storied self.

Pain more than he'd felt . . . long, long, long time.

Ssshh, whispered through him, and a wisp of alive-ness inside him but apart from him whisked through him. It trailed energy that soaked into each of his fibers. Riveted, he watched himself mend and grow stronger.

He's aware!

Then we must withdraw. He can Heal himself.

A while later, he turned his attention back from his beams and stones to understand a kick did it, brought him to full awareness and kept him there. The kick on his slammed door. *His* door, part of him. His main portal to the world *outside*. And odd that he sensed a *world* outside.

A different type and temperature of air against his rough

outer walls than the smooth inner ones.

He began to sense many things, put them in order. Think.

Live.

Primarily, hurt. The smashing of the door hurt. He whimpered and *strained* and the small pieces rose and set back in place. Still aching, he sent . . . energy . . . into it, soothing himself.

Better.

But still the door didn't quite fit, and a gaping crack let the cold winter air in.

Now silence lived within him instead of the noises, the mumbled words that he'd been aware of for a while and that had stirred him, reminding him of other times and sounds and voices of beings that moved around inside him, vibrating on his floors.

Yes, he *remembered* other voices, a snatch of back and forth between two beings long ago . . . *conversation.*

His oldest memory—words echoing through him, bouncing off his interior walls instead of soaking into them, then. *"If I am debris, then you must be detritus."*

He turned over the syllables, again and again, began to get meaning from them.

Debris and Detritus. He liked those words. Said often within his walls, the words fit him because they'd shaped him.

Now as he *thought* them, he tried to form them in sounds. Odd creaks, not like the smooth facility he'd sensed from those who'd originally made the words. But those sounds, the first words said by his own self, echoed through his walls, sank into his stone, seemed to anchor his being.

He was *Debris and Detritus.*

The concept of self floated through his mind, new and sparkly thoughts.

A vibration outside his walls, *outside,* heavy, stopped near his broken door—oh! from a *mobile being!* Additional ideas tumbled through Debris and Detritus's mind-self. He was *not* a mobile entity.

That odd being forced the door in, scraping and hurting. Debris and Detritus let wind whistle through his rooms, giving noise to the pain.

"Huh," the mobile *person* grunted, bootsteps stomping on the floor, through the tiled hall of the entryway, into the round mainspace of marble. *"Yep, definite squatters here. Kicked in the door. Left a lotta trash. I'll call in a report that I'm doin' a sweep of the house. That'll keep me here and out of the police guardhouse until end of shift. Good."*

The new being mumbled a word, one with weight that fizzed the air around it. And Debris and Detritus experienced another recently-remembered sensation; the inside of the mainspace chamber held less dark, became brighter with *light.*

He liked that.

"What's this? A hundred silver coin?" The new person made a series of deep sounds and radiated . . . *amusement.* Another concept came to Debris and Detritus's new thoughts. Laughing.

"Those fliggering squatters left something besides trash here. They'll

sure miss that. And I've got it! Only fliggering thing of value in this cruddy building."

More laughing. *"Huh. Will come in handy. I'll stay to end of my shift, do my regular thing so they don't look at me for stealing that brooch. Only twenty more minutes. But then gotta get out of the city with the jewel. Immediately. Live good for the rest of my life."* The bright white bathing his walls vanished from the mainspace.

He felt the air in his rooms change as the mobile entity traversed every chamber, light coming and going. As the being thumped up his staircase, Debris and Detritus *listened* to the words coming from the entity.

"Stupid, trashy place."

That made an odd and different pain inside.

The person kicked more *stuff* from the center of chambers to along his baseboards. *"If it weren't for finding that silver piece and for giving me a good excuse to hide out alone until end of shift, I'd be long gone from this abandoned and rotting house."*

Debris and Detritus creaked in surprise at more insulting words. He checked, fast. No rot lived within him.

Vibrations back from his third floor down the stairs and into the mainspace, then a ping sounded, a non-being-made noise. Then came a wheezing huff. *"That's it. Shift over. Will report in, then teleporting straight outta Druida—"*

Mumbling, then a whoosh of once-occupied-air, and the being vanished from Debris and Detritus's space. But as he left, a clink sounded as something fell onto the marble floor.

Fascinating object, full of pulsing energy, giving a heavier *feeling* than the true mass of the worked minerals. Debris and Detritus drew it toward his essence, his *thinking stones*, and surrounded it with energy, kept it safe. He liked the feel of it.

Then no more sounds or vibrations, either inside or close to his outside walls. Silence and not-light, *dimness and dark*, gathered within him, and he had much *time* to recollect the other noises and beings and conversations past, from long ago.

He considered time: minutes, septhours, days, weeks, months, a year.

Terrible *event* happened perhaps four years ago. Something he disliked—*hurt*—recalling. The end of the sounds and warmth and light of mobile beings, the beginning of emptiness.

Thoughts feathered at the edge of his brain, that portion of him he understood consisted of his *stones*.

There had been two mobile beings, persons, people. An old couple who had . . . talked to each other? Communicated?

He knew that word now, conversation and *communication*—ideas sent to other intelligent beings.

He scoured his memory and it flickered like . . . like the fire in his fireplace in the mainspace he had once felt, close to his stones. And he felt, then *considered*, things he'd heard and what the people had read aloud and those words that had echoed in his walls

Debris and Detritus recalled the last deliberate touch of those two, near his stones, and their words. *Shouldn't be long now; other Houses are Awakening*, the higher voice had said, smoothing a hand over the fireplace surround.

The other part of the couple replied in a deeper voice,

He will reach critical mass soon, of Flair that has sunk into him from this ground and atmosphere of Celta, of all the Flair his inhabitants have given him over the centuries.

Like us. We've shared, said the first.

Like us.

A loud breath from the higher voice. *We won't be here.*

Maybe, maybe not.

That conversation went around and around in his mind. He had much time to be, and remember and contemplate.

To come to decisions.

He needed . . . people.

He needed *Family*.

Somehow he'd get them. He would *keep* the next ones who came.

* * *

One night later

Zane Aster had heard a whisper of treasure . . . a treasure lost in Druida City.

While on duty, a venal city police guardsman had pinched a jeweled brooch from a GreatLord—a stupid deed. From that Lord's sentient Residence—an even more unintelligent action, since the Residence eventually figured out who'd stolen the item. And, the worst and final idiocy, the guardsman-thief had misplaced the brooch.

Reward money had been offered.

As he stared into his thick, expensive brew mug, Zane wondered if he'd been supposed to hear that rumor. If it had come to his ears because his Family worried about him.

He sat in a luxurious noble social club frequented by all

but the highest of society, his ass cradled by a thick cushion that conformed to his butt, the furrabeast leather chair tilted slightly to accommodate his wretched back.

If he'd been whole, he'd be down in a low-class tavern frequented by sailors and other treasure hunters like himself, but his pride wouldn't let him go back there in his crippled state.

Glugging down the last of the brew, he acknowledged his Family *should* worry about him. With his sight fading along with his *finding* psi-power, his Flair, he wouldn't give himself good odds of making it to spring.

He might not actually commit suicide, but he wouldn't take care of himself, and there were plenty of ways to perish if you just didn't give a damn whether you ate or how much alcohol you drank or what streets you wandered down drunk and wearing expensive clothes.

What he had to look forward to tomorrow was another Healing session. Maybe the Healers would break his spine again or plump up the pads in his spinal column or something equally nasty he didn't want to contemplate. The Healers could fix his back . . . eventually.

They had no clue how to stop his blindness.

Or the diminishment of his Flair.

And he couldn't just stay sitting on his ass and contemplating a very bad future.

So he called for a hot toddy to go—and exited the warm social club by the main door into the snowy night instead of calling for a glider to take him home.

The wind cut into him despite cloak over jacket and

tunic. He didn't have enough Flair, psi magic, to bend a weathershield over himself. He barely had enough power to activate the warmth spells on his clothing.

As he walked through the streets no more than a half kilometer from his own home neighborhood, he acknowledged that he'd made a mistake in not summoning a vehicle. Even his clothes and the false warmth of the alcohol in his blood didn't keep him from shivering.

Unless that was just another symptom of the damage he'd gotten in the underwater accident.

Still, when he reached the crossroads where he should turn left, instead he angled right, tripped over the curb of the sidewalk, then slid his foot to test the height and stepped onto it. Because he heard the faint wispy notes of a melody that called to the heart of him, to what had once been his primary Flair. A whiff of an odd but compelling tang curled into his nostrils . . . the scent of treasure.

He plodded in the blue gray evening, ignoring the warm yellow or white blurry rectangles of lit windows as he passed still-open businesses and apartments above them. He should go home to GraceLady Aster's Residence, his MotherDam.

Where he'd be fussed over and nagged, and he'd hate every minute.

But he could not ignore this final opportunity to hunt for this last treasure before his talent failed.

Time to accept that the large and drifting flakes of snow in the evening light weren't what dimmed his sight. That deteriorated all on its own. And the sensation of his Flair for finding a prize should have been a lot stronger, sizzling through his nerves, buzzing along his skin, especially since FirstFamily GreatLord Ivy's recently stolen bauble was more than a brooch, some sort of magical Family artifact.

Zane simply continued to put one foot in front of the other, following the whiff of energy and magic of that power-imbued treasure, calling himself foolish with every step. And he traveled from an upper noble-class part of town to an area of deserted streets devoid of inhabited houses.

The colonists from Earth had built Druida City, sure their descendants would populate it and the world beyond the walls.

But Celta was a tough planet for the humans. Though individuals lived longer, the sterility rate was high, the birthrate low, and the colonists' grasp on life still slippery.

So the city had never been full, and this part was empty.

Finally, he stopped in front of a tall, narrow house in a row of tall, narrow houses. His vision cleared for a few instants, and he saw rounded bowed windows on both the first and second floors, a balcony on the third, and a whole facade embellished with elongated designs.

A very elegant and beautiful building. And if his eyes and back and feet didn't throb with aching, he might have been able to call up from memory the Earthan architectural style this row of homes had been modeled after.

But his sight did flicker from the dim evening of reality to gray fuzz to a blank darkness, and he couldn't quite make out the exterior sculpture.

He *could* see that the tall and narrow door with a half-round top showed a large, and recent, gaping split. Zane sniffed, flexed his fingers, stomped his feet to move his sluggish blood a little faster and stimulate his Flair, and used his talent. Yes, the treasure awaited inside.

The icy wet of the iron door latch nearly seared his hand, and with a grunt and a shove of his whole body, he forced the thickly paneled door open. It scraped across the floor—a not-wood floor, unusual.

A spurt of anger zipped through him that someone had damaged the door, and he used the tiny amount of energy left to mend the wood fibers by feel, not by sight. Made the door whole, straightened it on its hinges.

His balance failed, and he windmilled and managed to set his shoulder, not his bad back, against the wall as he panted. Probably shouldn't have fixed the door, though he'd locked out the wind and weather.

He blessed the Lady and Lord for being out of the spitting weather if not out of the cold. He breathed and felt the warmth of his breath against his face as he moved forward through the entry hall, extending his senses. He passed doors on his right and left, he thought, then tripped on a low threshold from one room to another and stopped. A touch of sweat filmed his armpits.

His breath came ragged and harsh, sounding too loud. Did the material of the walls cause sound to echo? Or did he strain more to *hear* since his sight faded?

The drips from his clothing plopped around his feet, and since standing in a puddle didn't appeal, he scuffed his toe around and found even and solid ground.

Dark filled the interior of the abandoned house and he hesitated. On one hand, he could pretend his sight didn't decline in a night-black room. But he cherished even the slightest haze of pale gray that he could see. Which might vanish during the night.

Find the treasure and go.

So he stood tall and probed the room with his senses and pushed at his psi-power to *work*.

Oddly enough, the room felt circular, with a bank of colder, tall glass windows curving some meters ahead, looking out on the back. Not that he could see.

He tilted his head, noticing that the reverberations of the small noises he made sounded unusual. Slowly stretching out an arm, he touched a smooth pillar. Ah, more small columns must grace the room. Probably marble. He sniffed. Smelled like marble.

And yes, something not of the house, new to this environment, throbbed in slow and heavy pulses. A great magical artifact indeed. After inhaling through his open mouth, he tried to taste the essential magic of the artifact, thought he got a tang of bitter ivy. More overwhelming was the flavor of the house—sweet like golden honey, another peculiarity.

Blinking, he peered into the darkness, saw nothing, no glow from the brooch, which should blaze to his Flair-sight. He swallowed the despair coating his throat, shuffled a couple of steps in and past the pillar. Turned in the direction of the ivy taste, the whiff of Flair, the tiny hum of a magical artifact out of place. The jewel that needed to be returned to the Ivy Family, where it belonged and would be cherished.

"Just get the brooch and go," he muttered.

So he ignored his blindness and strode to the right into the room. A chill breeze whisked through the place, his foot came down on a piece of thin papyrus, and he slipped, toppling backward. His head hit the column, definitely stone. His mind spun dizzily as he fell, then his wits got swallowed up by a more gentle darkness than that of blindness.

* * *

The mobile being with male genitalia—a *man*—lay too still on Debris and Detritus's floor. An unfamiliar feeling, a rising sting, pulsed through his walls. He did not know the name of the emotion and did not like it. His windows on the third floor shivered as his air pressure increased due to the emotion.

No, he did not know this feeling and needed this man, his new Family, to explain it. Explain a lot.

The empty time before the man had come had stretched into an infinity of quiet moments, and Debris and Detritus began to realize how much he did not know. Did not understand concepts he should be able to grasp but made no sense.

Debris and Detritus *did* know of time intervals. The brick courtyard with a sundial behind his not-street-facing walls measured time. The previous mobile beings had told him of time and the sundial when it had been built. That instruction, and the bit of Flair they'd sent him at the time, had made a strong enough impression that he could access it.

But when the man had come and moved so quickly, Debris and Detritus had not been prepared. Especially since the man wanted to take away the powerful sparkling thing the last person had left. Debris and Detritus had swept a piece of flat stuff under his foot to slow him down.

Now the house had two sparks on the floor, and it appeared that the one from the worked minerals—the brooch!—was stronger. That did not seem right.

He did not know what to do, and he let out distressful creaks until the man made a terrible sound.

* * *

Lady and Lord his back ached! Worse than his head. Bad enough that Zane couldn't deny that he'd awakened from the chill of pain tears on his cheeks. Taking stock, he thought he'd be able to move; he hadn't torn any muscles or broken any bones. Just wrenched the damn thing.

Concentrating on keeping his breathing even and gentle, he let input lap at him and sensed the Flair of the Ivy brooch. The last treasure he could ever hunt and find.

It lay on the floor to his right about two arm-lengths away.

When the pain faded a bit, he rolled, and that didn't seem to tweak his back as badly as he'd anticipated. He came up against a slight ledge. The odor of old smoke and soot filled his nostrils. Extending his fingers, he touched cold metal. He traced it, discovered a fancy pattern, realized it was a fire grate.

His fingertips tingled this close to a great artifact. He refused to recall other times when his hands had nearly burned at the proximity of power.

Stretching over the grate and into the fireplace, he tried to touch the brooch, failed, and felt the sweat of pain coat him. That would chill him fast in this cold house; better to keep his exertions normal.

Rest again and wait. Don't hurry and use energy he didn't have.

Greet. You, said a mature male voice.

Zane jerked in surprise, let himself subside. "Who's there?" But his own words echoed through the chamber, so he felt foolish. "Anyone?" The harsh grating of that word emphasized that the salutation had been telepathic, mind-to-mind.

A Fam! His heart thumped hard. An intelligent animal companion. Lord and Lady, what a blessing, a being to help him get home.

"Fam?" he croaked. "FamCat? FamFox?" He called out the most common Fam species.

What is Fam? came the question, along with a long creak as punctuation, and his hopes plummeted. The building. This place had become intelligent, as happened to some after a couple of centuries.

Lady and Lord. He couldn't send the House to get help. And it sure wasn't hooked into the network of intelligent dwellings, Houses and Residences, or it would know of Fams.

Hope left him, and the chill pain of his body returned. He closed his blind eyes, let dampness ease the aching dry.

Greet you. Hello. Debris and detritus. Please respond, mobile being . . . man.

The odd phrase rang through his head, debris and detritus, usually leftover stuff after he'd finished a treasure hunt. Usually swept out to sea . . . or claimed by small ocean beings as dwellings. Odd bits that floated away.

Couldn't stay helpless on his back; he scooted to a pillar a few centimeters beyond the fireplace, propped himself against the column. Not an ungodly amount of pain, though his back did crackle during movement.

The sound of rustling surrounded him.

Finally, he croaked aloud, "Debris and Detritus?"

YES! That is me!

Definitely a telepathic voice, maybe not a hallucination, since he would never have imagined that phrase. Eh, he could talk until the last of the pain subsided, take the brooch and leave.

"Debris and Detritus is you?" His voice sounded harsh and with an edge.

Yes! Another creak punctuated the word.

"Why Debris and Detritus?" Everyone else on the planet had botanical names, following the lead of the FirstFamily colonists who'd paid for the starships and the trip. Those colonists had formed the culture after what they knew of the Celts—and the twenty-five sacred trees.

But the House replied, *My former person . . . people . . . one, two, three, four . . . no, only three, I think. One, then two. They were scholars and studied . . . studied legends. Ancient legends of the foreland. The place not here.*

"Ancient Earth?"

Yes! That place, and a place of that planet, Greece.

Zane grunted. He knew a multitude of legends but barely recalled those.

This notion of planets is odd.

His throat tickled as Zane began to answer and he coughed. His chest hurt, felt a little soggy. Not good. "The humans—ah, mobile sentient beings like myself—originated on the planet Earth and came through space from there to here, this planet we named Celta."

The atmosphere around him thickened with heavy silence.

What am I?

"You are a House. Capital 'h' because you are becoming intelligent—that is, self-aware and able to communicate in a rational manner with other sentient beings."

Oh. A House. Long pause. *What IS a House? Or a house?*

"A house is a building made by us mobile creatures to protect us. A dwelling."

I have a purpose! To protect a Family.

"That's right. From what I know of houses becoming Residences—" he cleared his throat where the damp fog had congealed, "HeartStones are placed when people—ah—mobile beings, want their homes to become sentient. The stones are blessed and, ah, given energy during rituals and such—" he pulled a hand out of a warm pocket to wave vaguely, though he didn't know whether the House could sense the gesture, perhaps a ruffling of his atmosphere. "And after a time, a critical mass of energy or knowledge or spirit or something sparks, and you, ah, become conscious and intelligent." Sounded good to him.

So I was WANTED.

"So I believe."

And as Debris and Detritus contemplated that in silence, Zane understood he, too, had been blessed. His chill lips curved in a self-mocking smile. He'd been more than blessed. He'd been arrogant. Had considered all the blessings of his life—his Flair, his career, his *sight*—as his due as a member of a Family who'd become noble within the first three decades of landing on Celta.

What is a Fam?

"A Fam is an intelligent animal companion who bonds with a person. Cats. Foxes. Dogs. Raccoons, I think, a couple of birds."

Animals.

"Yes."

I know of this. A pause. *Not humans and usually smaller and not bipedal.*

"Usually smaller. Think a horse or two has become a Fam." Gradually, he began to stretch his muscles, test them, especially his back as he sat up straight, shoulders over hips. Easy does it.

I am Debris and Detritus, the House said with a note of confidence not formerly in its tones.

"Greet you." If he licked his lips, the cold would crack them, but his mouth was dry. He rubbed a hand across it. "I am Zane Aster, of the GraceLady Aster Family." Though the lowest of the noble ranks, 'Grace,' the early founding of his Family gave them better status. "And Debris and Detritus is a mouthful of a name; I'll call you D and D."

That sounds . . . acceptable. A pause. *Greet you, Zane of the Aster Family.* Now the House sounded wistful. Another pause. *We have exchanged names. What comes next?*

Suppressing a grunt, Zane began moving in increments. He pushed himself to a squat, crab-walked back to the empty space he sensed of fireplace instead of wall.

Extending a hand trembling with cold—had to be cold causing the shivering, not more futile despair—and his fingers touched a stone, rounded, no doubt a fabulous gemstone, for some reason the facets under his fingers, and the way it . . . resonated . . . made him believe the gem was a great round ruby. It pulsed like heart's blood.

Yes, now that he relaxed a little, analyzed his senses—undistracted by Flair—he *felt* glimmerings of the treasure that had brought him here.

Zane Aster? What comes next?

"Next I take this nice little bauble and hand it back to T'Ivy and collect the reward."

No!

The whole house shuddered with a force that knocked Zane back on his ass, jarring his damn spine again so he sucked breaths through his teeth.

You can't go. You MUST stay! the House insisted.

"Why?" he asked.

I need a person. A Family. We belong TOGETHER.

Zane paused. "You're lonely." He had a big, nosy, and noisy Family, all ready to mend him, though he couldn't be fixed.

I will think on that word and concept.

Creaking to his squat again, Zane reached for the brooch.

NO! Static electricity snapped through the room. Zane's fingers curled reflexively, protectively.

"Give me the brooch." Gritting his teeth, he stretched, nabbed it. No electric jolt of pain that the intelligent Residence he lived in would have given him. Guess the House didn't know it could do that.

Drop a brick or a ceiling on Zane.

Good.

Bit by bit, Zane straightened to stand—hunched but upright. Soon he'd uncurl from that posture.

Eyes open, he saw nothing but black but recalled the door opening. He glided one step toward it then the next.

You can't go!

Impatient with being told once more this month what he could and couldn't do, he barked, "You can't make me stay." Naturally, he didn't have the strength to teleport. "I can kick in that door I mended." He didn't want to, and his physical strength felt subpar, his back ached.

If you go you will— Debris and Detritus broke off.

But Zane listened hard, knew the immobile being had nearly said something it might regret.

I can tell you a secret.

"Yes?"

A long pause.

The secret may make you stay.

More quiet, until Zane broke it. "All right, I'm a treasure hunter, so I'm a curious man, tell me."

When the answer came, it was a feathery whisper in his mind. *All who leave me leave something behind. It is the nature of . . . me. My being. My . . . Flair.*

That had Zane straightening to his full height, barely aware of his hurt back. His mind played with such a scenario a dozen ways, then he insisted, "That's not all of your secret, is it?"

No. If the person treated me ill, he loses what is most important to him. Loses more than if I like him.

"I don't understand that," Zane replied curtly, but that sure explained finding the brooch here. "You just became aware," he added.

It just happens. I don't do it on purpose. A pause. *I don't think, but if I'm upset—*

Maybe.

"This always happens?" Zane's voice cracked. He couldn't lose the last of his sight, of his Flair, of both, and survive. Could not. Not today. Yes, the House had trapped him.

He turned and pounded a fist on the wall, hurting his fingers. Didn't care.

Why did you do that? D and D asked.

Zane refused to answer.

I feel . . . heat from you.

"It's the heat of anger. You know of anger, ire, fury,

don't you?" Zane snarled. "Why don't you think on *that* concept."

But he couldn't stay still. If the House had been aware longer, Zane would have thought it bluffed. Couldn't count on that.

As he shuffled to the doorway, turned at the threshold, and walked down the entry hall to the main door, he strained to see. And to feel the object in his fingers as more than a brooch, a true treasure.

Gray-shading-into-black sight. Nothing but shaped metal holding faceted gems.

Face it. He'd already lost his sight and Flair.

Today. *Fligger.*

The tiles under his feet squeaked then the House said, *You will lose the brooch and the reward if you leave.*

Minor compared to what he'd already lost. Almost he let his fingers release the thing. His lips curled before he replied, "It is not an honorable act to constrain someone against his or her wishes. To imprison them."

It is not an honorable act to abandon someone! the House shot back.

"I'll come back," Zane grated out.

I do not believe you. This time D and D's voice whispered, so tiny Zane couldn't catch any emotion from him.

"Keep the brooch, then." Zane let it fall. A wind whisked the artifact away. Setting his hand on the latch, he braced, shoved the door open, and followed it into a blizzard.

His caught breath sucked icy air into his lungs, wind

whirled around him, pelting him with snow. He saw white, and thought even if he'd had his vision, it would have been the same.

MotherDam? he called with his mind.

Nothing.

No sense of how to go. He'd turned right into the house, but how many blocks had he walked since the last turn? How many times had he jogged left or right? He couldn't recall because he hadn't paid attention. First rule of treasure hunting, know where you were and how you got there, and he'd ignored that, sunk in despair. Big mistake.

And if he stood out here more than a few minutes, he would die.

If he tried to find his way home, he would perish.

Turning in place, he sensed the quietness of the open door of Debris and Detritus, and returned, shutting it behind him.

The lock clicked shut. He didn't care. Didn't even care when he heard inner bars slide across the door.

You DID come back, the House said tentatively.

"The weather is too bad. I can't make it home in a blizzard. I have to wait it out." He returned to the pillar and slid down it.

* * *

Emotion radiated from the man in wild pulses beating against Debris and Detritus's walls; small heat from that emotion sank into the House's floor where Zane sat.

The man did not speak to him further.

What could the House do to interest him again? To

make him think about the non-mobile being Zane shared space with?

He had said he was a curious man.

Debris and Detritus stretched his mind, considered all of his contents—the things transient people had left and those items the people who had made him had stored near his HeartStones, his brain.

Papyrus instructions, ancient books, audios that D and D had not the skill to access. Memory spheres, but they were too odd and strange for D and D, experiencing the world as a human did. Vizes—recordings of his man and his woman.

He could run a viz for Zane.

Straining with the effort of a new ability, D and D *projected* the viz from one of the stones in his walls.

There, there, three dimensional holographic images formed.

"If I am Debris, you must be Detritus," the man said.

"What's that?" demanded Zane.

A viz, D and D replied.

An ugly, spiky noise came from Zane, harder emotions flashed from him. "I'm blind, House, I can't see a viz."

Oh, terrible that he'd hurt Zane. *I am sorry,* he whispered in his tiniest voice. *I just wanted you to see my naming.*

The House sounded like a child, and its words stopped Zane's futile and ironic laughter. He wiped his sleeve over the wetness on his face, lingering from the storm, his runny nose. Anything remotely like civilized manners were lost to him.

The future looked—*was*—dim. Ha, ha.

So may as well while away the time with the past while the blizzard raged.

"Go ahead," he said gruffly. "Play it, I can hear the dialog, *listen.*"

Very well, Zane, came the high childish voice again. But then, in any terms, Debris and Detritus was a child, even less, a baby with only a full day's awareness. The House's first tones of mature and male were wrong.

"Watch where you're going," boomed a woman's voice. "You've broken the last vase. Left debris all over the floor. Well, I am not going to clean it up this time. It can sit until you do it!"

"No, you're a lump of *in*energy aren't you? If I'm debris, you're detritus. The detritus that life has left of a woman," said the man whose voice D and D had copied.

A gasp, then a sniff. "Well, Mister Papadakis, I don't think that's very nice of you."

In a lofty tone, the man replied, "We are no longer Papadakis. We are the Family Parietaria, and I missed being a GraceLord by one percent."

Zane snorted. That sounded like an old excuse to him. The whole scene sounded well-worn, though it kept his mind off his aches and his future.

The woman grumbled, "But you spend your days researching and writing about that ancient heritage of yours and too much time at night, too."

The man gave a sharp gasp, and Zane wondered if he'd gotten an elbow in the ribs.

He found himself smiling; more, his back had loosened

up, and he'd relaxed against the column. His shivering had subsided into occasional shudders, though his exhaled breath still felt warm against his face.

"Fascinating stuff," the man said. "I'm pretty damn sure that primal energies tagged along with us on our starships." Followed by a hiccup that sounded drunk. Then words continued, "Small and large entities. Why not? Our main religion of the Divine Couple is not exclusive."

"An inclusive religion is a very good thing," said the woman. "The easiest way for humans to pick a fight is to base it upon religious intolerance. We brought our religious fervor with us in many forms—"

"Our beliefs. Energies might stick to those, form into what we thought," said the male, more ponderous.

"Or the major energies of the Divine Couple are real," whispered the woman.

"Who knows?" he grumbled. "And since you complained . . . " A wet smooch . . . kissing?

Zane straightened from nodding off and cleared his throat. "Very educational." he said. "You can stop that now." He drew in a very cold breath, and warning bells alarmed in his mind.

Then he knew. The house was too cold. He would not make it until morning.

Despite the shelter, the cold would invade, and he'd freeze to death. With eyes open to dark gray, he contemplated how long it would take for his Family to find him.

Worse came to worst, they'd hire one of the Blackthorns

to track him—the FirstFamily GrandLord with great Flair and an equally great price, or one of that man's distant cuzes with a minor gift. In any event, it would only be to find his corpse—and the Ivy artifact, of course. If D and D allowed them to leave with the brooch.

Zane's whole body curled as he laughed. Now that his doom had come, he realized he didn't want to die.

Why do you make those noises, Zane? asked the House.

"I'm dying."

What!

"My lifeforce is being extinguished by the cold. Sort of amusing. You came to life yesterday, and I die today."

No!

Zane leaned back, kept his eyes open to blackness. "I have no Flair," he croaked. "Not even to call my Family. Not even to light a fire. I'm blind; I can't teleport when blind. I can't leave into a raging blizzard outside; I would not find my way home."

No, no, NO! said the house. *I will not let you die.*

The House was full of 'noes.'

I cannot have another death within my walls, another decaying human shell. It is terrible. Vermin come. They burrow into me and gnaw on me and bad stuff coats my walls.

That gave Zane pause. "Huh. If you prefer me to die outside your walls, I can stagger some meters down the street." He coughed. It racked his body, lasting longer than he'd anticipated. Well, it wouldn't bother him tomorrow.

No! I want YOU as my Family, the voice in his head sobbed.

Coughing again, Zane said, "There is a fireplace in this room. If you have wood or coal and you can light the fire, I might survive the night." And maybe he should stop talking and just *think* words at the House.

This is why you mobile beings constructed me! I am failing in my duty!

Uh-oh.

Not your fault, Zane projected mentally to Debris and Detritus. *You don't feel the cold, didn't know I needed more warmth than you can give me.*

The ceiling split. Zane heard plaster break, felt chunks rain just behind him. A thump hit a few centimeters near him, and he coughed from the dust.

WOOD! cried the House. *A beam, use it for fire!*

Lady and Lord, Zane matched the moan of Debris and Detritus, *why did you do that? I don't want to hurt you.*

It is done. The pain of the lost beam does not hurt me as much as my . . . fear . . . for you.

"Sorry," Zane managed aloud, through numb lips. But he scrabbled toward the beam, got slivers as he found the broken edge, ignored his back pain as he hauled the thirty-centimeter beam to the fire.

Then he panted and rested. Even such a short exertion exhausted him. His mind fogged as he wondered how to light the beam. *Too* awful to make the House set fire to one of its bones for him.

Fumbling in the belt pouch his nearest sister had equipped and fastened on his belt herself, he touched various objects then found a bespelled firestarter that would work even underwater. No additional Flair needed.

He lit the beam, feeling ghoulish, and rolled to the fire, but began to sink into a sleep he knew he wouldn't awaken from. *Sor-ry, Debris and Detritus . . . just too late. I am glad of your companionship, though I am sorry I cannot spare you the distress of my corpse.* He paused and listened to his slow and ragged breaths, the only sound he made. *Debris and Detritus, I think if you REACH OUT mentally, you could contact other intelligent Houses and Residences. You are not alone.*

I AM! You are leaving me alone! The entire House seemed to contract in the wail that trembled through Zane.

Not enough, the House wept in creaks around him. *Not nearly enough. Please do not die, Zane. Please, fight. I do not wish to stay sentient if another one of my beings dies. I cannot bear it.*

A child, no, baby's cry, that Zane could not ignore. He couldn't summon his Flair, but he could gather all the strength he had. *We . . . will . . . work . . . together.*

A pause in the lament.

How?

Zane struggled with sluggish thoughts. Think or die.

You have Flair. As you were constructed, they gave you strength and energy throughout your lifetime until you became aware.

Yes!

If you can share a little of that with me . . .

I can! I WILL!

Right. I don't know how we can share. Maybe if you run some energy down the beam in the fireplace—

*We will work together! *I* know how we can share energy. My HeartStones—*

And I WILL NOT hurt you further by messing with your HeartStones.

You cannot hurt me through them. I have much untapped energy that I can share!

Maybe he shouldn't put his trust into a newly aware House, a baby, but he had nothing left to lose. Zane found himself clearing his throat, mumbling, "All right then. Tell me what to do."

Stand up and face the fireplace! The order rang in his ears, reverberating oddly as if there was more than one being addressing him.

Nearly beyond him, he forced himself up, staggered, each step jarring his back, making his lungs bellow with breath.

Place your hands on the heads of the sculptures flanking the fireplace. Your reach is wide enough, a high snappish voice instructed, not the House's usual tones.

Zane blinked, saw only blackness, but now that the House mentioned it, he *could* feel the irregularities of sculptures. He moved forward, reached out, and found the tops of the heads of two figures, one male, one female, in the same style as those on the front of the House.

Not just your fingers, curve your hands around the facial features of Debris and Detritus, too! A deeper voice intoned, but now the atmosphere around him seemed to seethe with energy. Heat rose from the fireplace as the beam crackled, burning.

He palmed the faces of the figures.

NOW!

Lightning sizzled, arcing through him, and he yelled.

He'd tapped into the centuries-accrued energy of the House.

Pain zapped down every nerve, slid over his skin, sank to his marrow—raw power.

He screamed as the force filled him, overflowed, heard the shriek of the House, too. Definitely felt the whoosh of the beam as it zipped away from the fireplace, lifted to the ceiling, creaked into place.

He connected with the House; they melded together for an instant, and his own ribs shivered as the beam became whole, the burned end augmented with Flair and other . . . bits of wood left in the rooms. Plaster ladened the air as the ceiling mended to better than new.

He and the House groaned together. As the energies blew through him, he went toppling when his hands lifted from the statues of Debris and Detritus.

He crumpled, stunned.

I love you, said the House. *I will always shelter and protect you,* D and D said in the tone of a solemn oath.

Loving Zane? That was too damn quick, but he didn't say so. Words formed slowly as darkness tugged at the ragged edges of Zane's mind, complete sincerity, *I will always cherish and preserve you. My . . . vow . . . of . . . honor.*

* * *

The man, Zane Aster, Debris and Detritus's *Family,* lay still. D and D stayed quiet himself so he could sense all Zane's life indicators. He breathed, evenly, steadily. His muscles lay relaxed against the House's mainspace floor, his body *warm.*

They had saved him. Zane would live.

D and D's inner trembling receded. He felt as if he, too, could breathe. Odd that he began to think of himself in mobile entity—human—terms, but so it was.

* * *

Zane awoke to heat, and he *felt* that he lay in a patch of sunlight. Even with his eyes closed, he could delineate the ragged swatch of light on his body. He snorted. Eyes closed, right. From what he remembered of the evening before, he wouldn't see anything with his eyes open . . . or straining all his Flair.

Both gone forever.

But . . . he felt that sunlight. And his normal senses fed information to him, his skin, his brain, with a nearly painful acuity. As if those senses had expanded, no, magnified. Expanded exponentially. He smiled at the alliteration and opened his eyes.

Not darkness, but gray. A wavery gray like smoke. He didn't know what that meant other that he remained blind.

"I survived," he croaked aloud. "*We* survived."

Yes. We survived, the House whispered in his mind. *The sunshine on my outer walls has heated them warmer today than many days lately.*

"The storm has passed, and the weather is better."

Yes, Zane.

He could hear all the creaks and soughs of the House, some slight scratching of glass like branches on windows. But not on this level. Straining his ears, he realized the sounds emanated from one of the back rooms of the third floor.

His breath caught with a gasp that became a cough. But this cough didn't emanate deep from his lungs, racking him.

No, he continued to feel good—in muscle and bone, skin and tendon. No frostburn or windburn on his face.

He simply had no sight and no Flair.

But his senses seemed greatly augmented, a conundrum. Something that had occurred when he'd linked with the House the night before? Or the continuing strange results of the underwater accident that had almost killed him and taken his sight and Flair?

Who knew?

Who cared about the why? He didn't.

With an easy move, he rolled to his feet, stretched, popping joints. Yep, felt good.

"The room is warmer." He turned toward the fireplace, could sense the dimensions of the open interior, the individual pieces of charcoal in the pile, glowing red or white.

His hands recalled the feel of the two carved statues on each side of the fireplace with enough detail that he could form the images, male and female, in his mind's eye.

Slowly, he turned in place. His sight yet showed a dark flat gray. But the pressure on his skin, even through his clothes, told him where the columns were, the five tall rectangular windows in the back. He knew how far the ceiling loomed over his head and the dimensions of the doorway a few strides away.

Turning his palm upward, he commanded, "Lightspell!"

Nothing. Not a bit of Flair for him to draw on, the psi magic he'd felt pulse through his nerves all his life.

Blind and empty of Flair.

Zane? the House sounded nervous.

"I'm here," he said absently, still taking stock. Trusting in this new awareness, he strode across the room, stopped a few centimeters before a column. Raising a hand, he brushed it over the cool stone and frowned; it seemed to him that the pillar was of a light-colored marble . . . but not white. Odd.

This whole thing was odd.

The strangest days in his life. He whirled and jogged across the room and through the door, down the short hallway, noting another door on his left that would be the front room with the bow windows he'd seen yesterday evening.

Pretty much his last image was of the house.

ZANE, WHAT ARE YOU DOING?

Stopping at the front door, he lay his palm against it and linked with the House.

I FEEL you!

I feel you, too, he replied mentally. *You and I worked together to save me.*

You saved me, too, D and D said simply, *I'm glad you didn't die and rot on my floor. That is scary and nasty, and I couldn't go through that again.*

The atmosphere in the room trembled around him as if the air pressure suddenly dropped.

Zane grimaced. "I imagine so." Such a young entity

would have hidden his awareness from death and decay within his walls and perished if Zane had died.

Yes. We saved each other. He stooped and picked up the Ivy brooch-artifact, then added aloud, "I'm going to turn in this piece of jewelry for the reward, file a claim for you and your land so I will be named as owner."

Owner!

"I don't want the general public to know you're sentient yet. Not with your unique qualities. I want no harm to come to you. And I'll have to find out how other recently intelligent Houses became their own persons." He paused. "I think they are all associated with a Family."

You will be my Family? A tiny breeze scraped papyrus scraps around the room along with the equally tiny mental whisper.

"Absolutely!" He said it so loud it rang against the walls, more, so it sank into the House so D and D would believe him. "I'm also going to arrange the move from my . . . previous . . . abode to here, D and D. I'll be back within a septhour, seventy minutes."

You promise?

"My solemn vow of honor, and I have never given that to anyone before." He paused. "Except for you, last night. You should have memories of all the circumstances of a solemn Vow of Honor. I would suffer if I broke it."

I . . . care for you. You would hurt me if you betrayed my trust.

"I care for you, too. I'll be back." He paused. "One moment." He strode back into the mainspace, no stumbling or staggering now. He knew his surroundings. Oh, there'd be no deep-sea diving and treasure hunting for him anymore, but he had Flair. Maybe not. Not Flair, but he had some sort of talent or gift that mitigated his blindness.

He touched the stylized face of the male, Debris, then the female, Detritus, the sculptures flanking the fireplace. Gave and accepted a blessing.

Then he turned and walked to the front door, said the phrase he'd only given members of his Family before, but then, this House *was* his Family, now. "I love you, Debris and Detritus. I'll be back shortly."

I love you, Zane Aster of the House of Debris and Detritus. I will wait.

Zane chuckled and slid aside the bars, unlocked the door, and stepped into a cold, clear day. No doubt the sun shone, a white star in the deep blue sky; pain flickered.

Zane? asked the House.

"I'm all right," he murmured, though no one walked along the street for blocks. He couldn't see the sun or the sky, but he knew that. He took off down the street with a long stride. Someday he might learn how to teleport again; for now, he could walk the few kilometers to the GuildHall and turn in T'Ivy's brooch, file a claim for the House.

And he knew he'd left something behind after all.

Despair.

* * *

The House hummed to himself, a jaunty song his Family, Zane, had taught him. He tidied himself up as much as possible, found a button from Zane's jacket. He swept it into the pile of other small and interesting items next to the fireplace pillar of Detritus. He dusted and cleaned the entire house using the stored Flair he'd learned to tap.

His Family returned, as promised, within the septhour and pounded on his outside wall, to the right of his door. The House felt the warmth of his living flesh, and through that flesh the joyful emotions of the man. Then he felt a . . . brightness on the wall next to the door. A metal plate that someday he might be able to modify enough to see the street. Fascinating!

What is it? he asked his Family.

Zane said, "It is a name plate, designating you as an individual and an intelligent House."

Oooooh!

"It says 'Debris and Detritus House, Aware this Month of Willow, 424 Years After Colonization, Zane Aster Family.'"

YES! trilled the House, then welcomed his Family inside.

* * *

Like smoke rising, the minor gods, Debris and Detritus, removed themselves from the statues of the fireplace, their attenuated essence twined into the bedrock beneath the House, separating themselves from the newly intelligent being. They had helped the House become sentient, but now they wished to be individuals.

They'd linger, though. Rest and wait and grow stronger for a few decades.

Then they'd leave this sanctuary and run free.

* * *

About the Story

Celta is a planet of magic, telepathic animal companions, and romance . . . currently there are fifteen books in the series (including a novella collection). Throughout my Celta series, I've had walk-on (walk-INTO) characters of intelligent houses, sometimes minor, sometimes major secondary characters, arranging from the amusing to the grumpy to the obsessive. In this story, I wanted to show a House Becoming Aware.

Robin D. Owens

Small Gods

Chandaelaine Spurlock

"You bastard." Moira crossed her arms against her chest and leaned away from Tony to sneak a quick glance at her watch.

"Who took the jam out of your donut?" Tony tightened his grip on the pole as the train braked for the platform at Tottenham Court Road station.

The bifold doors sprang open with a hiss, and Moira stepped onto the platform without so much as a glance in Tony's direction.

"What?" Tony stumbled out of the carriage and into the path of a man in a tailored suit. The video feed on the suit's tablet flickered.

"Watch where you're going, mate! You . . . uh . . . " The words evaporated on the man's tongue under the heat of Tony's stare. "Sorry. My fault." He slipped past Tony with a watery smile, his hooded eyes fixed on the cement platform. "Didn't see you there."

Tony raised his right eyebrow and leaned forward, the charcoal gray lapel of the man's suit gripped tight in his right hand. "I think you did."

He wrenched himself from Tony's grasp, sprinted down the platform, and flung himself past the rush hour crush onto the train moments before the doors slid shut.

"Stop doing that to people. Not his fault you weren't paying attention." Moira frowned into the depths of her brown leather handbag, her cheek brushing the knuckles of her left hand as she gave the bag a violent shake. She popped up from her excavation, right arm buried elbow deep in the brown leather, only to be lashed in the face by her hair as the train pulled away from the platform. "Did you get his wallet?"

"Of course," Tony patted the breast pocket of his black wool trench coat. "Calfskin."

"That's all right then." With her left hand, she hefted the handbag back to her face and stumbled away from Tony toward the concourse.

Within two steps, his right hand rested on the small of her back to guide her through Tottenham Court Road tube station, past the construction barriers, and into the queue for the escalator.

She remained unusually silent throughout.

"Just showin' 'im I'm 'ard enough." In spite of hours of dedicated practice his new accent had more in common with Dick Van Dyke singing jolly songs with a broom than any East End wide boy.

Moira jerked her arm free of from her bag and held the Oyster up toward the overhead lights. "Found you," she said under her breath and stepped onto the escalator. "I don't remember waking up this morning with a fucking chav. A pompous ass . . . "

"Oi!" He stepped onto the escalator one riser below her, leaned forward, hooked his chin over her left shoulder. His posh accent purred in her ear. "Is this better?"

"Yes." She spun to face him, seized the lapels of his coat, and jerked him forward. Her lips brushed his as she said, "I don't sleep with chavs."

"Never?"

"Not ever." In one graceful motion, she turned, stepped off of the escalator, and flicked the hood of her black wool coat over her head.

"Whose Oyster card's that?" Arm looped across her shoulders, he kept her close and his face hidden from CCTV as they queued for the turnstile.

"How do you know it isn't mine?"

"Yours has a picture of St. Paul's and The Gherkin. That one has a picture of Kate and Wills."

He was rewarded with the beginnings of a smile twitching at the corners of her lips. "It's Hunter's alibi."

"Is that today? Too bad for Simon. We'll have to do flowers or somfing for the funeral."

"It'll be your funeral if you don't stop it with the Jason Statham-Guy Ritchie nonsense." She veered out from under his arm, cut into the queue to her right, and slapped the alibi-generating Oyster card against the reader. Careful to keep her face turned away from the CCTV cameras, she pushed through the gray plastic barriers and let them flap closed behind her.

Tony ducked his head into his scarf and pulled his driving cap low over his ears as he sidled through the barriers to rejoin Moira.

Buzzers sounded behind them. A wave of British Transport Police jogged past in a beeline toward the locked barriers. The low murmur of the crowd turned to the disgruntled roar of a mob as more people realized they were trapped inside the station. As Tony turned to look back over his shoulder, Moira snagged his right arm and dragged him toward the Oxford Street escalators.

"Don't look," Moira's whispered with a shake of her head. "We've struck again."

"You don't know that. Could be anything: system failure, hackers, strike."

"That's our fault," She threw off the hood and hooked her right thumb over her shoulder toward the station as they stepped out onto the pavement at Oxford Street. "We just broke the transport center of the Universe."

"Not this again." He rolled his eyes. "I'll stop with the Cockney if you promise not to bang on about our being cursed."

"You have yet to sound Cockney—like the Queen having a stroke, but not Cockney." She tugged at his arm with a tilt of her head toward Neal's Yard. "Come on."

"No." Tony set his feet. "I'm not going down there. I'd rather starve than eat another organic, vegan, three-bean and dirt salad, I don't care how good it is for me. Never again. No." His eyes lit up. "Look, Burger and Shake. Now that's what I'm talking about."

"After our appointment."

"You lured me away from the office with the promise of food, not mysterious appointments." His eyes narrowed. "Is it something to do with the wedding?"

"You'll see" failed to shift him toward Neal's Yard. She heaved a sigh and said, "I swear to God there will not be salad, three-bean or otherwise." There was a tight smile on her face, but the deep furrow between her eyebrows said, "I'm going to give you a kicking."

"Maybe this time the place won't burn down." Her brow smoothed, and she relaxed her stranglehold on his arm as they walked.

"That wasn't our fault."

"Their solicitor disagrees." She led him down the twisting passage, past the scattering of café tables on the pavement to where the brickwork for Neal's Yard Remedies met with Walk-in Back Rubs. "This is us."

"Which one?"

"Here." Moira pointed toward a narrow, arched doorway wedged between Walk-in Back Rubs and Neal's Yard Remedies. The hobbit-sized blue door stood open below a beaten wood sign which squeaked in the winter wind. Upon the sign were the words, "Madame Charisma's Psychic Services, Love Found and Fortunes Told." Below the telephone number, in small Gothic script which followed the curved bottom of the sign were the words, "Curses Removed Upon Request." Beyond the door, a flight of stairs climbed into darkness.

"That door wasn't here before." He did slow sweep of

the street with his eyes from right to left.

"The door's always been here." She started up the narrow staircase, turned half-\way up, and bent over to look back at Tony through the open door.

"That door," He leveled his index finger at the offending portal, "wasn't there two minutes ago." Hands balled into his trouser pockets, he rocked back on his heels, eyes fixed on the sign. "Where in the bloody hell did it come from?"

A broad grin spread across her face. "There's only one way to find out."

* * *

The office was covered in an array of rainbow-hued cushions, scarves, and throws and packed to the rafters with crystals, fairies, and other New Age baubles. Four uncurtained windows the height of the small room ran along one wall, allowing a weak winter haze to cast a gray pall over the blinding décor. The only surface not covered in cushions or crowded with fairies were the two bright orange fiberglass 1950s waiting room chairs upon which Tony and Moira perched.

"Completely ordinary office, is it?" The stale patchouli and sandalwood incense trapped in the room's thick air stung his eyes. He brushed tears with his knuckle and sniffled.

"Yep." From her handbag, she pulled a palm-sized, blue leather journal, a stainless steel Sharpie, and a tissue, which she passed to Tony. With the journal and the Sharpie safely gripped in her right hand, she pulled the bag's cross-body strap over her head and let it land on the carpeted floor between their chairs.

"You don't think there's something odd?" He crossed his legs, uncrossed them, and then slid forward to balance on the lip of the chair's seat. Resigned to twenty minutes of physical misery, he slid back into the beach ball-shaped seat indentation and tried to blink the incense out of his eyes.

"Could do with a clear-out." Her uncapped Sharpie hovered in expectation over a fresh page in the journal balanced on her right thigh. "The fairies look a bit evil."

"The fairies. Right." He stared at a small pewter figure on the corner of the desk, certain it was either Ian McKellen as Gandalf or Merlin as, well, Merlin.

A wisp of a middle-aged woman in full West End-costume-shop gypsy regalia, from her aubergine turban with gold lamé stars to her bedazzled slippers, slid into the room. Each of her pale arms was covered to the elbow in enough bangles to outfit a harem, which clattered as she moved across the room. She glided past them in a cloud of rosewater and threw open the window at Moira's right.

"I'm your psychic, Phyllida. Sorry about the smell, the place doesn't half-reek. It's all the hippies, you know, trying to dispel ghosts or spirits or some such shite."

"Where did she come from?" Tony scowled at Moira, his arms crossed tight against his chest.

Moira blinked at him once, twice, then said, "Through the door in the paneling, you nonce." She turned to Phyllida and asked, "Don't you believe in ghosts?

"Of course I do, pet, but a load of good it will do to try to gas them out of the place. That'll never work. Now, what can I do for you?"

"We have an appointment with Madame Charisma," Moira tapped her pen on her journal, "at 1:15."

A cheeky grin spread across Tony's face, and he raised his eyebrows as he peeked at Moira out of the corner of his eye.

"I bought the business from her years ago now, flower; kept the name for continuity like. Keeps the older ones coming round, if you know what I mean. So, why are you here, luv? Is it 'cause of him?" There was an amused glint to her eyes as her sharp glaze flicked to Tony. "£150 to know the true love of your life. Small price to pay to be shot of shifty here." She blinked and vanished for an instant, reappearing as though nothing out of the ordinary had occurred.

Tony shot forward in his chair, eyes riveted on Phyllida. Startling shades of neon pink, teal, and yellow eyeshadow were slathered across Phyllida's eyelids, each blink a testament to the effectiveness of urban camouflage.

To Moira, Phyllida said, "Special discount rate of £75, flower. He's pretty enough—" she leaned forward across her desk and said in a conspiratorial stage whisper "—but he's got some issues, dear."

"We're cursed," said Moira.

"He's not as bad as all that, like I said . . . "

"Your sign says, 'Curses Removed Upon Request.' Well, we would like to be uncursed." Moira's pen ratta-tat-tatted against the journal page. "Whenever you're ready."

Stunned, Phylllida's head bobbled about on her neck.

"Why do you think you're cursed, dear?"

Tony scratched his nose to hide his widening grin from Moira.

"Well . . . " Moira launched into a blow-by-blow account of the past twenty-four hours, starting with the morning's accidental stoppage of the London Eye and ending with the Oyster card failure at Tottenham Court Road.

Phyllida blinked in the silence, her brows knit over her nose.

Tony flung his right hand up in mock exasperation and began to stand. "Fantastic. We can go now. I wonder if Burger and Shake is still serving lunch?"

"You're not going anywhere without me." The tight look of certainty on her face brooked no further argument. Moira sat back in her chair and studied her nails. "And then there is the wedding to think of."

"Are you sure you don't want that address, flower? I'm sure you can get most of your deposits back, and the dress will keep for the right one."

Tony dropped back into the chair and turned to Phyllida, all humor wiped from his face. "We're cursed. Fix it." He caught Moira's eye and said, "I've paid a plum for this wedding, and I'd like to see it go off."

"And it's affecting our work." Moira turned to Tony, "Like that thing with Petrov's video files."

"Oh, no——" Tony definitely waved his right index finger in the air "——that had nothing to do with me. He wanted the jump drive. I got him the jump drive. Not my fault the damn thing was blank. Just bad luck's all."

"You can't blackmail someone with a blank jump drive; now he wants us to—" Moira lapsed into a slurry Russia accent "—make it right."

"Oh, so you're police then?" asked Phyllida.

Both Moira and Tony's eyes locked on her.

"Ah, no," said Moira.

"Not exactly," said Tony.

"But . . . " Phyllida's voice trailed off. "Oh. Right. So, no blackmail for Mr. Petrov. Okay, I take it that's bad. Right, uh . . . right." She nestled back in her chair with a waggle of her hips, pressed her palms together in front of her chest, closed her eyes, and began to hum. Mere seconds later, her left eye flew open and fixed on Tony. "I have consulted with the spirits."

"Really?" was Moira's incredulous answer.

Phyllida's shoulders relaxed and her right eye opened; with a dismissive wave of her hand, she said, "Of course not, luv. It's just what the punters expect. Got to give the people what they want."

"Well, that was £200 well spent. Right then, let's . . . " Tony tilted his head toward the door.

Moira bent down to retrieve her handbag.

"Have you consulted the London Guild of Minor Gods?"

"Pardon?" said Tony, who thought Phyllida looked a little smug for someone who talked complete bollocks.

"Sorry?" Asked Moira as she sat up with her bag in her hand.

"The London Guild of Minor Gods." Phyllida's mouth

dropped open. "Oh my, that's what the problem is. Well—" her left hand fluttered to her chest "—that explains everything." She dove under her desk and, after much bangle-clanging, reappeared and heaved a massive leather tome-onto the desk.

On impact, two crystals, a pendulum, Gandalf/Merlin, and an untold number of fairies all jumped two inches to the left into the cloud of dust which exploded from between the book's frayed leather covers. Several small, weathered pieces of paper were blown from between the book's pages, fluttering to the carpet like dead moths.

Phyllida dropped into her chair and threw open the book's cover, the poison green nail of her right index finger flying down each page. The finger stopped. She gnawed her bottom lip as her index finger tap-tap-tapped on the ancient paper.

"1832. Well, it has been a while, hasn't it?" Elbows propped on the pages of the open book, she leaned forward to say to Tony and Moira, "Debris and Detritus are two halves of the same whole. But now you have met. Lovely. And you won't stay the hell away from each other. Perfect. We have gone 183 years without you two showing up. Let your reign of destruction begin."

"What in god's name are you on about?" Slack-jawed, Moira gawped at Phyllida.

"Oh, you two are Debris and Detritus, darling, Greek gods of destruction or chaos or something or other. I knew it the minute you came through the door. Now, being invited to join the London Guild of Minor Gods is quite an honor. There are a number of gods who have fallen out of fashion during the past few years, but everyone is going to want to know about the two of you, yes, they are. Now—" a dash of smugness crept into her voice "—I am, myself, the Romanian Goddess of General Bookkeeping and the guild's registrar, but you won't know it by looking at this lot." She smacked the ledger with the open palm of her left hand as her guffaw turned to a snort.

"You're a fucking nutter," Tony whispered in awe.

"Now—" Phyllida swayed back and forth in the universal signal for 'bad news.' "There is a small fee to register."

"Of course there is," said Tony. Money was firmer ground for him, at least until he glanced at Moira, who tilted her chin up—her way of saying "yes" to something he wanted to say "no" to. "Which I am happy to pay?"

"Excellent! The sooner we have contact information for the two of you, the better. You can start by signing here." Phyllida spun the book around to face them.

Tony stood and took the bright pink quill pen Phyllida thrust his direction. On a blank line near the bottom of a page labeled "Gods: Greek: DETRITUS" wrote, "Tony Johns" and watched as "Johns" morphed into his actual surname of "Carlton-Wheeler."

"Nice try, shifty." She took the quill from the stunned Tony and offered it to Moira. "It's your turn, flower. Right here under the label 'DEBRIS.' Lovely, dear. Now, there are a few things you need to know." From her right-hand desk drawer, Phyllida pulled a pamphlet made from a single sheet of tri-folded A4 and laid it on the desk between Tony and Moira.

"You and Your God-Like Powers: A Guide for Modern Deities," read Tony aloud then bit down on his tongue to keep his laughter at bay.

"Pull up your chairs, and we'll go through it together," said Phyllida. She took them through it line by line, placing a tick mark next to each point as though they were opening a high-yield checking account. Once she was satisfied the perfectly silent pair understood each of the salient points, which included: monthly meetings (mandatory), a direct debit membership fee (mandatory), and registration with the Ministry of Small Gods within the next 30 days (also mandatory), Phyllida collected the £175 registration fee and sent them on their way. Albeit with a reminder that the next Guild meeting was the following Thursday at 8:00 p.m. at the Neal's Yard Meeting Rooms. They would not want to be late.

They remained silent as they climbed down the steps and walked through the twisting passage of Neal's Yard and to the intersection of Monmouth and Shaftesbury Avenue.

In front of The Diner, Moira pulled the carefully folded pamphlet from her handbag and read out, "At no time shall any deity carry out an unauthorized (i.e., rogue) smiting. See Section A, Paragraph 16c for instructions on acquiring an Application for General Smiting, Type A22."

"My particular favorite is Item 14a, Paragraph 2g, Guidelines for the Proper Care and Feeding of Hellhounds."

"Worth every pound," she gasped out between bursts of giggles.

"Talk about commitment to the part. Jesus." He wiped away his tears of laughter with the back of his hand. "I didn't think I was going to make it."

"I am never getting rid of this; it's worth it just for the laugh." She jammed the pamphlet back into her handbag. "Do you know where I could get a gypsy rig? Don't think I would need it for long."

"Are you kidding? You in that outfit, with a few copies of that pamphlet, we would make all our Christmas money in one go."

They crossed Shaftesbury Avenue enraptured with the economic opportunities provided by a cheap room, a piece of tri-folded A4, and a gypsy costume so did not notice the signal failures in their wake.

* * *

TWO WEEKS LATER

Moira padded barefoot down the front hall and ripped open the door to a stupidly tall, lanky git in an ill-fitting suit holding a beaten briefcase and leaning into the buzzer. She cocked her head to the right, took in his too-wide tie, white button-down, and plastic rimmed glasses, and pegged him for either a low-level clerk or a missionary.

The lanky git pushed his glasses back onto the bridge of his nose with a long index finger, cleared his throat, and said, "Hello, I'm Reginald, your liaison with the Ministry of Small Gods. May I come in?"

"Tony's never going to believe this." She stepped out of

the way to let Reginald into the house.

* * *

Twenty minutes of internet searches, document checks, and telephone calls to two of Tony's former schoolmates who did secret sneaky things in the name of Queen and country confirmed Reginald was, in fact, Reginald. The Ministry of Small Gods was his domain.

Reginald, for his part, could not stand still. He bobbed, weaved, shifted from foot-to-foot, twitched, and once, even did the cha-cha while sweating bullets under an unhappy Tony's gaze.

"Well, you see . . . " Reginald pushed his glasses back into place, bobbed his like a chicken, cleared his throat, and then said, "as newly identified deities, I am here to help you—" he shrugged his right shoulder "—ah . . . inform you what you can do for your country."

It was his third run at the speech.

It was not received any better than either of the previous attempts.

"This'll be a laugh. Go ahead, son, show us what you've got." Tony crossed his arms against his chest and waited.

"Well . . . okay. Right." Reginald spun in circles, his head snapping from side to side.

"Stop before you hurt yourself. What are you looking for?" asked Moira.

"I put . . . here!" Reginald fished his tablet computer out of his briefcase and hit the home key. "We're not heathens, so no worries, you won't need to start until after your honeymoon, which will be in Dorset."

"No, we're going to Italy for two weeks." There was a hint of laughter in Moira's voice.

Reginald wrinkled his nose, bobbed liked a cork, then said, "Sorry! Your passports have been canceled. Bad luck that, but we can't be having any unscheduled plane crashes, now can we? No, of course not. Oh, and sorry about this, but of course, if you refuse to do this small gift of a lifetime of service to your country, both of you will be prosecuted for a variety of crimes against the state." His toothy grin failed to amuse. "Okay. Right. Shit. Okay, well—" he flicked his index finger across his iPad screen twice "—stopping the Eye, causing an Oyster reader failure at Tottenham Court Road, signal failure at Shaftesbury Avenue and Monmouth, theft of a Matisse from the exhibition at the National Gallery . . . "

Moira shot a hot glance at Tony. "I thought it was a print."

"Ours is a print."

Reginald continued. "The theft of three sheep from an Inverness market, multiple car thefts, interference with twenty-three ongoing police investigations, and—" his right eyebrow crept into his hairline "—a rash of cat shavings in the East End."

"He can be prosecuted alone for that one," said Moira with a scowl.

"It was your idea." Tony scowled at her in return.

"And that is just what you have been up to the last fortnight. Need I go on?" Reginald looked up from his iPad to find two pairs of angry eyes staring back. Nerves frayed raw, he did a neat little box step cha-cha combination, pushed his glasses up his nose and his mop of curls off his forehead, and then dropped into a gray linen club chair.

"How is Dorset this time of year?" Moira asked Reginald.

A broad grin broke across his sweat-damp face, and his shoulders sagged in relief. "It's lovely."

* * *

About the Story

"Small Gods" is the first story in the new series: "Ministry of Small Gods." Stay tuned for more Moira, Tony, Phyllida, Reginald, massive system failures, crap accents, and seriously shifty business.

The grift will continue in: *The London Guild of Minor Gods,* coming in June, 2017.

Chandaelaine Spurlock

Queer Eye for the Dead Guy

Rhonda Eudaly

"WHY? WHY? WHY ME?" Hades slapped his palm against his forehead in time to the questions. "I became the god of the Underworld to get away from those two! How could Zeus do this to me? I haven't done anything to him . . . lately."

"You know what this place could use?" A highly chipper and bubbly voice echoed through the reception area.

"Besides a good scrubbing? Did you see that river?" A nearly identical voice answered. Both voices giggled.

Hades vaulted off his throne and frantically scanned the room for an escape route. He had too many choices, too many doors. One headed to Tartarus. One was the gateway to the Elysian Fields—which few people realized was actually a small town in East Texas. The third door led back to the rivers and the Gates to Hades. The fourth led to Hades's personal living quarters. Unfortunately, most of the chambers in this part of the Underworld were made of stone, so there was no telling exactly from which route the voices came.

"Hades! There you are!"

He froze—something most thought impossible in the Underworld—as the two annoying minor gods approached from the rivers. He turned and forced himself to smile through clenched teeth at the immaculately coiffed and attired twins. "Debris. Detritus. What can I do for you?"

"Do?" Debris cocked his head, puzzled.

"For you?" Detritus echoed. They looked at each other and laughed. "Oh, my Olympus, no."

"It's not what you can do for us, dear Hades." Debris made a grand, sweeping gesture. "But what we can do for you."

"Oh, yes, Hades, Zeus sent us just in time. This place needs a complete makeover. It's so . . . so. "

"Last Millennium?"

"Exactly."

"Do you have to do that?" Hades demanded, rubbing his temples.

"What?" the twins chorused.

"Do that weird twin speak, finishing each other's sentences thing," Hades said hotly. "It's giving me a headache."

"Your headache is probably because the Feng Shui in this place is all wrong!" Debris flung his arms out to include the whole room.

"Or it could be the dust." Detritus flicked a linen handkerchief and dabbed his nose. "It's a more common and insidious allergen than most people know."

"Give us a week," Debris said. "You won't recognize the

place, and you'll feel better. We guarantee it."

"What are you going to do?" Hades enunciated every word.

Detritus puffed out his chest. "We'll do for you what we did for Olympus. For Zeus. It'll be fabulous. You'll love it. Just think of how much better this place will be with a few potted plants!"

"Throw pillows!" Debris' eyes glittered. "Can't you see this place with big, colorful throw pillows?"

"Pillows? Why do we need pillows?" Hades's headache bloomed brighter, bordering on migraine.

"And you know, a nice light wash on the walls would really brighten up this dreary room." Debris completely ignored Hades, and his gestures grew more flamboyant as his excitement rose.

Hades ducked more than once to keep from getting socked in the jaw. If anyone was going to be hit before all of this was over, it wasn't going to be him. "Though something to throw might not be so bad." No one heard him.

He finally cleared his throat. "Excuse me, what about me? Don't I get a say in this? It is my Underworld after all."

"Darling, why would you want a say?" Detritus asked, without looking at him. "You had your chance. Now it's our turn. Zeus decreed, and we must obey."

"You have got to be kidding me." Hades rubbed his temples a bit more. There was a vein in his forehead starting to throb. "I've got to do something about this headache."

"We'll be here." Debris pulled out a tape measure.

"There's *a lot* to do."

"That's what I'm afraid of," Hades said as he fled to his quarters. He could still hear them.

"You know what I'm seeing here, Debris?"

"I think I know where you're going, Detritus."

"Curtains!" they chorused.

"Persephone!" Hades bellowed.

* * *

"Well, they did say you wouldn't recognize the place," Persephone said uncertainly a couple of days later.

"It hasn't been a week yet." Hades raked aggravated fingers through his hair. "What else could they do?"

"It's not that bad, Hades, and I think the cushions on the thrones are nice. I didn't like sitting on cold stone all the time. It was hard on the posterior. And if you don't stop pulling your hair, you're going to go bald."

"But *this?* This isn't so bad?" Hades yanked his fingers out of his hair and gestured at the River Styx. "Just look what they did to Charon and Cerberus! At least they have the decency to look embarrassed."

"Yes, Master," Charon picked at the gold-trimmed sleeve of his new white uniform.

"Well, it's a bit classier than that old black shroud," Persephone tried to find the bright side to things. "Welcoming, even."

"Welcoming?" Hades voice rose in volume and timbre at the thought. "We're not supposed to be welcoming! No one's supposed to want to come here—not even the ones who make it to the Elysian Fields!"

"Well, Charon does look like a refugee from the *Love Boat*; maybe that'll scare some souls off."

"There is that," Hades grudgingly admitted. "But what about poor Cerberus? Look at him."

The Hellhound guardian hung all his heads in shame, his serpent tails tucked between his legs.

"What's wrong with him?" Persephone asked.

"He's been *groomed!* They've put bows around his necks," Hades stormed while pacing the banks of the Styx. "And what did they do to his tails? Have they molted? How's he supposed to turn back unwanted souls looking like that? Wait, what are you doing?"

Persephone looked up from scratching Cerberus's ears. The hound had rolled over on his back with all his tongues hanging out in pure doggie pleasure. "What? I'm sorry, honey, but I couldn't resist. He's cute!"

"Oh, for Olympus' sake!" Hades threw up his hands and stalked off. "I'm going to have words with those neatniks. Where are they?"

"I think they were going to tackle Tartarus today, dear."

"No! Not Tartarus!"

Hades took off through the Underworld at a dead run.

* * *

"This has got to go, don't you think, Detritus?"

"Oh, absolutely, Debris."

Hades slid to a halt and couldn't hide his complete horror as his jaw dropped open. The brimstone smell was gone. So were the open pits of lava. He couldn't hear one scream of everlasting terror, not one whimper of unending regret. "What's going on? Your changes to the Elysian Fields were one thing. The Fields are supposed to be nice. Souls are supposed to strive to go there, but this is Tartarus. What have you done? Where's the fire? Where are the tortured souls?"

"Oh, all that stuff had to go," Detritus said with a flick of his wrist. "It was all garbage, and trust me, we know our garbage. Renew. Recycle. Reuse. Resale! We made a bundle in that rummage sale over in the Elysian Fields. Those good souls know a bargain when they see one."

"Though to some people, we do unearth treasures," Debris added. "Did you know you had a full collection of world dictators down here? You could make a fortune on the collector's circuit. On eBay alone."

"Oooh, eBay? Not eBay. It's so passé." Detritus tapped his chin while he thought. "I know! Craigslist! We could unload some of the picked-over stuff that way."

"That's a fabulous idea! Detritus, you're brilliant."

"Why thank you, Debris. I thought so myself."

"Why can't you just leave everything alone?" Hades finally lost his temper.

"Where did we put those Asian wall hangings?" Debris asked. "Those would so go in this space. Those bloody battle scenes would be perfect in here."

"Battle scenes, Debris? I don't *think* so. Take a look around you! This place doesn't want more blood and gore. It wants contrasting themes. Flowers. Bunnies. Puppies!"

"You know, Detritus, you may be right. Some nice fluffy kittens, maybe. What do you think of chihuahuas?"

"No, not chihuahuas. They can go feral, you know."

"That would be bad, but I see flowers."

"What are you . . .? How . . .? Chihuahuas? Bunnies? Flowers?" Hades couldn't make the words come out. "This is Tartarus. It's not supposed to be . . . Excuse me . . . I have to go . . . "

Hades didn't see Persephone when he stormed into their quarters. She looked up from the basket she was rummaging through when he started banging around. "Problems, dear?"

"I need something for a headache. Then I need to talk to Hermes. Zeus has to take them back before someone dies."

"That's nice, dear. I assume Hermes won't be staying for dinner," Persephone said absently, bouncing a ball in her hand and heading for the door.

"Not unless you want him underfoot for the rest of time." Hades finally focused on the ball. "What're you doing?"

"Cerberus wants to play."

Persephone closed the door behind her, cutting off Hades' frustrated scream.

* * *

Hades slumped at the table with his head in his hands.

"Dude! That must've been some party. You should've invited me, man."

Hades dragged his head toward the young voice, glaring at the messenger god.

Hermes took a step back and lifted his hands in surrender. "Whoa, dude, sorry. Guess it wasn't a party. Wassup?"

"I need you to get a message to Zeus. I need him, *now*."

"No can do, Hades." He looked around. "Something seems different. Have you done something to the place?"

"Why can't you deliver my message to Zeus?" Hades asked.

"He's gone to ground. Mortal ground." The messenger god looked around puzzledly. "Hera's in one of her Moods. Dude, what's different?"

"Great. Just great. It's going to mortal ground that puts Hera in those Moods. Now what do I do?" The god of the Underworld slapped his forehead repeatedly with the heel of his hand.

"Dude, why're you doing that?"

"Because if I bang my head against the wall, it would leave a bloody mess, then I'd never get rid of them."

"Get rid of whom?"

"Debris and Detritus."

"Oooohhhhh." Hermes nodded knowingly. "Enough said. I wondered where they went. I'll do what I can, man. But you know how Zeus gets when Hera's in one of her moods."

"Why do you think I took on the Underworld instead of staying on Olympus?" Hades shuddered picturing Hera's tantrums.

"I hear you, man. I'll see what I can do."

"Thanks."

Hermes was on his way out when he looked back. "By the way, who're the serious babes I saw coming in? Usually I get a bunch of grief from the Furies, but I didn't see them, just some hot chicks . . . "

"No! Not a makeover on the Furies! They didn't!" Hades took off at a dead run. "That's the last straw! Find Zeus before I do something drastic!"

* * *

Hades paced on the edge of the mortal realm when he saw Zeus coming. "It's about time you showed up. Didn't Hermes tell you it was urgent?"

Zeus shrugged. "I came as soon as Hermes found me. And you know if he can find me, Hera's not going to be too far behind. She's still in the breaking-things mood, and that usually means me. So let's make this quick, okay?"

"Hera's not the one you need to be concerned about, it's me."

"What're you talking about?" Zeus asked.

"Debris and Detritus. You have to take them back. Now."

"Oh, come on, what's got your chiton in a twist, Hades? They're good kids. Besides, they're good at what they do, and they were getting bored. They've done all they can with Olympus. I had to do something before they started trashing things just to have some garbage to deal with, though with Hera, there's almost always something in pieces."

"So you sent them here? Without warning and without asking? Gee, Zeus, I know you're in charge and all, but wasn't that a bit harsh? I haven't done anything to you . . . lately. Just wait till you see what they're doing with the place. It's not the same anymore." Hades dragged Zeus into the Underworld with him.

Debris and Detritus were oiling the hinges on the Gates of Hell when the two major deities found them.

"No!" Hades rushed forward, totally forgetting Zeus was with him. "You're going too far this time! You can't oil those hinges!"

"Why not?" Debris and Detritus asked together. Debris looked particularly puzzled. "What's wrong with a gate that doesn't squeak from all the rust and corrosion? A well-oiled gate is a long-lasting gate. And who says the Afterlife has to be an unpleasant experience?"

"I do!" Hades shouted. "I say so! I have a particular ambience set up down here, and you're ruining it!" He turned to Zeus and gestured madly. "Back me up here, Zeus. You have to take them back to Olympus with you. They're driving me crazy."

"Maybe they have a point?" Zeus shuffled uncertainly. "I never really did like the noise those gates made. It was an awful lot like that fingernails-on-a-chalkboard sound."

"That was the *point!*" Hades was losing ground. "You have to see what else they've done. This is no longer the Underworld mortals have come to know and fear."

Hades took Zeus on a thorough tour of the "new and improved" Underworld. The god of the Underworld felt his rage build to epic proportions as he discovered further changes. Debris and Detritus had been busy while his back was turned.

"You should do something about your anger issues," Zeus said as they toured Tartarus. "That vein in your forehead is about to burst. And trust me, the results aren't always that pleasant."

"But *look* at this! There's no fire, no brimstone!"

"Well, wasn't that all hot and stinky anyway?" Zeus looked at the twins. "What *did* you do with the fire and brimstone?"

"We have all that routed into the saunas now," Detritus said proudly. "All those renewable, reusable resources were going to waste. And if the immortals don't set the example . . ."

"Gah!" Hades couldn't get any words out. "What's going on with the souls doomed to Tartarus? You never told me what you did with them. Where are they? It's too quiet in here."

"Oh, we've put them on a rotating schedule. The noise was just awful, all that weeping and gnashing of teeth. Just awful. Had to go," Detritus said. "So we've taken care of that. The souls are either in the HDTV theater watching endless reruns of *Gilligan's Island* or being the animatronic children in the *Small World* ride at Disney World. They were just cluttering up the place hanging out here, anyway."

Hades screamed.

"There goes that vein again. I hope you do better with whatever comes out than I did. Athena's a real handful. And those weapons and armor of hers really hurt." Zeus rubbed his own forehead as he looked around some more. "I don't see the problem here, Hades. It seems like they're doing a great job getting this place clean and organized. Olympus has been a paradise since they got done with it."

Hades felt his eyes go so wide, he thought they'd pop right out of their sockets. "You've got to be kidding. How many times do I have to say it before it gets through to you people? This is the Underworld! It's not supposed to be a paradise. Why is this concept so hard for people to comprehend? I thought it was pretty clear!"

Hades thought his head was finally going to explode until he realized Zeus wasn't kidding. He grabbed Zeus' arm and dragged him out of Tartarus. He didn't stop until they were in Hades' receiving room, where he had to blink in the brightness of the lights.

"Why in the Underworld is it so bright in here?" Hades demanded at the top of his lungs.

"Oh, that would be the lights reflecting off the Hell's Bells," Debris answered.

Hades whirled, not realizing the twins had followed them. "What did you do? What. Did. You. Do?"

"We polished the Bells, and it's about time, too. It doesn't look like they had been cleaned since the beginning of time. Now, they're shiny new."

Hades turned to Zeus, eyes flashing with psychotic rage. "Get rid of them, Zeus! I'm telling you, if you don't, I'm going to commit deicide! Put them among the mortals if you have to, but get them out of here!"

"Come on, Hades, I don't see the problem here," Zeus said.

"I'm getting really tired of repeating myself, Zeus! The Underworld is supposed to be ugly and dirty and nasty. We have an image to maintain, and it's *not* this! The poster boys for Scrubbing Bubbles don't have any place in my realm! How are souls supposed to abandon hope if the Gates have flowerbeds around them and the Guardians of the Underworld wear ribbons and bows?"

"Well, you don't have to be so mean," Detritus said in a huff. "We were just doing what we were born to do! Weren't we, Zeus?"

Hades didn't wait for Zeus to answer. "Get rid of them, Zeus, before I go totally insane, and I don't think this world is prepared for that!"

He saw the possibilities whirl through Zeus' eyes and finally click. "That would be worse than Hera on a bad day, wouldn't it?"

"Think every bad monster movie ever made from every culture gone crazy at the same time, live and in person." Hades's calm, even tone was scarier than his shouting. "Teenagers running in high heels, the pointless screaming, going through obvious doors with death behind them, stupidity running rampant . . . "

Zeus waved him down. "I get the picture, Hades. You've made your point." He turned to the twin deities. "Pack up your squeegees, boys, we're going back to Olympus."

"But we're not through here!"

"Oh, yes, you are," Hades lunged for their necks. "One way or another, you're out of here!"

Zeus grabbed Hades before he could reach the two lesser gods. They looked at him in uncomprehending horror. Then, as they realized their peril, they broke and ran.

Hades herded all three unwanted guests out of the Underworld ten minutes later. Just as soon as they were out of sight, he sighed deeply in relief and turned back. He took great pleasure in slamming the Gates closed behind him. His first step on the road to normalcy was to rip the ribbons off Cerberus's multiple necks. The Hellhound thumped his tails gratefully, leading Hades to scratch behind one set of ears.

"I have to admit you do smell better." Hades stopped and shook his head. "No! I'm not going to find the good in this."

Hades let Persephone rub the tension out of his shoulders and temples when he finally went to bed that night. When he was just about to drift off to sleep, he heard her say softly, "You know, a housekeeper's not such a bad thing. Maybe we can get them to come back once a week or so."

Hades sat bolt upright, screaming.

* * *

About the Story

"Queer Eye for the Dead Guy" has been one of the most amazing journeys of my writing career. If you read the Foreword, you'll see we've had quite the road to here. It's a tribute to humor, to people now gone, and frankly is kinda the basis for my part of Redheads of the Apocalypse. Find out more about the journey, the stories behind the stories, at my website.

RHONDA EUDALY

Used Goods

Toni McGee Causey

IT WAS A ROUTINE day inside the skinny three-story building that housed the Used Goods store near the heart of the French Quarter . . . until the sword starting singing to Miranda.

Swords did not ordinarily sing to her, you see, and this just would not do. A customer might come in and hear it. People were usually rattled when they stepped inside, compelled, she had begun to suspect, by something they didn't understand, and a singing sword was just one notch of crazy too far for many of them to handle.

She told the sword to *hush*, but the sword kept singing.

Off key.

It really was quite irritating. People passing right there on the sidewalk would sometimes pause, confused, looking straight into the little bay window displays that Griff had set up, baffled by the terrible singing, she supposed, not guessing it came from the sword in the window. Not that all of them could even *see* the window, but that was another bag of worms entirely.

Miranda dusted the haphazardly stacked merchandise on the back wall behind the counter, wary of the little tin soldier who liked to try to stab her with his bayonet when she wasn't looking. She couldn't *prove* he was trying to actually stab her. She just kept finding him awfully close to her arm with his bayonet positioned menacing-like, even when she would have sworn he was on a different shelf not five minutes earlier.

"Not today, Lt. Birnbaum," she told the little soldier as she swiped over him with her feather duster, because it was just ever-so-slightly easier to think she hadn't completely lost her mind if these things had names. "Maybe tomorrow you'll have better luck. Off you go, back in your box." And she scooted him back into the tattered Birnbaum Shaving Kit box where she'd first found him and Griff had said he was supposed to stay, but apparently, Lt. Birnbaum had felt quite differently.

The sword in the window sang a little louder, somehow more irritatingly out of tune, though it might have been aiming for some sort of Irish ballad, so maybe it was singing it correctly.

"Please stop it," she told it again, and it ignored her. Again.

"Under no circumstances are you to touch the weapons," Griff had warned her on her first day. *"Never. Ever. For any reason. Not even a little bit. I will know, and you will lose your job immediately."*

"If you don't stop it," she told the sword, "I'm going to tell Mr. Warm-and-Fuzzy. Maybe he has a nice vault somewhere."

The sword got a little quieter, though it didn't cease altogether. She rolled her eyes and hoped no one came in and complained about the noise.

Of course, customers rarely wandered in, at least not of their own volition. Which was weird. She had no idea how the store managed to stay in business.

The front of the store looked all of its 200 plus years in age—paint of an indeterminable color had faded and flaked off to the point where most of the original stucco was exposed, grayed from dirt and grime. The building might have once been glorious with its balconies (two floors of them) and wrought iron balustrades, but now it only sagged there like a once-formally dressed old lady who'd been struck with leprosy and only wore rags.

In other words, it was exactly the kind of place tourists looked for and swarmed like gnats. She checked the doorknob to make sure it was unlocked.

Yep. Definitely unlocked. Not a single customer all week.

She glanced back at the stack of thingamabobs she'd just dusted, and she blinked. Every item was in a different place than they'd been five minutes earlier.

"It's not like I actually *plan* for the weird things to happen," she told the fat little elf statue that clutched a four-leaf clover over his head as if hiding from the world. If she tried to remember what she'd thought he'd clutched yesterday, she'd have said a gold ball—clearly her powers of observation were on the fritz, or there was another one of those figurines around the store somewhere. "Odd things just happen around me. It's not my fault, right?"

She could have sworn, for just a split second, that the elf shrugged.

The sword got shriller, though she hadn't thought it possible.

"No kidding," she said, stomping over to the display in the bay window, "I may not be able to touch you, but I can surely find some sort of tongs and use *those* to toss you into the oven. There's a kiln just two blocks over."

The sword switched to something that sounded like a fight song, but the volume had gone down a couple of notches. If she had to guess, she'd say it was seething, which really, that was nonsense. It was an inanimate object.

Inanimate objects *do not seethe.*

Honestly, this was more crazy than even she was used to. Maybe the shrinks had been right all those times they tried to put her on medication when she was in the foster care system.

But some of the meds made her quite sick, and the rest knocked her out for entire days. She couldn't finish school, sleeping her life away, and she couldn't get a job, or get out of the foster homes, if she stayed sick. Sometimes the side effects had been hideous, like hives and swelling and horrible acne, though she didn't tell a single soul about the one time she developed something that she swore to herself looked like scales. Actual *scales.* Which probably explained her addiction to cheap body lotion that she smeared all over her arms when she felt herself beginning to lose it.

She looked down and realized she was holding the lotion bottle right now that was usually tucked in her pocket, smearing like crazy, covering her arms.

Damned singing sword.

* * *

She'd first been aware that the store was stalking her three weeks ago.

It was her second year of living on the streets. She'd gotten out of jail after a slight misunderstanding over who exactly possessed the jewelry she'd been found to be carrying while traipsing out of a house where she'd not—strictly—been invited to visit.

In all of the times she'd stood on that corner, trying hard to play her slightly battered, wholly stolen violin for money and passing up opportunities to pick the pockets of lazy tourists, there had never been a skinny, three-story building facing her from across the street.

She'd been playing some random piece that came into her head—it was always some random piece of music that wouldn't let her be, so she might as well make a few bucks off it—when between one blink and the next, the store was there with a battered sign in the window that read:

DEBRIS & DETRITUS
USED GOODS

She'd stopped playing and stared, and a honeymooning couple who'd been listening to her threw her worried glances, along with a five into her hat, and she didn't even bend down to grab it and shove it in her pocket, lest the gutter punks snatch it and run with it like they had last week.

Miranda might only be twenty-three in physical years, but she was at least forty on the street and had seen more crazy than anyone ought to, and *even that* didn't seem to brace her for the surprise of a building being where it was clearly not supposed to have been.

There were now seven buildings on the block, when there had only been six before. It didn't have an address on the front, which, really, how silly of them, and she wondered what type of Used Goods they sold.

Not that she had any money for that nonsense, because she was barely holding her own at the shelter as it was. People didn't know how much it cost to be homeless. People were right daft sometimes.

Miranda had shaken herself from her reverie, picked up the tune where she left off, and when she was done, glanced back over, and the storefront . . . was gone.

She blinked, closed her eyes, and then looked again, but nope, the street was perfectly normal. Well, as normal as the French Quarter gets.

It happened again the next day. She'd riffed on a song, thrown in something random, then realized the building had appeared. This time, sporting a HELP WANTED sign.

She was standing on a different street corner than the day before.

Miranda squeezed her eyes shut, and by the end of the song, it was gone again. Her playing suffered, because it was just a little difficult, you might agree, to concentrate on playing well when a building was pranking you and you were wondering if you wandered into an ER, if they'd bother giving you an MRI or skip all the paperwork and just go ahead and ship you off to the crazy ward. Probably the crazy ward, since she didn't have insurance, she decided, and so she packed up everything, determined to look unruffled, and sauntered back to the homeless shelter. She hung out a couple of hours before they opened for the night, listening to the others to see if anyone else had noticed anything weird.

After overhearing three conversations about sparkly aliens and another guy talking (to himself) about how dinosaurs needed to quit stealing his blankets, Miranda gave up hoping for enlightenment.

She refused to look at any of the buildings.

The third day, when the building appeared between two famous restaurants that Miranda knew actually shared a wall, she wasted no time. She needed money, and she wasn't letting some stupid stalker of a junk shop screw with her again.

She cut her song right there in the middle, scooped up her hat and her violin case, and marched past two corners——one with a sax player who made her want to linger and one with a short, drunk guy laying out knives to juggle that she carefully avoided—until she finally found another unoccupied corner.

She set out her hat, primed her violin, and started playing.

Miranda felt it before she saw it: like ants crawling into her hairline.

When she looked up again, mid-song, the blasted Used Goods storefront had followed her.

She was being stalked by a skinny-ass building that didn't—couldn't—exist.

The July heat was scorching, and she was surely coming down with something. Insanity, probably. She ignored it, and then when she looked again, the HELP WANTED sign was back, with a big sign next to it:

Yes, you, Miranda.

"That's not even funny," she muttered under her breath.

It's kinda funny.

. . . the sign read, and when she blinked again . . .

You've passed the interview.

"Oh, hell, no, I haven't," she grumbled, flinging everything into the fiddle case, her head bent over it.

The sign stretched so low, it almost skimmed the sidewalk, where she couldn't help but see it.

1 bedroom apartment

Food

Clothes

Low pay (hey, you can't have everything)

Apply within.

She stared for all of two seconds before she irritably hiked up the case and stomped across the street.

"You should have said so in the first place," she muttered as she stormed through the door.

She waited at a filthy counter for more than an hour,

and when Griff showed up, hostile and snarling, he said, "Well, I guess I don't have any choice about it. You're hired."

He looked as mean as he sounded; tall, with a craggy face that looked rock-hard and angry.

"Really. And here I thought it was just me who had no choice in the matter."

"Clean up. Everything." He glanced around as if really noticing it for the first time. "That should keep you busy."

She looked over the massive stacks of antiques, bric-a-brac, and items so long past their usefulness date, they were practically moldering on the spot, and saw enough dust and grime that a backhoe would be necessary.

"You're kidding," she deadpanned. "I can see why sales are so brisk."

"If a customer comes in, be polite, but *do not sell them anything* unless I say it's okay. We don't sell stuff."

"But . . . this is a store, right? Not a museum."

"Of course it is," he muttered, as if just now discovering that fact.

"Well, here's a nutty thought: if we sold some of this stuff, it would be a lot cleaner in here."

He looked back at her, and she almost could have sworn his face looked like . . . actual granite . . . and there was this strange *hush* in the place, as if all sound had drowned.

"We don't sell things to just anyone," he said, revising. "I decide who, what, and when. Not you. You shouldn't even be in here, but that decision's out of my hands. So clean."

"So . . . clean stuff. Stuff that we're not going to sell. How again is this a store?"

"Feel free to leave."

Food. Privacy. Money. For that, she could put up with almost any amount of crazy. Even this.

"And try not to be stupid."

Crazy did not have to include insults. But still. She bit her tongue.

"Okay, got it. Clean. Don't sell. Do I leave it all jumbled like this?"

He looked around again and sighed.

"You can try to straighten up. Not that it's going to do any good. And don't touch the weapons. *For any reason.* Under penalty of death."

She'd smiled and offered him her hand. "Deal."

Smiling always drove them crazy in the group homes.

That was three weeks ago. Now Miranda stood, straightening up the cupboard next to the bay window, the one which housed all of the pieces of a knight's armor, wondering (not for the first time) why anyone would think used armor would sell. It was tarnished and bent, and she was afraid that the brown stains might have been blood.

The sword started screeching another tune. She could not imagine that it could have managed to sound worse, but it did.

"Oh, for the love of all that's holy," she muttered in the sword's general direction, "Have you no pride? The *least* you could do is try to mimic an actual *song*, if you're going to torment a body."

The shrieking grew, making Miranda's bright red curly hair stand nearly on end, and she moved near the sword, careful not to touch it, and shook the velvet-lined saxophone case where it was lying, in all its ugly glory— why something that plain was in a fancy velvet case was beyond her, but maybe it was a sales tactic—and it screamed louder still.

"Hush!"

And then, in the blink of the next second, the front door . . . vaporized. Or seemed to, and there was someone standing there, someone in a horrible looking costume— complete with demon horns and two spare heads. It wasn't Mardi Gras or anywhere near Halloween, which gave her pause, until she realized that someone had very likely meandered in when they were looking for a private costume party.

"Can I help you?" she asked, cringing as the sword seemed to bray and cry. Maybe the person couldn't hear it—maybe it was all in her head—because he didn't seem concerned about the noise. He didn't answer, and he hadn't looked fully at her. At least, not that she could tell. She was pretty certain the center head was the real one—though the costume eyes on the other two heads seemed to rove around the room. She silently awarded points for a Very Good Costume, even by New Orleans' standards.

"Sir?" she guessed, wishing for the first time Griff would show up and deal with this customer. He'd made the last one cry and run back out in five minutes flat. "Do you need something in particular?"

The man turned to her. One face held what she might have termed a quizzical expression, only the head had tilted forward at a 90-degree angle to the body, and a tongue had slithered out, tasting the air, snake-like. "Great, uh, look. Is that a from a movie filming around here?" she asked, and he took a step toward her.

Fear flashed all over Miranda, a sudden freeze of icy cold racing up her spine, and without thinking, her hand closed . . . and the hilt of the sword was somehow in her palm.

The screaming stopped, and a song—something Miranda knew in her bones—came welling up from the soles of her feet, through the bone and flesh and steel blade of the sword. For the first time in her life, she didn't feel . . . alone. The music washed over her and seemed to cloak her, like a cape, and she couldn't tell if the costumed customer could hear the music, but he paused, as if concerned.

She chanced a glance around, hoping for Griff, and saw, instead, at least a dozen little . . . gremlins. Goblins. All manner of creatures. All frozen, shocked at the sight of her holding the sword. All of their mouths hung open, paused there as if she wouldn't see them if they didn't move.

One blinked.

The elf, who now held something that looked eerily like a small hand grenade.

"You!" she pointed the sword at the elf, who blushed but tried vainly to pretend he didn't notice her. "I *see* you."

"All hail," the customer whispered, sarcasm dripping

from every word, wrenching back her attention, his gravelly voice a rasping sound that shivered her every nerve, "The Queen of Dragons. The Griffon thought to hide you here. How clever."

She looked around just to be sure there wasn't some statue he might have been referring to.

"Hi," she said, thinking he might have gotten another step closer when she'd glanced away. "My name is Miranda. I work here. I dust, mostly. There aren't really many customers. Could I interest you in that cauldron over there? It looks like it would go with your costume. Really great look, by the way. What movie are you here for?"

One of the other heads cocked, like he found her puzzling, and really, that was one autonomous head too many.

"He thinks to disguise you," the guy said.

So the cauldron wasn't the way to go. "We have a sale on elf statues," she suggested, pointing at the row of elf statues which seemed to have grown to a couple of dozen in the last few minutes, all of whom looked aghast and affronted at her spontaneous offer.

She was absolutely certain she'd never dusted more than three at any given point. "Just this morning, in fact. 50% off. They're really cute. And they will bring you good luck."

"Has your keeper left you?" the guy wondered, tongues now slithering out of the two non-speaking heads. "Does he think to fool us? We will not be swayed from our path, Queen of Dragons. You will never reign again."

And he *moved*, slicing across the air with talons Miranda

had not fully seen but had leapt backward from on pure
instinct. She raised the sword in defense, something that
would have made absolutely no sense to her ten minutes
earlier.

And it SANG as lightning sizzled along its edge and it
seemed to throb with music. *Angry* music.

"Ohhhh," she marveled, pointing at the sword with her
left hand, "I don't think it likes you. I think you need to
leave."

The man—or creature, she had about given up hope
that there was something normal at work here—sprang
forward, claws out. She blocked with the sword again, but
apparently, she'd waved it, too, and off went one of the
hands, green blood spurting as it rolled across the floor.

Miranda had enough time to think:

"Ewwww!"

"Oops!"

"Sorry?"

Before the creature regrouped and came at her, green
blood spraying the walls, the elves (who all ran, screw this
pretending we don't see you thing). One elf was slimed
with blood and ignited! Three goblins grabbed a nearby
tapestry, probably expensive, and started beating him with
it to put out the flames. Or they had some interpersonal
issues.

The demon spun, spraying more blood *everywhere* and
then his freaking hand regenerated, and now?

Now he looked pissed off.

"Ohmygod, *run!*" she yelled to the other . . . elves and

goblins and gremlins, holy crap, meds were looking pretty good right about now, because *clearly*, she was losing her mind, trying to fight off an acid-bleeding demon in a Used Goods store that didn't even freaking *sell* anything.

Swinging a sword? Not nearly as easy as they make it look on TV. She missed the demon (twice), the sword was screaming out of tune, and she lopped off the arm of a statue (dear God, let that one actually be a statue) like cutting through butter, but she was losing ground and fast. The store just wasn't very big, with that many aisles to run down, and the demon seemed to be . . . growing.

"Low pay my freckled ass," she muttered, wondering if there was a hazard pay clause in the form that Griff had made her fill out.

The sword screamed a warning, and she ducked just in time, cornered now, and something large and fast *whooshed* into view between her and the demon—

The air exploded.

Something with giant black wings swooped down in front of her, and she flew backward, landing with a hard crack as the demon's three heads rolled one way, and his body started bubbling as it fell into a chaise longue that was definitely going to have to be reupholstered now.

Blech. She had not even had *caffeine* yet.

The massive wings expanded and stretched, blocking her view of the body. Idle thoughts like *police, jail, accessory to murder, maybe I can plead insanity as a defense* ricocheted in what was left of her mind as the immense . . . person's . . . *wings* continued to stretch, practically touching each wall, they were so tremendous. They shook, shivering, almost vibrating and then suddenly: calm.

The calm was far, far creepier.

Miranda scrambled to her hands and knees and up to her feet, heading for the back door. Not again. No way. She was out of there.

The huge beast landed in front of her, and the floor trembled under the impact.

The midnight-black wings folded back in, lying flat, and she heard Griff's voice, somehow lower and scarier, though how that was possible, she did not know.

"I told you, Miranda, *do not touch the weapons.*"

Griff has wings? Holy shit!

"I swear, that was not my idea. It was the sword's. It just showed up in my hand when creepy three-headed guy came at me."

Griff turned then, and Miranda nearly went dead at the sight: he was beautiful, terrifyingly so. Everything in her screamed *run, he will kill you* and the sword hummed a loud, hostile chord in her head.

"Shut *up,*" she told the sword. Then she saw the anger flame in Griff's eyes and she backed up a step. "Um, not you. The sword. It won't shut up. It's really really annoying. Here—take it. I'm sorry I touched it."

Griff glared at the sword as if he'd like nothing better than to hoist it into outer space.

"I didn't mean to touch it, honest. It kept screaming." She looked down at it. "I think it was lonely. I mean, the singing was a tip-off, and that was bad enough, but the screaming was just a bridge too far."

"It's singing to you." He was clearly unhappy about that. So was Miranda because obviously, she was the only one it could torment. She'd like to share that little fortune with him, the way he glared at her, like this was somehow her fault.

"Where was it?" he asked, like this was a trick question.

"What do you mean, where was it? In the window, where you put it. In the velvet case."

She wanted to add *duh*, but thought it best not to push the angry guy *with the wings who just killed a demon.*

"The saxophone," he said, to himself, disgusted, which made absolutely zero sense. "Sonofabitch."

"Am I fired?"

He frowned, grim and resolute. "No."

She was unexpectedly and quite unreasonably relieved.

"Now we are at war. And unfortunately for you, you're the leader."

"I quit!"

* * *

Miranda could have sworn actual steam wafted from his nostrils.

She backed up another step and set the sword down on its velvet box.

As soon as her hand let go, a crashing wave of wrongness flooded her, and the sword screamed so loudly, she thought for a moment her eardrums would shatter. She touched it, and it paused, quiet, waiting for her to decide what to do next.

"Back away from it," Griff said, the weight of authority in his voice so strong, it practically had a gravitational pull.

And yet. She couldn't quit touching the sword. She wanted it. Badly. She'd never actually wanted anything, besides food, a place to sleep safely, a shower, and she wouldn't say no to some shiny jewelry (she looked fondly over at the pristinely clean jewelry case), but the sword? Belonged to her.

"I don't know why it's screaming when I set it down." She picked it up again. "Does it have an off switch?" she asked her boss. It must have some sort of electronic proximity gizmo, and she searched the hilt. She hadn't remembered the hilt being quite that ornate, and quite that shiny of a silver, or why she'd thought it was ugly before. "Was this a film prop? Because they did a pretty good job. I don't see any 'Made in China' stamp, either."

She looked up to see Griff had covered his face with his hands, as if he needed to keep them busy to keep from strangling her. It was that distinctive *strangling* vibe that made her take another step back and look away.

"Anyway, if you'll show me how to turn it off, and give me my wages, and by the way, an extra two weeks severance would not be at all out of order here. I'm sure there's a ton of OSHA violations I could report."

Griff *roared* and the glass shook, things fell, lots of little elf and goblin and gremlin faces peeked out of hiding spots and then snapped right back out of sight again.

"Oh, you know, on second thought, I'll just leave leave. Um, real quick. I'll go get my clothes and violin."

She peeked up at him again. The wings had disappeared. But his typical *I'm so exasperated with you, I could squash you* expression was firmly locked in place, only now that she knew what he was—she laughed wildly in her own head— the expression looked far less annoyed and far more murderous than she'd realized before.

He just killed someone. Three feet away from you. Get out!

The body and the heads were gone. The elves and gremlins and goblins or whatever they were, were now out of their hidey holes, and all pretending to be frozen in different positions.

"Um . . . what happened to the body?"

"The portal absorbed it," Lt. Birnbaum replied from the counter as if that was a perfectly rational thing to happen. She squinted at him, and he doffed his little hat. "The store—Ma'am, as it's called here."

"That's enough, Michael," Griff snapped, and she peered back up at him. "As you can plainly see, there are more things here going on than you understand. Unfortunately for you, I'm not allowed to explain them."

"There are rules, but you can't tell me? Why not?"

"Cursed," said the elf with the grenade—and really, was that a real grenade? That couldn't be a good thing. Should she take it from him?

Griff flicked a small motion toward the elf, and he was frozen—unable to speak or move for real.

"We can hint," Mr. Birnbaum stated, rather argumentatively, she thought. "But we cannot explain. To do so brings on ramifications. You must learn and grow on your own, and if you don't, you die."

"Wait, what? I *quit* already. I don't have to keep following rules, although if you ask me, telling someone they'll die if they don't is just a little harsh. I'm sure there's some sort of harassment code against that . . . " she saw Griff's glare and her voice got smaller, "um, somewhere." For heaven's sakes, she was arguing with a statue and something that had wings. Maybe he'd drugged her food. That had to be it.

"Look, I'll just set this down . . . " And she tried to set down the sword again, but it screamed so loudly, the glass in the windows cracked, "or maybe not. How much does it cost? I think it's lonely. I'll just buy this with whatever's left of my paycheck after room and board and I'll be on my way. Not dying today, though, thank you for the job, and, um, place to stay when I needed it."

"You need to learn," Griff ground out as if it was painful for him to talk to her. "You are untutored, unaware of what is going on, and unable to defend yourself." He buckled to one knee, as if fighting against some sort of torture as he pushed out the rest of the words. "Take the sword, at least. If you call me, I will come. But know this . . . if you call me, you are committed."

Huh. I'd have to be committed to call you.

"Do you have a scabbard? I can't exactly walk around the Quarter with a sword."

"It will . . . disguise . . . itself," Griff ground out, going down on another knee, one hand braced against the floor. She could see his shudders, his muscles knotting and flexing and rolling and wow, did that look . . . awful. It made her stomach flip, and her knees felt gooey with fear.

"*Go!*" he yelled, and she ran for her things in the upstairs apartment, grabbed her little stash of money, her violin, her clothes, and not having a clue what to do with the sword, stuck it in her belt, then hightailed it back down to the store. Griff had gone somewhere else again, and all the little elves were frozen, all the little thingamabobs were still and quiet and not the least bit suspicious. Mr. Birnbaum was back in his shaving box, looking forlorn as usual, and there was absolutely no reason to stay.

It broke her heart.

"Goodbye," she whispered, and not a single sound whispered back. "Be well."

When she stepped outside into the heat of the summer in the Quarter, the Used Goods store wavered and disappeared. She glanced down, and the sword had become a bright purple parasol, its hilt now a curved handle, its blade now frilly and sparkly where it lay at her thigh.

"That cannot be a good thing," she thought, as the crowds dodged around her, not a soul seemingly surprised that she had materialized out of a wall where no door now existed.

* * *

On the upper balcony of the Used Goods store, if you'd been able to see it, (and it's not your fault that you cannot; there are things at work here you are yet to understand), two men reclined in beautiful chairs, a lovely tea service set between them. One, Debris, who was the more practical of the two, sipped his mint tea with a frown on his unlined face. He was ancient, though he looked as dapper as any young fifty-year-old might, and he was quite proud of that fact. You could see his confidence in the cut of his seersucker suit, the sweet bow tie, the white chinos, and the high polish of his two-toned shoes.

Detritus was practically slovenly in comparison, in his too-currently-popular shredded jeans, tattoos covering whatever he felt like should be covered today, long hair wadded in a leather tie, falling out haphazardly, with some of it tucked behind his ear. He ignored the tea and drank beer, instead, and though he looked more like a thirty-something rocker who'd lived a very hard life, he was actually slightly older than Detritis, by a century or two. Possibly more, though no one had ever gotten the truth out of them, least of all Griff.

If Griff had bothered to look behind him at the building, he'd have seen it glowing like a jewel box—stunning cobalt blues on the outer walls, pristine white trim, perfectly gorgeous windows that led to rooms so welcoming, you'd have sworn some master interior designer had plucked your favorite style from your mind and strewn it before you like diamonds. Griff, frankly, was sick of this shit and wanted to kill them both.

It was nigh on impossible to kill demi-gods. He'd tried for a few centuries, so he should know.

"Do you think, dear boy, that she'll stir up quite a lot of trouble?" Debris asked him, and Griff ignored him.

"It's going to be a blast, either way," Detritis said, and

he was probably composing some song or ode to the impending disaster. Just another one to add to the thousands he'd accumulated.

Griff's anger raged beneath the surface because he knew they didn't care. Miranda was alone, out there in the world again, and they were going to enjoy the apocalypse from a front row seat, and there wasn't a damned thing he could do about it.

"Yes," Debris agreed with his partner, smiling into his tea. "Yes, quite."

They watched as Miranda hiked up her backpack, which held most of her worldly goods, her violin case in one hand, the sword now appearing as a parasol dangling off her other side. Oh dear Jupiter, she didn't even know to put it on the correct side where she could get to it quickly with her right hand.

"Please try not to kill her again so soon," Debris added, almost as an afterthought, but Griff knew nothing Debris said was an afterthought. "It's so delicious to watch this, knowing now she's found the sword. She hasn't found it all of the other times."

"How many thousands?" Detritus asked him.

Griff continued to ignore them both, watching her disappear into the crowd on Royal.

"Oh, hundreds of thousands. I've lost track of the millennia. You're getting soft, Griff," Debris teased. "You never let her live long enough to get close to the sword before. What's changed, I wonder?"

He didn't answer. He sat like a gargoyle on the

balustrade, watching her, knowing his other half walked away into certain death. And if she managed to live, he would have to kill her again.

He was so tired of having to kill her.

She'd made him promise. All those millennia ago. Part of him wanted to let her live long enough to remember him, to remember that damned promise, just so he could strangle her for having made him make it.

Part of him knew she'd been absolutely right to do so.

Why had things changed this time?

Griff didn't know. He couldn't put it into words.

Loathing, perhaps. Loathing of what little of himself he had left.

Maybe that's all it was.

It sure as hell wasn't hope. He knew better.

* * *

About the Story

One of the best things about dear friends who are also writers is that they understand your particular brand of Crazy. One of the worst things is that they generally encourage it. Pooks knew I'd been noodling with a fantasy dragon series. Something fun and action-y and crazy and set where I live, in the French Quarter, and then she upped the Crazy by suggesting I add these two not-quite-prime-time Greek Gods to the mix. All I had were the names, and they popped to life for me and were absolutely perfect for the story. That almost never happens with others' suggestions. (Thank goodness Pooks isn't into pushing crack, or I'd be a goner.)

What you see here is pulled from what will be the book. Join my newsletter (www.ToniMcGeeCausey.com) to see exclusive offers, snippets, and general fun news, including contests.

TONI MCGEE CAUSEY

GARBAGE IN, MONSTERS OUT

IRENE RADFORD

DETRITUS SCURRIED BEHIND HER older sister Aphrodite across the manicured lawns of Mt. Olympus. Aphrodite discarded an orange peel without looking at the "No Littering" sign Zeus had placed deliberately along the path his divine daughters and immortal sons usually walked, neatly circumventing the sacred fountain at the center. When that didn't keep the lovely children from dropping food, used handkerchiefs, decorative shawls, and feathers from their headdresses, Zeus assigned his youngest children, the half-mortal twins Detritus and Debris, to pick up after their older siblings.

"Spoiled brat," Debris whispered to his sister, younger by two minutes and therefore inferior to his superior knowledge of their world.

Aphrodite had to have heard his comment. Instead of acknowledging the insult, she waved joyfully at Apollo, just coming off his chariot ride across the skies. He slapped his driving gloves and gauntlets together and tossed them vaguely in the direction of the twins.

"That's debris," Detritus told her brother. "They need to be saved, cleaned, and put where he can find them again."

Debris shrugged. "Here comes Herakles and his apple core. That's yours." He ducked the flying bit of garbage so his sister could catch it in her drawstring bag and not have to touch it. Aphrodite wasn't so polite. She dropped the rest of her orange peel off to the far side of the path, sending Detritus scurrying to pick it up.

"How come we get stuck with the suckiest job Pops could think up?" Debris grumbled.

"Because by the time we were born, he'd run out of beauty to bestow upon us. We're the youngest and the ugliest, therefore we are garbage and thrown away," Detritus replied.

"We never had garbage before the Romans drove us out of Greece to this refuge," Aphrodite said. "We had mortal servants happy to pick up after us. It was getting pretty ripe around here before you two came along to help us out."

"At least now we have a job instead of drifting about doing nothing. Pops can't deny us a fair share of ambrosia anymore," Debris said, looking toward the athletic field where Herakles showed Hades the fine points of a discus throw. The ghost of Xena looked on, tut-tutting at every mistake.

"We get a servant's portion, not a family-sized bowl." Detritus stared at Aphrodite's handkerchief. The goddess of love, the epitome of beauty, had blown her nose on the fragile piece of woven cotton with a needle lace trim.

Detritus wondered if the immortals ever had to blow their noses in the before times or if her sister did this just to make more work for the unappreciated twins.

"Hey, sis, you dropped something," Detritus called after Aphrodite.

"Go trip over it," Aphrodite sneered. Then she smiled up at Apollo, and the entire world stopped breathing in awe. The sun, Helios, froze in place at the horizon, lingering to limn her in glorious light.

Sure enough, a compulsion to obey washed through Detritus, and she politely tripped over the fragile scrap of cloth. Mud and grass stained her chiton, her knees, and her chin before she could right herself.

Debris laughed raucously, pointing a finger at her supine figure. Their divine siblings tittered as well.

"I'm going to get you for that. All of you," Detritus snarled.

"Shshsh," Debris hissed at his twin. "This is a good gig. We don't want to get Pops angry. He'll give this job to someone else!" He delicately retrieved the soiled hankie and put in his recycling bag. He'd wash, dry, and press it along with other debris cast off by his siblings.

"Who else would take this lousy job?" Detritus snarled. She brushed off grass blades from her short draperies. She'd scraped her knees, and her jaw ached from having bumped her chin, and she'd bit the inside of her cheek, and it bled onto her teeth. Now she was truly the ugliest of them all. She grabbed her collection bag and stomped toward the edge of the warm pocket of paradise Zeus had created for their playground. Playground, humph! Everyone else did as they pleased. Detritus and Debris had to work day in, day out.

At the edge of the green, lush growth, she paused and braced herself for the worst part of her job. All she had to do was close her eyes and think about a door leading outward. A portal would appear in mid-air. Easy for the other immortals, if they thought of a need to exit Paradise. So far, no one else had thought up a reason. Detritus was always exhausted when she did this. She waited until the end of the day so she only had to do it once.

Then, when she had an opening into the rest of the world, she must thrust her arm out into the frigid air of the mountaintop and upend her collection bag. Two minutes' work.

Two minutes of bone-numbing cold. On top of bone-numbing exhaustion.

It was snowing out there in the world of mortals. Snow blowing nearly sideways and piling up into huge drifts. She could barely see the outlines of stunted trees only a few yards away from the portal.

"Just this once, I'll wait. Maybe it will be warmer tomorrow." Determinedly she looked around to make sure she was alone and unobserved. Some of the cold leaked through the barrier. None of the beautiful children of Zeus would come this close to reality to notice. Detritus upended the bag behind a laurel tree. "We'll see how long that takes to smell up the old place."

Whistling a jaunty tune of defiance, she returned to the

open meadow, where daisies bloomed eternally and butterflies flitted about to the delight of the immortals.

"Detritus," Debris said on a relieved sigh. "Apollo's gloves are hopelessly stained. You know how he is, always demanding the most pristine accoutrements. There is no way even Pops could get out these stains. They look like he dipped them into a tar pit," he wailed.

"Does he have other white gloves and gauntlets?" the younger twin asked.

"Of course he does. Dozens of pairs. I don't even know if he knows how many pairs he has, only that it's supposed to be my job to retrieve them, clean them, and place them back in the temple where they belong."

"Well, if he won't miss them, then throw them away," Detritus replied, quite annoyed at her brother's inability to think beyond the narrow dictates of their father's instructions.

"Where? Do you know what they'll do to us if anyone finds them? We'll lose our jobs. We won't get any ambrosia. We'll become—" he gulped and his throat apple bobbed in his skinny teenage neck "—we'll become mortals." He blanched with dread.

"I'll show you." She led him toward the barrier but didn't stop at the portal. A dozen yards to the right, still close to the invisible wall, she found the laurel tree with its thick and spreading branches. She lifted one of them to where she'd earlier dumped the garbage. The sweet smell of fresh oranges wafted upward. The spiral peel rested on top of other bits and pieces of discarded food. Had it been so big and substantial a few moments ago? Or smelled so strongly? Sweet it might be, but not this overwhelming. Apollo's white kidskin gloves should cover it and mask the perfume. Apollo had big hands.

Still, the gloves barely obscured the peel and the apple core and other garbage.

Over the next several years, the autumnal and winter storms outside raged with increasing intensity. Spring and summer passed without comment.

The cycle of life continued inside as it always had, with little or no change anywhere. Who knew what happened beyond the barrier. Were the dreaded Romans still in power over Greece?

Detritus continued to dump her garbage beneath the laurel tree. Debris added more and more of the discards of the immortal children of Zeus. The pile grew. And so did the tree, while all the others remained the same size. Even the grass failed to grow and need mowing.

The fountain continued to gush upward and flow downward. The overflow channeled off into a stunted copse, where it pooled and Debris washed the soiled artifacts of his siblings.

The sweet perfume of fresh oranges grew sour. The twins had to hold their noses whenever they approached the dump. But a few feet away, beyond the protective branches of the laurel, they smelled only the usual mix of flowers and trees that never died, never withered, never discarded their leaves. Never grew. Only the laurel tree changed. And the fountain flowed.

* * *

"Pops wants to see you," Apollo said, one evening, staring down at the unwanted twins.

Detritus bobbed a curtsey to her older brother.

"Did he say why?" Debris asked. He didn't dip his head or salute or anything. Unheard of! The compulsion of respect hadn't compelled Detritus's curtsey. Only long habit.

Detritus cringed behind Debris, not willing to be caught in Apollo's wrath at this lack of respect. She didn't think he deserved anything more than what one immortal owed another, but he thought all of the Olympians should grovel at his feet.

"How am I supposed to know?" He tossed another pair of soiled gloves at Debris, expecting the boy to catch them and deal with the filth that might infect all of Mt. Olympus if left untended. "He spoke, I heard, I passed on the message, though someone else should have that lowly job." He moved away to perform whatever duties he had. Did he even know why he drove his bright chariot across the skies every day?

"Whatever he wants, it won't be good for you two. You were born to do all the dirty work, including be the brunt of his temper. He's been throwing tantrums a lot lately," Herakles said coming up behind the bright and shining Apollo.

When they had both passed out of sight and earshot, Detritus smoothed her freshly washed chiton. It looked grey rather than white, no matter what she did to cleanse it.

The washing pool had grown colder and didn't clean as well as it should. Her face also had a permanent streak of dirt across her nose and down her cheek.

Debris smoothed his hair. A cowlick stuck up at the crown of his head, despite repeated attempts to tame his mane. He, too, had developed the dark stains across his nose and on the opposite cheek as his twin.

Inside the largest marble temple on the mountain, Zeus looked as he always looked, tall, broad-shouldered, strong, and imposing with jet black curly hair and full beard. He sat forward on his golden throne, bracing a golden spear against the ground as if ready to leap into action.

Was that grey salting his hair and beard? Detritus thought her father looked older. No, never that. More mature. He was immortal, after all. As were they all. But his long white and gold robes looked a bit tarnished.

Everything within Mt. Olympus had faded from pristine and glowing white to dustier shades. But the change had been so gradual, Detritus didn't think anyone had noticed.

She gave her father a full and respectful bow. So did Debris.

"You two are doing a marvelous job at keeping our home and refuge clean. I award you an extra portion of ambrosia tonight and every night. You may return to your duties with the full knowledge that your loyalty and good service are appreciated." The elder god dipped his spear tip in dismissal.

The twins backed out of the temple, never turning their backs on Zeus the almighty.

"He never noticed our good work when we dumped stuff outside the barrier," Detritus mumbled once they were free of their father's exclusive enclave.

"Maybe because we aren't opening the portal, even when it's summer outside, and therefore keeping all the warmth and beauty inside," Debris said.

"Maybe. I'm going to enjoy my ambrosia as long as it lasts." She had an awful feeling, like a vast emptiness in the pit of her tummy that something awful, or very exciting, was about to disrupt the same old same old routine of immortality.

Years passed. The trees and grass and flowers lost some luster. The temples began to sag.

Detritus noticed a haze in the air.

"Yeah, it's there," Debris admitted to her. "Sort of like an orange mist in the distance. But up close, everything looks the same."

But it didn't.

Later, while Mt. Olympus slept and the moon hung motionless in the sky, Detritus crept out of her little bed— she was always a young teen, never aging—to see what about Mt. Olympus was different, damaged. Dangerous.

The night air chilled Detritus more than she thought necessary. Part of living in Paradise was the comfort of constant temperatures. It was always sunny in Paradise. If it ever rained, that happened at night, replenishing the plants without disturbing the immortals. The difference between night and day should only be enough to require the comfort of a light blanket for sleeping. She wished she had something warm to cover her toes within her sandals.

"I'll make this quick and be back inside before anyone discovers I'm gone."

"Wrong," Debris said from right behind her. "I heard you leave. Where are we going?"

Detritus shrugged. "Something is not right. I figured now would be a better time to discover it than during the day, when everyone watches us."

"No one watches us. We are beneath their notice unless something goes wrong, and then they blame us, even if it isn't our fault."

"True. But I think something is really, really, really wrong. If we don't find out what and fix it, then everyone will find out and maybe kick us off Mt. Olympus." That had happened before. Long, long ago. She couldn't remember who. But her siblings only spoke of it in fearful whispers. She thought it had something to do with a Roman spy, but she could be wrong.

"Well what is different?" Debris asked. He looked taller in the moonlight, with broader shoulders and the hint of a dark beard. He was growing up. Immortals didn't do that. Zeus needed his youngest children to be teenagers forever. They should stay teenagers forever.

A quick glance at her own silhouetted shadow and she saw the willowy curves of a young woman. *An illusion of moonlight and shadow*, she told herself.

She wasn't convinced. Now was not the time to discuss that change. Better to show her brother though he wouldn't see anything but the most obvious.

"The luster is gone."

He scratched his head. "Now that you point it out . . . yeah. How come white clothing, white marble temples, even white leather doesn't glow anymore?"

"The only thing that we've done differently is to not open a portal when we dump the garbage. Have you noticed the pile lately? Have you seen how big it is growing? Could it be draining Mt. Olympus of whatever makes things glow?"

"I haven't lingered or looked. It smells bad. I get in and out as fast as I can."

"Same here. That's why I think we need to really check it."

Together they walked as fast as they could, without making any noise, to the far reaches of the meadow, toward the now enormous laurel tree. A light rapping noise made them freeze in place. A light came on in Aphrodite's temple. Then they heard their sister sigh contentedly and giggle as she blew out her little lamp.

Detritus wondered who graced her bed this night. It didn't matter. Her sister's job was to spread love to all.

The laurel tree loomed ahead of them, dark and menacingly.

"What are you afraid of?" Debris asked as he urged his sister forward. "Pops would never create anything dangerous, and the barrier keeps everything else out."

"There are stories left over from when before we were born and Zeus and his children roamed the Earth. People worshipped them. The stories speak of monsters and demons, and . . . humans trying to kill us so they wouldn't have to worship us. Romans ruling the world instead of gods."

Debris blew a raspberry. "They're just stories." He marched ahead of her and brazenly lifted the lowest branch of the laurel on the far side of the tree. "Ewww." He held his nose and dropped the branch.

Detritus spotted something that didn't look right. She lifted a different branch.

A long white foot wearing one of Apollo's sandals laced high on a shapely calf stuck out from the shadows.

Detritus jumped back, gasping for air. Then she leaned forward to examine the foot. It glowed with the lustre of an immortal.

"Debris?" she asked hesitating to move, even to drop the laurel branch back into place. "Who . . . who is this?"

"Who? Where?" He looked all around, over his shoulder through the barrier—the rocky landscape showed hints of blurry green, must be spring out there—back toward the temples and the vast moonlit meadow.

"Down here," Detritus said, with more courage now that she had to direct her stupid brother.

"That looks like a foot and a lower leg." He shrugged it off, then stilled as the implications set in. His sister could almost see his mind working.

"It's big. Bigger than Herakles. Maybe even the size of a Titan," Detritus whispered.

"Who does that foot belong to?" Debris asked. "And . . . is the rest of the body there too?"

"Only one way to find out." She pushed aside a higher branch, holding it away from the foot with her body. "I see the rest of the leg and another foot. It's still gray and doesn't have a sandal."

"Is anything moving? Like breathing?"

"I can't tell. Hold back some more branches."

Debris sidled closer, careful not to get too near the foot. When he backed away, taking three levels of branches with him, they could see all the way to the tree trunk. Propped up against it, sat a man. Sort of. A rotting melon formed his head, without features. Bits of tattered cloth, discarded handkerchiefs, and torn robes covered his mushy torso. His arms appeared to be handless sticks, pruned branches from the apple tree—more evidence of unplanned growth.

"He hasn't finished forming yet," Detritus whispered, almost afraid to wake up the man made up from the garbage and cast offs by the immortals.

"What's going to happen when he does finish?" Debris asked. "Will he be alive? Will he hurt us?"

"I don't know. Pops created this place for himself and his children. It stays lush and green, growing food profusely all year long. Everything grows here except us. We are supposed to stay the same."

"So, like the apples, and oranges, and olives that grow and ripen all year long, the remains of our food keep growing too."

"And we've added soiled clothing to define the shape of what keeps growing."

"What should we do?" Debris kept staring at the vague

and unfinished body.

Detritus thought the wisest thing to do would be to break the thing apart and chuck all of it out the portal. If it continued to grow and eventually animate into a . . . very large person, then it could find its way down Mt. Olympus to where people lived and let them deal with the giant.

Then she remembered how her older siblings treated her. At first, they'd shunned her, ignored her, and insulted her. And then when she and her twin had duties to benefit them all, the beautiful ones treated the youngest of them all as if they were the same as the garbage they collected.

Would the humans who lived in the real world reject this giant? She didn't think anyone deserved that.

"Let's leave him for a bit to see what happens."

"If you say so. How much more garbage do you think he needs to finish . . . finish whatever he's doing?"

Detritus shrugged and eased out of the tree, though the branches and trees tried to ensnare her clothing and hair. "Behave," she admonished the tree, as if it could hear her. "I will not be treated as garbage by you or anyone else."

She marched back to her sleeping quarters with her head held high and shoulders back, presuming her twin followed her lead like he always did.

Time passed, as it always did, days of endless summer followed by moonlit nights. Outside the barrier, Detritus watched the seasons progress from gentle spring to hot and sere summer to colorful autumn and back to stormy winter. The man made from garbage continued to coalesce and refine. His nose grew straight, his mouth gentle, his stick arms filled out and grew hands and stubby fingers. Indentations for eyes remained closed, devoid of lashes or brows or even eyelids. Nothing to indicate he was anywhere near to waking.

* * *

"Pops, you have to do something!" Aphrodite wailed, kneeling at the feet of Zeus the father of them all. "My gowns are tattered and grey. They make me—" sob "—look ugly."

She did indeed look faded and tattered. The hemline was frayed. Her once glorious mane of blonde curls had become lank and dull, even worse than the drabness of her gown.

Detritus slunk back into the shadows of the exterior Ionic columns, watching her older sister become more and more like the youngest siblings.

"Pops, you have to do something," Aphrodite pleaded. "Whatever you do to create new clothing and endless portions of ambrosia isn't working anymore. If only you'd allow me to bathe in the fountain."

"You dare criticize me! No one may use the fountain except me!" Zeus shouted, the words reverberating around Paradise. His angry words became a roar of thunder inside the barrier and outside, all the way down the mountain to the humans living below.

Detritus cringed and clapped her hands over her ears. She slammed her eyes shut, knowing that when Zeus pounded the butt of his spear on the marble floor that lightning would launch outward like a volley of arrows.

No one deliberately angered Zeus.

"Well, someone has to bring this to your attention, Father," Aphrodite sneered. She alone among the immortals dared speak to him so. She was his favorite and the most beautiful of the beautiful.

And then, Detritus watched her father rise from his golden throne, not as tall or imposing as she imagined, and stomp toward the fountain at the center of their home. He stepped into the pool and let the water cascade over his head. It didn't shoot as high as it used to, or flow with as much water. Layer after layer of accumulated dust and grey discoloration sloughed off Zeus. An ugly layer of scum collected on the water's surface.

But mighty Zeus himself had regained some of his luster. And he didn't look down at the dirty water he used to create new things.

"Is that all we have to do to regain what has faded?" Aphrodite giggled, her laughter sounding closer to tinkling bells than it had for some time.

"It usually works for me," Zeus said.

"So why have you forbidden your children to partake of these waters or even splash and play in the fountain? We could take care of ourselves."

"Because this is the water of life. This is what keeps our home a paradise, lush, green, full of warmth and love. For anyone but me to stand here and bathe in this water would give you the power of creation. Only I have the wisdom to know how and when to create." *And if you had access to the fountain, you would not need me anymore. As mortal people have no need for us anymore.*

Detritus almost heard his unspoken words and knew the truth.

Zeus stepped out of the fountain, still dripping water. He cast off his wet garment.

Debris appeared as if summoned. He placed his collection bag beneath the sodden garment before it could touch the ground. His duty complete, he retreated to the shadow of the same column that sheltered his twin.

"You know what we need to do with that," Detritus whispered.

Debris nodded solemnly in reply.

As they scuttled away, Aphrodite dipped a toe in the fountain. Then she jerked it out, looked around guiltily. Her gaze landed on the twins. "You two, you did not see anything. And why haven't you cleaned my clothes adequately of late?" She marched toward them, anger creasing her face into a fearsome mask, making her uglier than her discolored and fraying clothes could ever do.

Detritus nodded her head and bent her knees in curtsy out of long habit. Strangely, the compulsion to obey did not wash through her. Nor did she forget what she had seen, as her older sister commanded.

"We clean your cast-offs as we have always cleaned them, in the runoff pool below the fountain." Debris pointed to the north.

The laurel tree and their garbage dump lay to the south.

"Well you aren't doing a very good job," Aphrodite pouted. "I will report your slackard ways to Zeus."

"It isn't that I don't try, sis. The water is missing whatever special energy Zeus gives it to clean and repair things, and restore the natural luster given it at the moment of creation."

"Impossible. Zeus has lost nothing of his power since we retreated here after the Romans deprived us of worshippers. He protects us." She turned abruptly and followed the path to her own temple, not that of Zeus beside the fountain.

"So, are we going to do this?" Debris held up his collection bag with the sodden robe Zeus had cast off. It shone through the bag, nearly as bright as the waning moon.

Detritus looked up at the silvery orb. "The moon is always full. Why does it wane now, after all these years?"

"Because Paradise is waning," Debris replied. This was the first wise thing Detritus had ever heard from him.

"Come. The time has come to do what we are destined to do."

"Why us?"

"Because . . . I don't know why. I just know that this is something we must do."

Resolutely, she led the way to the laurel tree that had now grown almost as tall as the sky. Outside the barrier, spring flowers dotted the rocky landscape.

Spring, the time of rebirth and new growth.

As she drew closer to the tree, the foot protruding from the shaded shelter twitched. She jumped backward, nearly knocking over her brother. "Did you see that?"

"Yeah. It recognizes us."

"Do you really think it is alive?"

"I think it's coming alive. Do you want to do the honors?" He shoved the glowing bag toward her.

Detritus cradled it against her no longer skinny chest and walked the final six steps to the foot that now was clearly visible outside the circle of leafy branches. She drew in a deep breath and held it as she went through the familiar routine of holding branches back with her body and upending the bag on the almost human figure—if one overlooked the collage of discarded food and grass clippings and such that made up the garbage man's skin. The still-dripping robe landed in his lap.

Instantly, he opened his eyes and stared at her in wonder. His mouth opened and closed, but no sounds emerged. He reached for the robe, spreading it out to cover himself and absorbed the water dripping from the cloth.

A clap of thunder and a bolt of lightning split the skies.

Cold air rushed down, sending chills up and down Detritus's body. She wrapped her arms around herself in a useless effort to warm herself.

The roofs on the distant temples cracked and their foundations groaned. Immortals erupted from them, streaming outward, screaming and wailing in bewilderment and despair. The beautiful, immortal people looked old and haggard.

The garbage man stood up, donning the robe as he stretched his limbs and twisted his head right and left.

Another earsplitting crack and the air grew colder.

"What is happening?" Zeus demanded. His voice could not compete with the cracks and claps of different airs clashing in an all-out war.

In that moment, Detritus realized the barrier had split open, revealing the cloudy night sky with only a glimmer of the waning moon above them.

"Paradise is dying!" Aphrodite wailed. Her voice creaked and she bent double in a long racking cough. When she righted herself, all the beauty of the ages had collapsed into an ancient crone with more wrinkles than hair, her back slumped as it twisted into a hump. Apollo, Adonis, and Dionysus withered as well. Herakles lasted a little longer, being only half immortal. He wasn't robbed of all his heritage all at once, as were the others. The ghost of Xena, beside Hades, laughed silently, until she faded to mist and vanished.

Before their eyes, Zeus aged and failed. His thick mane of dark curls thinned and fell off. His rippling muscles sagged into flab. His hands twisted with arthritis. His spear turned to dust, the gold flaking in to the fountain.

Seeing the destruction of all the people she knew, Detritus look a hasty look at her hands before putting them to her face to check for wrinkles. Smooth skin. Her brother, too, had matured but not aged like their siblings.

The fountain stopped flowing, the marble foundations cracked and spilled the collected water. Another booming crack, and Zeus's temple collapsed. One by one, all of the others finished falling apart as well.

The air grew colder yet.

"Paradise is dead," Detritus said.

"Paradise might die, but we are still alive," Debris said on an awestruck whisper.

"But why?" Detritus asked the universe. "Why did it have to end? They were happy here."

"You weren't," a deep voice said from behind her.

She whirled to face the garbage man. He stood as tall as Zeus used to, not as handsome perhaps, but just as imposing.

"I'm Detritus, the youngest of Zeus's children, I'm not supposed to be happy." That sounded all wrong to her own ears. She repeated them in her mind. The same words she'd been telling herself all her life. The same words Zeus and his children had been telling her and her twin.

They were still wrong.

"Their time has passed. Long ago. All this is but an illusion," she sighed.

"I was created to carry you and Debris out of here," the strange man, made of detritus and debris, said. He punched the barrier and watched it crumble, leaving a rough doorway shape open to the rest of the world.

"Why us?" Debris asked.

"Because deities come and go, but garbage lives forever."

* * *

About the Story

When the anthology theme was first presented to me, the characters popped into my head and asked, "What took you so long to find us?"

Irene Radford

SHABBY CHIC

MARK FINN

INDIVIDUALLY, THE TWO MEN wouldn't have drawn more than a passing glance from the harried pedestrians of San Cibola. After all, it was a town known for its inherent strangeness, and an unshaven man, wearing rumpled and dirty clothes and bearing scraggly, shaggy, unkempt hair would have registered on any urban traveler's survival radar as "homeless lunatic" before they moved ahead to the next potential hazard.

But together, walking side-by-side and arguing like twin brothers at a dysfunctional family barbecue, they were somehow greater than the sum of their parts. Their rumpled trench coats flapped behind them in unison, and random bits of trash and refuse spilled out in their wake, tumbling from under the coats, bouncing and clattering onto the concrete as they walked.

To the more civic-minded citizens they passed, this created a cloud of benign hostility behind them, a collection of scowls, sibilant "tuts," and muttered admonishments that never reached the pair of men, lest an actual conversation or worse, a confrontation occur. They were, after all, in California. So the concerned citizens that dared not voice their objections merely picked up the pair's trash and dropped it into the trash can and resumed their lives, aglow with the knowledge that while they didn't make the world a better place just then, they at least didn't help make it a worse one through their privileged inaction.

The two men didn't notice, or if they did, they didn't care in the slightest. They were deep in discussion, loudly debating and gesticulating as they strode with great purpose down 34th Street, one of the three major thoroughfares in the Arcadia district, a neighborhood that boasted a mix of upscale residential and light commercial real estate. On the weekends, the sidewalks filled up with tourists and visitors and crowded into the bistros and artisanal shops to tweet where they were and take pictures of food with captions, "This is what a nine-dollar muffin looks like." Mid-week, however, in the early afternoon, it was mostly full of locals and those who had real business to transact in the light retail and commercial shops.

"They'll never agree to it," the older homeless man with bushy brown hair said bitterly. "They don't do do-overs. 'Gods don't make mistakes.'"

"It's around here, somewhere," said the younger homeless man with wavy blond hair, ignoring what was clearly on old argument.

"You don't know that," said the older homeless man. "You've never been here before."

"Well, no, but I know the apartments in this area are all

over the businesses." He scanned the numbers above the stores as he walked. "So, we're looking for an 'A' or a 'B' or an 'and a half' or something like that."

"This is bullshit," said the older man. "We should have called first."

"He won't talk to us on the phone, you know that."

"He might."

"He wouldn't!"

"You don't know that!"

And so it went, for almost the length of the block. Finally, the blond homeless man stopped in front of a floral delivery shop called Pan's Garden.

"See?" said the younger man, pointing. "3249, here, and right there—" he shifted his attention to the left of the floral shop to an innocuous-looking door "—is 3249 A."

"Or B," said the older man. "Or 'and a half.'"

"Right," said the younger man. He walked up to the door and tried the knob. "It's locked."

"Huh," said the older man. "That's weird. It's almost as if, you know, he doesn't want visitors to just walk up to his apartment and bang on the door. So strange."

"Will you shut up and come give me a hand?"

"This is a bad idea," said the older man. He touched the doorknob, and it suddenly sprouted a patina of green age and separated into two parts. The knob on the other side of the door hit the welcome mat and bounced once. The other half with the shaft slid out from the hole in the door, and the younger man caught it. The door seemed to buckle and warp slightly, and then it swung inward on now-rusty hinges.

The younger man scooped up the other half of the doorknob assembly and said, "Why didn't you say something before?"

"It's all I've been saying to you," said the older man. "You only hear what you want to hear."

"Well, it's too late to back out, now." He started up the steps. "You coming?"

The older man sighed and started climbing. "Yeah, yeah. But when this blows up on us, I am going to say 'I told you so.'"

"I know you will."

* * *

Gary Meade sat in his tastefully uncluttered study, on the piano bench, and stared at the handwritten sheets of musical notation. He could read it with his eyes, and he could hear it in his head, but something was not coming together. He wadded up the last page and tossed it in the trash can to join the other failed attempts. His coffee cup steamed on top of the piano, untouched. It was the fourth cup this morning. He rarely drank more than two cups when he was working. Caffeine made him jumpy, and when he got jumpy, his strings all started playing *pizzicato* instead of *allegro*, and that just didn't work, unless you were writing for Bugs Bunny cartoons. Carl Stalling he was not.

So, what, then, was that irregular beat that was running through his score? He could hear it when he sang the woodwinds part. It was driving him crazy, and he went back to the beginning of the movement and started over, and son-of-a-bitch, there it was again. No, wait. It wasn't in the music. Someone was knocking on the door.

That got his attention. What the hell? How could anyone knock on his door without first ringing the bell downstairs? This was why he had an intercom installed. He got up, took a sip of his coffee, and approached the door as if it was alive.

"Who is it?" he called out.

"Ganymede? Is that you?"

Gary slumped. Of course. Of-bloody-course. Olympians. They were the only ones who called him Ganymede. Even members of the underground supernatural community in San Cibola known as "the Neighborhood" called him Gary Meade. Even if they knew who he used to be.

"Who is it?" he said again, only now his trepidation was replaced with anger and resolve.

"Um . . . I don't know if you remember us . . . "

Us? Who the hell was an "us" these days? The dozen and a half remaining Olympians made a point of not congregating because of their tendency to revert to form. Old habits died hard. Curiosity got the better of him, and Gary Meade opened his door and stared.

"Who the hell are you?"

The younger, blond-haired homeless person spoke up. "Oh, hey, there you are. Hi . . . "

"The name is Gary Meade, now, okay?"

"Right, Gary," the blond said. "Well, I don't know if you recall, but we're . . . "

"Debris and Detritus," said the older, brown-haired

homeless man.

"Oh, shit. Yes. Of course. How could I forget?"

Detritus said, "Clearly, you must have forgotten. Otherwise, you would have already extended to us the hospitality of Olympus that is our right, so long as we still draw a breath."

Gary Meade sighed and swung himself to one side. He hadn't forgotten. Rather, he'd hoped they didn't know about the Compact. "Come on in."

"Thank you," said Debris, the blond. He handed the doorknob to Gary as he moved past.

"That was not our fault," said Detritus.

"Right. Well," said Gary, "Look, I'm in the middle of something very important, so why don't you tell me how you tracked me—you know, on second thought, I don't want to know. Just tell me what you want."

Debris and Detritus stood in the living room, openly swiveling their heads around, taking in the apartment. "Nice," said Detritus. "A little Spartan for my tastes, but nice."

Debris said, "It needs some color."

"And more bric-a-brac."

"Hey!" Gary snarled. "I'm right here, boys, and you're using your outside voices."

Debris smiled and bobbed his head. "Sorry. No offense meant. We're just used to people not paying any attention to us."

"You currently have my undivided attention. I'm giving you two minutes, and then I'm kicking you out of my house, Compact or no Compact. I do not—repeat—do not—need this today." Gary put his hands on his hips. "Go."

Debris opened his mouth to speak, but Detritus beat him to it. "We want a Comeback."

Gary let out a short, sharp braying laugh. "What? You two? Are you fucking kidding me?"

"Why not us?" Debris looked wounded.

"Because, guys, unless you're one of the big names, you don't get a Comeback, and more importantly, you don't get to decide for yourself."

"Look, I know we're not Hercules or Cupid, but you've made a life for yourself," said Debris. "Others have, too, right? We're just sick and tired of walking the Earth."

"Frankly, I'm surprised to even see you," said Gary. "I had no idea you were still hanging around."

"We got a big boost from that show, 'Hoarders,'" said Detritus.

Gary nodded. "Okay, I can see that. But the fact remains . . ."

"Come on, 'Bris," said Detritus. "Fuck this guy. He's not going to help us. I told you he wouldn't. He probably doesn't even know Hephaestus."

They turned to go, but Gary stamped his foot. "Excuse me, but I do so know Hephaestus."

"I stand corrected," said Detritus. "We didn't mean to intrude. We'll just be on our way. Sorry about the knob." He pushed Debris out ahead of him and turned to face Gary. "By the way, that piece you're working on would sound better in E-minor." He closed the door, leaving Gary staring at the space the pair had just occupied, suddenly running the music through his head. Eight bars in, he knew Detritus was right.

Gary ran out the door and caught them on the sidewalk, arguing. "How did you do that?"

Detritus reached into his pocket and pulled out a crumpled sheet of paper. "You threw it away, didn't you?"

Gary took the wad of paper from Detritus. He looked at the trash in his hand and then at the pair. Someone walked by and gave Debris a dollar. "What do you want with Hephaestus?" Gary asked.

"We think he can help us," said Detritus.

"Actually, we have a brilliant idea," said Debris.

"It's pretty good," said Detritus. He smiled, showing crooked teeth.

"Gods and Monsters, what is it, for shit's sake?" Gary stamped his foot again.

* * *

Hephaestus wasn't called Hephaestus anymore. He hadn't been Hephaestus in a long time. Currently, he was going by Hal Festus, and he lived and worked in converted warehouse on the edge of the Financial district. San Cibola was his home, had been for over a hundred years, though he didn't seem to age appreciably. His balding, graying hair was clipped short, and his beard was likewise neatly trimmed. His blue, long-sleeved work shirt was open at the collar and hung down over the top of his faded jeans. No one would have ever guessed from his appearance that he was one of the more affluent Neighbors in San Cibola. His cane, a sturdy wooden and brass affair, was hooked to the back side of his desk. He didn't need it for walking as much, but he felt strange without it, so he carried it more as an affectation these days.

The two men sitting in his dingy and crowded office on the other side of his desk had tried their best, but they still looked like they'd gone ten rounds with the Keystone Cops. Every time the older one straightened his tie, it would slowly, deliberately loosen and list sideways, to the right. Every time. The younger one wasn't wearing a tie, but his turtleneck was slowly, visibly becoming more dirty and disheveled. It made it hard to concentrate on what they were saying.

"I'm sorry," said Hal. "Could you please repeat that?"

Detritus scowled. Debris nodded and said, "Okay, we think that if more people are reminded of us—you—us, that is to say, I mean . . . we're wanting out of this job. We've had enough."

Hal coughed. "What makes you think I can help you?"

"You're in that field, aren't you?" Detritus said. He plucked a battered business card out of his pocket, one of Hal's own, and waggled it at him. "This is Vulcan Forge Design, right? 'Innovative designs for modern living?' We need to be set up as interior decorators. That way, we can bring back the old Classical Aesthetic. The more they get used to seeing Olympian design, the more power we all get back."

"And once we have enough power, we can get a Comeback."

Hal started to voice his objections, but despite himself, he was fascinated. "As what, exactly?"

Debris leaned forward, all smiles. "Well, we've been thinking that maybe we could step in and take over some of the muses. Rework a few of the out-of-date ones, update them. That sort of thing."

There was so much wrong with what Debris said, Hal didn't know where to start. "You know it doesn't work like that, right? I mean, you don't get to pick what you end up doing. It just happens. Sometimes it takes years. Over a long-ass period of time, right?"

Debris looked at Detritus and hit him on the arm. "See? I told you it wouldn work!"

"We don't have a decade, you dumb-ass!" Detritus hit Debris back, and there was a brief scuffle as they attempted to out-frog each other. Hal watched for a few seconds and then said, "Hey, boys?"

They dropped their fists and looked at him.

"Do you have any experience as interior decorators? Any at all?"

Debris said, "No, but honestly, how hard can it be?"

Hal looked down at his desk for a second to keep from laughing. "It's harder than you think. People go to college to learn how to do it."

Debris was undeterred. "I've been watching HGTV for a year, now. Trust me, I can stage a room."

"Well, you've got the lingo down, I'll give you that." Hal folded his arms in front of him. "But seriously, now. You're Debris and Detritus. You are the gods of trash and rubble."

"I'm trash, he's rubble," said Detritus.

"Whatever. You can't possibly think that you're going to have any aptitude for this work."

Debris' voice went up an octave. "Give us some credit! We're not just pulling this idea out of a hat! We've given this a lot of thought!"

Detritus added, "We're going to rebuild Olympus, one living room at a time. All of that is up here," he said, tapping his forehead. "I can recall every square inch of that place."

Hal leaned back in his chair. "No offense, but if you're so familiar with the old digs, how come I've got no recollection of ever seeing you there?"

Detritus started to say something, but Debris cut him off. "We came after you . . . left. Sir."

Hal nodded, understanding splashing across his face. "Romans."

Detritus spoke around Debris' obvious physical attempts to silence him. "What the hell is wrong with being Roman?"

"Nothing, not a thing," said Hal, his hands up in conversational surrender. "It's just that . . . your, ah, version of Olympus may not be quite the one that I remember."

Detritus started to stand up, and Hal realized there was a terrific likelihood of the homeless man climbing across the desk to slug him. To stave that off, he said, "Okay, I guess we can give it a try. But no promises. And if it doesn't work out, we'll go our separate ways. Our Compact at an end. Our business concluded. This is your one shot. Understand?"

Detritus straightened his tie and sat down, mollified. Debris smiled. "You won't regret it," he said.

"We'll just see about that."

* * *

Gary Meade stepped out of the cab. "Wait for me," he said to the portly driver. His phone was ringing inside his pocket. He ignored it. He knew who it was. It was Hal. Again.

He walked up along the carefully-manicured walk that neatly bifurcated the lush green lawn. As Eden Park mansions go, this was one of the newer models, built in the late 1940s, a tastefully ugly blend of art deco and mid-century modern sensibilities, managing to typify and excuse the best and the worst qualities of both styles. Clearly, this was the least desirable house on the street, priced at one-point-seventy-five million dollars. A starter mansion for any number of *nouveau riche* Neighbors, new to San Cibola and desperate to acclimate themselves.

It should have been a perfect assignment for the two of them, but, as Gary Meade walked up the brick steps and into the house, he knew that for anyone else, they would have made it work. Not these two. Not Debris and Detritus.

"Hello?" he said loudly, stepping into the arched entranceway. "Guys? It's Gary."

"We're back here," Debris called out.

Gary walked through the trashy-looking sitting room and

into the equally trashy-looking dining room, where Debris and Detritus were currently standing, ready to come to blows. Debris was dressed in tattered blue jeans and wearing a light blue T-shirt that said *2D Design & Decorating* across the chest. Detritus wore a knit shirt with the same logo embroidered on the right side of his chest. The clothes were brand new, but both of them looked like they had slept in a dumpster.

"What's happening?" asked Gary.

"Did Hal call you?" Detritus accused.

"Yes, he did, you lunatics. He called me because your client, who he recommended you to, is freaking out."

"Jove's Thunderbolts, 'Bris!" Detritus snarled. "You're going to screw this up for us! I told you to let me take the lead."

"For the thousandth time, we cannot paint the entire fucking house Dumptruck Gray!"

"And we cannot paint this room Snot Yellow, either," Detritus said. "I know you think it's Lemon Yellow, but it's not. Here." He swung around sharply, a paint swatch in hand, and thrust it at Gary. "Tell him."

Gary took the paint swatch and looked at it. He hated yellow. None of the colors on the battered and bedraggled cardboard strip appealed to him, but this wasn't his house, either. "Honestly, I can't tell you one way or the other what to do. But you need to get started, because you're about to lose another client."

They both looked at him. "Get started?" Debris said. "What do you mean, 'get started'? We're nearly finished."

"What?" Gary was flabbergasted. "How is that possible?"

"Look," said Detritus, leading him back into the sitting room. "See? Just stop for a second and take it all in."

"It's very subtle," said Debris.

Gary looked. The sitting room, the first formal room in the house, was a shambles; four mismatched bookshelves crammed to the gills with dishes and platters, decanters and goblets, all tucked in behind a pair of sideboards that had been intentionally distressed to the point of looking ready for the dump. A late Victorian fainting couch was positioned at oblique angles to two faded wingback chairs, each one a different color from the other, and none of them in harmony. Underneath all of the furniture was a rug made from vintage angora, snow white, giving the impression of a giant skinned Persian cat laid out like a hunter's trophy. A mid-century coffee table cut from a slab of diseased driftwood and polished to a glassy sheen held it all down somehow.

It was the worst, most God-awful room Gary had seen in decades.

"I think it may be *too* subtle," said Gary, searching for a way to better express his displeasure.

"You don't see it? The bar, the glasses, the decanters . . . ?" Debris looked shocked. "You really don't see it."

"No, I don't see it. Walk me through it."

Debris took a step into the room and threw his arms out wide. "It's the Sun Room from Mount Olympus!"

Gary blinked and for an instant, he got a flash, like a

half-remembered dream, of a grand salon with light streaming in from Apollo's chariot as it moved through the sky, and all of the Gods of Olympus were gathered around, drinking Ambrosia from the golden pitchers and decanters at the white marble bar, and Zeus lounging on his bed, attended to by a small throng of servants who passed morsels of food on golden platters under his nose as he told embarrassing, filthy jokes that everyone laughed at, as Dionysius raised his glass and called for more wine . . .

And it was gone, replaced by the rude shapes of the hand-me-down furniture and strange color combinations. It was all in the same place, technically, but it was a lot like looking at someone trying to duplicate the Mona Lisa with an Etch-a-Sketch. Gary couldn't help it; he snickered. It was a tiny sound, involuntary, but it cut deeply into Debris. This had clearly been his idea.

"Oh, shit. Shit shit shit shit *shit!* It happened again, didn't it?"

Gary shook his head. "I'm sorry. I shouldn't have done that. But . . . yes. It did."

Detritus put his hand on Debris' shoulder. "Hey, don't beat yourself up. We'll just rebrand again. We'll call it 'shabby chic.'"

Gary shook his head again. "This isn't an issue of rebranding. You're not chic enough to be chic, and you're way past shabby to be considered shabby. This is . . . "

"It's fucked," said Detritus. He was resolved. "Look, 'Bris, we tried. We're going to have to face facts; we can't pull this off. Everything we touch turns to shit."

Gary was torn between backing up Detritus's unflinching honesty and softening the blow to prevent Debris from breaking out into uncontrollable sobs. It had happened before. Despite the massive time sink that they had been for the past six weeks, he was starting to root for them. Then he spied something laying askew on the ugly coffee table. He walked over and plucked it off.

A heavy ink fountain pen, the kind with a nib on the end. He uncapped it to verify that it was all in place. "Where did you get this?"

Detritus looked up, distracted by Debris' pre-hysterical warm-up. "Huh? Oh, that. Someone left it behind at an estate sale."

"How do you know that?" Gary asked.

Detritus shrugged. "If it's left behind, thrown away, or forgotten, I know about it and can access it. It's my thing."

"Do you know what this is?" Gary asked. They shook their heads. "It's a Parker Duofold fountain pen from 1923. It's highly collectible. I'll give you a hundred dollars for it."

"We'll take it," said Debris.

"Wait, how much is it really worth?" asked Detritus.

"And how do you know that?" asked Debris.

Gary started to speak and then hesitated. It was a fraction of a second, but it was enough. "Aha!" Detritus said, shaking his finger at him. "You're trying to fuck us."

"Okay, okay, it's worth about a thousand dollars. But you'd have to sell it for that, retail, and I'm not paying you that much money for something you just found in your fucking pocket." He grabbed his wallet and shook out a handful of twenty dollar bills. "Here. Two hundred. Take it."

Debris and Detritus did not move. They stared at one another, and for the first time in a long time, they were both smiling. "What?" asked Gary.

"You wouldn't pay a thousand dollars for it," said Detritus.

"But somebody will pay a thousand dollars for it," finished Debris.

Gary realized what they are getting at, and he started smiling, too. "Or more."

"Or more," said Debris and Detritus together.

* * *

Gary set them up. Well, he and Hal both did. They structured it as a business loan, since Debris and Detritus had used up all of their favors with their fellow Olympians. Hal found them some retail space, a thousand square feet in the middle of the Tenderloin. It made more sense to put a resale shop there, anyway. Gary made them lists of things to look for—high end antiques, collectible glassware, designer label fashions, and so forth. For the first few months, he would bring a separate set of friends to Shabby Chic, their store, and all of Gary's friends would gladly empty their wallets and leave, loading with kitsch or cool, depending on their tastes.

The pair paid Gary and Hal back their original stake in two years and moved the shop to the edge of the Tenderloin, where more tourists could get to it. By then, Shabby Chic had a reputation as the place to go for that thing you were looking for—but be prepared to pay a handsome price for it.

They had been at their new location five years when Gary walked in one day and found a woman behind the counter.

"Gary!" she said. "It's been forever!" she wore a rumpled blue work shirt and paint-spattered jeans. She slipped around the counter and hugged him. Only when she got to arm's length did he realize who she was.

"Debris?" he asked.

She beamed. "It's Bree, now. It happened! Just like Hal said! It just—happened."

"Well, great," he replied. It suits you, I think."

"I know, right?!"

The curtain to the back room parted, and Detritus came out.

"Trite, look who's here."

"Hey, Gary," said Trite. He wore a vintage linen shirt, badly in need of an iron, and an old silk tie, currently askew. He shook Gary's hand, smiling. He was still sloppy, but he no longer looked homeless. "What? Do I have something on my shirt?"

Gary smiled and shook his hand. "No, nothing like that. But Bree here, she got her . . . "

Trite smiled back. "Yeah, I know. We're not sure why I haven't . . . or if I'm even going to, at this point. I'm kinda hoping it doesn't happen, now. The business is doing great, you know?" He chuckled, clearing the throat of the conversation, and made his face bright. "What brings you out?"

"Not that you need a reason to pop in," Bree said.

"Well, this is something of a long shot, but . . . a friend of mine has gone missing."

Trite cocked his head. "Your friend?

"It's Dawn."

"Oh, wow." Bree leaned against the counter. She was a much better looking woman than man. "Heavy."

"What you're asking . . . " Trite said. "I don't think I can find her."

"Maybe all you need to do is find what she's thrown away."

Trite nodded, lost in thought. "I'll give it a try."

"Thanks."

Trite walked back into the office and emerged a minute later with his old trenchcoat on. He put his hands into his pockets and came up with a couple of handfuls of paper and spilled them on the counter. He and Gary looked through them—receipts, half-started Dear John letters, notes, and doodles of curved penises. Trite finally fished a scrap of paper out and handed it to Gary.

"Selene," said Gary. "Duh. I should have guessed." He pocketed the paper. "Thanks, Trite. I owe you, big time."

"Forget it," said Trite. "We're square."

"Listen, I've got to run," he said. "Someone needs this info. But I'll swing by when I'm not so busy, okay?"

"It was great to see you," Bree said.

"You too. And hey, congrats on your do-over." He flashed them a grin, the kind of smile only an Olympian can deliver, and then he was gone.

Trite came over to Bree and his arms encircled her waist. "You didn't tell him?" he asked.

"He'll find out about it soon enough." Bree put her hands over Trite's, and then she moved them to her stomach. "We'll ask him to be the godfather later. There's plenty of time."

Trite kissed Bree on the cheek. "I've been thinking about names."

"Yeah?" she said. "What do you have for me?"

"How about . . . Diana."

Bree smiled. "I like it. It's a good family name."

They separated and went back to their respective duties. Trite pulled objects out of his trench coat for resale, typing each thing into his computer to check its rarity and value.

Bree went back to re-arranging things on the upper shelves and tried to quiet the voice she now regularly heard coming from inside her.

Mother, I don't like that name.

Hush, child, Bree said, touching her stomach. *You don't get to pick your name.*

But when I'm born, you're going to die.

Maybe not. That's not for any of us to decide.

No, Mother, I've seen it. It's about the act of Creation.

Bree frowned. *How did you get so smart?*

Everyone knows you can't have Creation without Destruction. That's how you get Debris and Detritus.

Bree let her unborn daughter prattle and tried dusting the glass countertops. No matter how hard they tried, the place never really looked clean.

* * *

About the Story

I've been playing fast and loose with Greek gods for a while, now, in my urban fantasy stories. The city of San Cibola as a setting is a perfect urban fantasy environment because magic is alive and well but carefully hidden from the mundane world. As such, it makes relatively easy to set magical and mythical beings into the real world, and the gods are the perfect funhouse mirrors of us: loud, proud, and locked into behavior that's not always healthy. In my story, I saw an opportunity to put these second-stringers to work, literally gluing together some things from my previous stories set in San Cibola. I like them so much, I'm trying to find a way to use them again.

Mark Finn

The Bovines of Bybanos

MJ Butler

Viewed in one direction, the Celestial Hall was everything Zeus desired.

Three ivory thrones decorated in gold rested between hand-carved columns atop the polished marble floor.

The problems started when he turned around: three additional thrones fought for space as the walls converged into an open doorway barely large enough to squeeze through.

Less a grand hall and more a twelve-foot-long triangle. And while the ceiling displayed an exquisite mural depicting their victory over the Titans, it hung so low that Zeus's head was inches away from his painted one.

He began to doubt his decision to have the Cyclopes build the Hall, given their lack of depth perception.

"A toast . . . " Zeus raised his cup to his brothers and sisters. Poseidon sat nearest him, while Demeter, Hestia, and Hades sat bunched together on the opposite end, shifting positions when their legs bumped together. ". . . to our new home. Mount Smolikas."

"My brother, this is Olympus," Hades said.

"Oh, I thought . . . " Zeus's voice trailed off as he looked at Hera's empty throne.

Crap. He had told her it was Smolikas.

He imagined her standing on a mountainside in a Celestial Hall consisting only of scattered rocks. While it would be far less cramped, she wasn't going to return happy.

"Yes, of course. Mount Olympus." Zeus waited for everyone to raise their cups then took a drink of nectar. "Also, Hera won't be making it. She had a thing."

Poseidon leaned forward. "Now down to business. Deciding who will be god of what."

"Yes . . ." Zeus said. "You, Hestia, are the eldest. You should be the goddess of the hearth, representing family and the home."

Hestia considered this for a moment then smiled.

Zeus turned to Demeter. "You should be goddess of the harvest. Each season's crops will succeed or fail based on your favor."

Demeter nodded. Zeus decided this was going well.

"Hades, you should leave our heavenly palaces to be god of the Underworld, a dark, desolate realm devoid of joy and hope, where you will remain for all eternity, accompanied only by the miserable souls of the dead."

Hades looked up from admiring the gold trimming on his armrest. "Um, wait . . . what?"

"Poseidon, you struck at our father with your trident. It's only fitting you be god of the sea."

"Can we get back to my thing for a second?" Hades asked.

"As for myself?"

Zeus paused to savor the moment.

"I will be god of all gods, ruling over each of you with Hera as my wife. Okay, good meeting, everyone."

Zeus smiled at his new subjects. They stared back at him, speechless, no doubt because they were impressed by his wise decisions. He stood to leave.

"Just hang on a moment," Poseidon said.

Zeus sat back down. "What is it?"

"It just seems like . . . we're getting the lesser of the deal here."

"Yes, why are you deciding all of this, anyway?" Demeter asked.

Zeus frowned, confused. "Well, I'm god of the gods. Why wouldn't I decide?"

"But you're the one who made yourself that."

"Also, as your sister, Hera might object to marrying you," Hestia said.

"Well, she should have bothered to show up, then."

At the front of the Hall, two servants struggled to bring a statue Zeus had commissioned of himself through the too-small opening.

"All of ours have something to do with who we are," Hestia continued.

"Mine doesn't," Demeter said. "What the Hades do I know about crops?"

"Really? 'What the *Hades*?'" Hades turned to Zeus,

frowning. "Well, that certainly didn't take long."

Hestia pointed to Zeus's nectar. "You are fond of fine cups! You should be . . . the god of ceramics!"

Zeus glanced down at his cup for a moment then back to the group. "No, I'm pretty sure I'm good with being god of the gods. But thanks."

Demeter turned to Hestia. "What of his glorious tunic? Surely, he should be the god of wool and/or linen!"

Zeus was starting to think this wasn't going well after all.

"No, that doesn't scream 'me.' I'm going to stick with the god of gods. That's me. God of the gods here."

"While I used my trident, you struck down Cronus with a thunderbolt. What if you were . . . the god of sky and thunder?"

Now *this* was worthy of consideration.

"Yes . . . yes, I like that."

Zeus grabbed the metal thunderbolt he had resting against his throne, stood, and held it above his head. "I shall be . . . the god of sky and thunder!"

His brothers and sisters also stood, applauding.

"*And* the king of the gods!"

Poseidon slumped back into his throne. "Oh, so now he's two unrelated things. Great."

"Is that possible?" Demeter asked. "Can I get a second thing?"

Hades raised his hand. "Can I just trade mine out for the god of ceramics?"

* * *

King Leotis stood on the rocky promontory, examining the scroll detailing all of the gods and their domains. When he was a young king, he could hold the unraveled scroll himself. In the decades since, the number of gods flourished due to a breathtaking amount of incest and occasional bestiality. Now the papyrus stretched out ten feet, requiring four servants to hold it. There had been only two last year, but a strong wind transformed the scroll into a sail and blew the servants far into the Aegean Sea.

As ruler of Bybanos, it was vital he knew each god and their domain. This was a lesson he learned when his father, the former king, was murdered by an angry Philophrosyne for not remembering she was the goddess of friendliness and kindness.

He turned to his entourage standing next to the statues of the two most important gods to Bybanos. As a fishing port, Bybanos depended on the good will of Poseidon for its economy, and as a sister city of Athens, Athena was its protector.

It was the new statue of Athena that brought them there. The old statue had fallen into disrepair from the ravages of time and weather. Leotis searched all of Greece to find an artist who could sculpt a new statue that would please Athena. The sculptor now stood proudly next to his creation.

He nodded to the sculptor, who then covered the statue. "Surprise" was something that pleased the goddess. He knew because it was written on the scroll.

Leotis raised his hands heavenward. "Blissful and

merciful Athena, come, for you are revered gloriously."

"Who summons me?" a voice boomed from the sea. It sounded both male and female at once, a voice born of thunder.

"It is King Leotis. Great Athena, the city of Bybanos wishes to honor you with a new tribute to your likeness."

"It looks like Poseidon."

The king turned to the two statues, the still-covered Athena resting next to the Poseidon. "No, I meant the—"

"What do you mean 'no'? It's clearly Poseidon, right down to the trident."

"If you would allow—"

"Cut off the sculptor's hands and have him fix it."

Leotis walked to the covered statue and removed the cloak. "Behold . . . "

"Ah, yes, I see. That's much better."

Leotis turned back to the ocean. "Then you are pleased?"

"Yes. Now cut off the sculptor's hands."

The king looked to the sculptor, whose smile had dropped. "But . . . I thought you were pleased."

"I am," came the reply from the ocean. "But I'm also infallible, even when I'm wrong. So I can't rescind any of my commands. Cut off his hands and have him make the Poseidon one look like me."

"Does . . . it have to be in that order? It would be difficult for him to change the statue once—"

"You're questioning my infallibility? You must now also reaffirm your allegiance to me by having all men in the city change their name to 'Athena' in my honor."

"Wouldn't it be more fitting for the women to—"

"I'll check back on the statue in a month."

* * *

Everyone stood to receive Athena in the same spot one month later. The Athena statue remained as it had been, but the Poseidon had been crudely changed, with the amputated artist standing next to it. It didn't resemble Athena as much as it did an unfinished version of the statue that did. Helpfully, a sign reading "Athena" rested at its base.

The king raised his hands heavenward far less confidently than he had in the previous month. "Blissful and . . . mostly merciful Athena, come, for you are revered gloriously."

The booming voice returned from the distance. "Who seeks council with the gods?"

"It is I, King Athena, formerly King Leotis, ruler of Bybanos. We wish your approval of our new statue."

"This is Poseidon, not Athena. Do I sound like Athena?"

The voice sounded exactly like Athena.

The king shook his head. "Um . . . no."

"What have you done to my statue?"

"Athena . . . she asked us to alter it."

"That accursed woman. Defiling my statue is an act of war! I will wipe your town into the ocean unless a sacrifice is made."

"What shall we do, great Poseidon?"

"Wait, did you say your name was Athena?"

"Yes." The king motioned to the other men in his entourage. "She also had the men in our town change their name to hers in a show of allegiance."

"Everyone named Athena is to march into the ocean."

King Athena looked to Athena, worried. All of the Athenas look concerned. Particularly Athena.

"And each Athena is to lead oxen into the sea," the voice continued.

"Could we simply slaughter the oxen? It would be very difficult to get them to—"

"Into the sea! I'll check back later."

* * *

Queen Peletta and her newly promoted female entourage stood on the rocky promontory. It had been weeks since the hundreds of men of Bybanos marched over the cliff into the sea, each with a cow or bull in tow, and the track marks from the great struggle were still visible.

The queen hesitantly raised her arms heavenward. "Blissful and . . . somewhat merciful Poseidon, please bless our nets with plentiful fish. Our city starves as we have far too few oxen to plow our—"

She was interrupted by a booming voice in the distance. "What was that about Poseidon?"

"Oh, hello great Poseidon. Thank you for gracing us."

"I'm not Poseidon. Do I sound like Poseidon?"

The voice sounded exactly like her late husband's description of Poseidon.

"Why . . . no."

"Poseidon retired. I'm the new god of the sea."

"Well, let us know your name so we can now sing your praise in prayer in his stead."

"It's—" The sentence was interrupted by thunder erupting.

The queen looks to the others. They all shook their heads. No one else heard it either.

She turned back to the sea. "Sorry, could you repeat that?"

"You dare have me repeat myself? I said my name is—" Once again, thunder erupted over the name of the new god.

The queen looked to the ground, nervously. "The town of Bybanos welcomes you, oh—" She covered her mouth and said something unintelligible that sounded much like "arrggbytoonie." Then she uncovered her mouth. "—new god of the sea."

"I am pleased with your statue of me next to Athena. It's a perfect likeness."

Peletta looked to the crude statue that didn't look like a person or god but more an abstract celebration of marble. Her steward helpfully stepped sideways toward it and put her foot over the sign reading "Athena" at the bottom.

"What town is this that fights sea battles with cows?" the voice asked.

"I'm sorry?"

"All of the dead people and cattle in my sea. Have your cattle mastered ship building? It looks like it was evenly matched."

"No, your predecessor commanded—"

"I see my first duty will be to settle this conflict you have with your people-cows. Bring forth representatives of both man and cattle so that I may mediate. You have an hour."

* * *

Within the hour, Peletta and her people had led a cow up the cliff with difficulty, but not with as much difficulty as pushing each one off the cliff had been. She and the cow were each given five minutes to plead their case. The queen argued passionately why humans needed to rule in order for the town to function. The cow was mostly silent during her allotted time until the final few seconds when she mooed.

The new god decided in favor of the cows.

"All positions of power in Bybanos will be turned over to them immediately," the voice said. "No action will be taken without the verbal consent of your cow overlords."

The former queen looked to her new queen, who was chewing grass, then back to the sea. "Oh most powerful . . ." She paused when she remembered she didn't know the new god's name. "Oh most powerful Most Powerful. Surely this would lead to the economic collapse of our town . . . the starvation of our people . . ."

"If you find this arrangement unsatisfactory at this time tomorrow, return here and summon me. You may do so—"

* * *

Detritus looked down at Bybanos from her Olympian

palace. "—by saying my name three times. Again, it's—" She picked up one of Zeus's plundered lightning bolts and threw it into the sky above Bybanos. "That is all."

"What was that about?"

Detritus turned to see Debris had entered. "Nothing. I intercepted a prayer meant for Athena from a town called Bybanos a couple of months ago, and I've been messing with them ever since. I even got them to deface a statue of Poseidon."

"Poseidon won't like that," Debris said.

"No. When he finds out, he'll send the women into the sea to join their men. And cows."

"Cows?"

"It's not important."

Debris pointed to the one remaining lightning bolt. "Don't you worry our father Zeus will miss his lightning bolts?"

Detritus waved it off. "No worries. Our father was away impersonating one of the bulls in Byblos once he knew the men were gone and it was ladies' night."

* * *

About the Story

I don't know much about Patricia Pooks Burroughs.

Other than that time she pulled me out of a burning building. Since then, she's been all "Hey! I know you! I pulled you out of that building!" And I'm all, "OKAY! I GET it! I'm thankful for you saving my life, but can we get over it already?" This story makes us even.

MJ Butler

After I chipped the polish on two nails dragging you to safety? I think not.

The Editor

SWEET DIRTY LOVE

JEANNE LYET GASSMAN

DETRITUS CLICKED ON THE next profile on ImmortalLoveMatch.com and sighed. "It's hopeless. There is no one out there for me."

"Nonsense," her half-sister, Tidy, insisted. "We just have to keep looking." She took a step back from the computer, tsk-tsking in her usual slightly disapproving tone. "We really need to do something about your hair. Perhaps if you put it up . . . ?"

"What? No." Detritus shook her head, ignoring the cracker crumbs that showered over her shoulders. "My hair is fine."

Tidy looked doubtful. "If you say so."

Although Detritus and Tidy were both daughters of the bawdy Greek goddess Baubo, the two of them could not have been more unalike. Tidy, a statuesque blonde, was the epitome of order. She worked part-time as a rep for Athena Lou Cosmetics, selling make-up to the female immortals who could no longer hold on to their beauty by magic and thus depended on artifice. Everything about Tidy was perfectly coordinated, with matching shoes and purse dog, immaculately groomed nails, and just the right shade of lipstick. In fact, Tidy had a saying about personal crisis: "You can fix anything with lipstick." And she stuck by that belief, too, until the first time she tried to give Detritus a makeover, and the lipstick ended up smeared on Detritus's chin. "How do you do that?" she cried.

Detritus grinned at her, exposing flecks of "Perfect Passion" on her teeth. "It's just my nature."

According to Tidy, her half-sister Detritus had "issues." Her tangled red hair stuck out from her scalp in disorderly coils, and she couldn't manage to stay clean no matter how hard she tried. Bits of trash seemed to attach themselves to her clothing, and her apartment was decorated with the strange collages she created from her forages through garbage bins, dumps, and walks on the beach. Detritus would never admit it to Tidy, but she found messiness comforting.

Baubo still kept in touch with Tidy's father, Janus, who liked to have "twice the fun" and met Baubo twice a year for a reunion tryst. Detritus's paternity, however, was much more uncertain. According to Baubo, she was the product of a wild party in Hades' lair, but Baubo claimed she had no idea who had done the deed. "After cruising down the River Lethe, my memory is Swiss cheese. I recall nothing." She had plucked a string of damp seaweed from Detritus's sleeve. "Be happy you were conceived in love."

And love was what Detritus wanted now, not absent-minded love from her wayward mother or even the grudging affection of her half-sister. Detritus wanted to experience wild, crazy love, the kind of love that makes your heart bounce out of your chest with lust and desire, the kind that makes your knees wobble at the sound of your lover's voice. Too bad no one wanted her.

After Tidy left, Detritus returned to the computer, clicking once again through the limited list of prospects Immortal Love had recommended. Despite the many times she had adjusted her profile, IL had managed to find only a pathetic three matches. Was she that undesirable? The first one on the list, a god called Plaman, brandished a mullet and a ton of attitude. In his photo, he leaned back in his chair, his thinning hair slick with grease and an index finger crooked at the camera, as if to say, "I want you, babe!" Detritus found his cocky grin unnerving.

The second choice, who went by the name of Orphistus because he was a devoted follower of Dionysus, posted he loved women and wine, in that order. But with his red-rimmed eyes and puffy cheeks, Detritus suspected Orphistus loved wine more.

Her final match, Deb, had a sandy beard that had been unevenly trimmed and an endearing smudge on his brow that looked like dirt. He referred to himself as a collector and a sculptor, something that appealed to Detritus, since she herself was an aspiring artist. During her long, lonely strolls along the shore, she collected broken shells, pieces of rock, sea glass, and other found objects and arranged them in her collages. Of course, she also brought home a few uninvited hitchhikers that managed to attach themselves to her as well, including fiddler crabs, sand fleas, fish hooks, empty water bottles, beer cans, and lost keys. Sometimes she added these items to her art. Baubo called Detritus's work "interesting" and hinted strongly that Tidy should hang one of the pieces on her own wall. But Tidy balked. "I agree. They have a certain . . . flavor. But they're so messy. And some of them have crawly things. No, thanks."

Now Detritus studied Deb's profile photo. No doubt about it. He was cute. She hesitated, then sent him a flirty wink.

He sent a flirty wink right back. She was so surprised she almost shut her computer. What should she do? She requested a date, and he accepted.

They agreed to meet the following Friday evening for coffee at the popular Elysian Brew Spot on Valhalla Ave. It was crowded, noisy, and most importantly, safe.

* * *

Tidy was beside herself when she learned Detritus had a real date. "I'll do your make-up, but you have to promise to sit still. No disasters."

Detritus paraded her wardrobe for her half-sister's approval. "What about the blue? It brings out the color of my eyes."

Tidy tapped a manicured fingernail against her pursed lips. "Hmm. No, the dress is, well, a little worn around the edges. Your hem is fraying, and there's a tear in the right sleeve."

"Then this coral number. It shows off my figure, I think."

"Is that a cheese stain on the bodice?"

Detritus was ready to send Tidy home. She was such a critic. "It's fine. I'll wear a sweater."

On the afternoon before her date, Detritus was so nervous she allowed Tidy to stay only long enough to apply mascara, blush, and lipstick. Shortly after Tidy left, Detritus received a text. Deb had cancelled their date.

Despairing and desperate for a friendly shoulder to cry on, Detritus phoned her half-sister.

"You're supposed to be having a great time," Tidy said when she picked up. "Not talking to me."

"It's off," Detritus wailed. "He dumped me, and we never even went out."

"What? I'll be right there."

Tidy may have been critical and disapproving of Detritus's lifestyle, but she was loyal. She breezed into her half-sister's apartment, immediately taking charge, snatching up dirty socks and a discarded dishtowel and tossing them into the hamper. In the kitchen, she scooped up a pile of dust bunnies and feline fur. "Do you have a cat?"

"No, I'm allergic." Detritus burst into a paroxysm of sneezing.

Tidy swept the dust and hair into the trash. "Now, tell me everything," she said as she rinsed out a mug and poured Detritus a fresh cup of coffee.

Detritus rubbed her eyes, smearing her knuckles with charcoal mascara. "He cancelled our date. Gave some lame excuse about needing to wash his chariot."

"Hmm. Well, it's possible. Men do love their vehicles."

"It's raining!"

Tidy coughed. Dabbing a tissue at the streaks on Detritus's face, she said, "Well, he's a cad, that's all. And what kind of name is Deb anyway? It sounds like a girl's name."

"It's a nickname. Short for Debris. He's a collector and an artist."

"Well, he's still a jerk by any name." She straightened Detritus's collar. "You know what they say you should do when you fall out of a chariot and break your leg."

"Get a splint?"

Tidy giggled. "No, silly. Get back in." And before Detritus could stop her, Tidy had opened the IL file. "So, who else is on your list? This guy Plaman looks promising . . . " She tapped the computer.

"No, wait," Detritus cried.

"Too late. You have a date for drinks at Bacchanal's in forty minutes." She dragged Detritus from her chair. "Let's get you cleaned up. And wear a sweater. That cheese stain is spreading."

* * *

Detritus spotted Plaman easily, as he was holding court in the corner, flirting with half a dozen young women. But none of them stayed long. They paused to listen to his patter then shrugged their shoulders and moved on. Dodging the crowd of females fleeing Plaman's overtures, Detritus edged past a morose-looking figure slumped at a table: Orphistus, who was nursing his third drink alone, judging by the empties. She stumbled on toward Plaman.

"Hello," she said, her voice coming out like a croak.

Plaman glanced up, his smile freezing and fading as he took her in. He clearly recognized her from the Immortal Love site but had obviously been expecting someone more alluring, Detritus thought. Without a word, he motioned for her to sit down.

An awkward silence followed. Then Plaman said, "So, you're the aspiring artist, uh, Detritus, right?"

She nodded. "Yes, I like to make collages."

Plaman waved for the waitress to take their order. He requested another "whiskey, straight," while Detritus asked for a martini with two olives, "leave in the pits." She planned to use the pits later in one of her art pieces. After downing his drink, Plaman turned to Detritus and stared. "Did you know you have a broken pencil sticking out of your hair?"

She plucked the pencil from her ponytail and dropped it on the table. "Those things happen to me all the time."

"Ah." Brightening, Plaman sat up and began to brag about his important connections. "Prometheus is my third cousin, once removed. I inherited his skill. I can light this candle with my fingertips. Watch."

Flames shot from his fingernails, igniting the strand of toilet paper dangling from Detritus's sleeve, which set her cocktail napkin on fire, followed by the roaring inferno of the tablecloth. It took three waitresses, two fire extinguishers, and a lot of screaming to put out the blaze, and that effectively ended their date.

* * *

After her disastrous encounter with Plaman, Detritus decided all men were losers. The only cure for her blues was shopping, and she especially loved shopping estate sales. While most of the patrons squabbled over furniture and china, Detritus liked to dig through the junk drawers and button jars. People threw away the most interesting stuff. The following Saturday morning, she hit the circuit.

The first two stops were duds and had been cleaned out of anything useful, but at the third place, she found a box crammed with scraps of fabric, thimbles, rubber bands, paper clips, crumbled erasers, unidentified keys, and various screws, nails, and fasteners. She was sifting through the box when she heard the homeowner say to someone behind her: "Just shove that pile out of the way. It's all garbage anyway."

"No," the person said. "That's okay. I want it. How much?"

Detritus turned around to see who was buying trash. Deb, or more accurately Debris, stood by the curb. His eyes widened as she faced him. Detritus set down her box and offered her hand. "Hello. We haven't met in person, but I'm—"

"Detritus. I know." He cleared his throat. "You're very pretty."

It was her turn to blush. "Thank you." She pointed to the stack spilling around his feet. "You're buying this?"

He scooped up a waterlogged magazine. "Isn't this great? I believe in dirt. It's good luck."

Detritus stroked the scrap of tattered paper, imagining

the possibilities. "It's lovely."

"Look, I'm sorry about the other night. I guess I panicked a little. I thought when you met me you'd . . . " He hesitated. "I thought you wouldn't like me. That you'd think I was a slob."

She smiled. He had cement dust caked on both elbows and a blob of paint on one shoe. "I think you're very creative." Gathering up her treasures, she added, "I was planning to visit two more yard sales today. Would you like to join me?"

He nodded. "And maybe I could take you out to lunch afterward? To make up for my rudeness?" Tenderly, he brushed a cobweb from her ear.

At his gentle touch, Detritus's heart bounced wildly in her chest, and her knees wobbled. "Ooh, I—"

Deb caught her elbow. "Have you ever been to the dump?"

* * *

About the Story

Debris and Detritus. These gods have a small shrine (collecting dust!) in my house. When I was asked to write a story about them, I was honored and delighted. How wonderful to be able to pay tribute to the value of messiness. My home is notorious for its clutter, dust bunnies, piles of books and papers, missing pets, and general disarray, but out of that confusion and disorder, I still produce art. Some of my writing is humorous, some of it is more dramatic, and some of it is downright intense. I write everything from essays to short fiction to novels, and I hope my readers find my work entertaining and thought-provoking. If you'd like to more know about what I write and who I am, please drop my website for a visit.

JEANNE LYET GASSMAN

The Groom Wore Wings

Melanie Fletcher

"There you are!"

The Greek god Debris lowered his Prada sunglasses, blinking at the sea nymph in front of him. "Lisa?" he said in unfeigned delight. "Sweetie, you look fabulous!"

His twin brother Detritus (also Greek, also a god) slid his own designer eyewear up just to be different, eyeing the leggy brunette. "Girlfriend, you are looking on point," he said in approval. "Kate Spade?"

"Kay Unger," Lisa said, glancing down at her dress. "But that's not important right now. I need your help."

It was common knowledge in the Greek pantheon that the Nereid Ligea, with her sisters Iaera and Pasithea, had made quite the splash in human society by founding It's Divine Event Services. The company had quickly become the premier party-planning service in south Florida, with the trio of sea nymphs (now known among mortals as Lisa, Jennifer, and Patricia) using their magic to fulfill the demands of the fussiest society hostess or whacked-out Bridezilla.

Debris and Detritus had recently helped the Nereids out on a particularly sticky wedding. The challenges had included a couple who were up-and-coming Hollywood stars with accompanying egos, paparazzi-piloted drones peeking into hotel room windows, the alcoholic mother of the groom who loathed the bride with a passion, a pre-ceremony fistfight among the bridesmaids over who was going to nab the Oscar-nominated and exceedingly well-hung best man, and floral table decorations unexpectedly infested by fire ants.

While the Nereids managed the engaged couple, drunken mother, and unwanted drones, Debris had whipped up stunning replacement table settings after a quick visit to Publix, and Detritus had spiked the bridesmaids' hopes by seducing the best man in the church's basement. It had been a ball.

Both gods leaned forward. "Is it another wedding?" Debris said hopefully.

Lisa settled on the end of Debris' lounge. "Sorry, sweetie, no," she apologized. "But all three of us are swamped so I really need someone to help out who can handle the supernatural."

Both twins' eyebrows rose at that. "Supernatural how?" Detritus asked.

"You'll understand when you meet my client. Please, just go and chat with her. If you don't want to do it, I'll understand, but I think you'll change your mind once you meet her."

The Nereid held out a Post-it note. Debris plucked the

pink paper out of her hand, frowning at the words written on it. "Shady Oaks Nursing Home?"

* * *

The old lady seated in the recliner gave them a sassy grin. "I know this must be a little unusual for a company like It's Divine, but—"

"Unusual is our forte," Debris declared, plucking the woman's spotted hand off the armrest and giving it a gallant kiss. "So you want us to throw you an eightieth birthday party."

"Yes. And I want it somewhere fun with a specific DJ to provide the music. I want my friends here to come, but I also want it to be open to the public. This needs to be one hell of a party, and not just for old farts."

"I see." Debris pursed his lips in thought. The request itself didn't sound too difficult. Putting together a rave was something he and Detritus could do in their sleep.

It was the person making the request who was unusual. Captain Margaret Henderson (Army Nursing Corps, retired) looked delicate and frail in the crocheted afghan wrapped around her bird-like body. But her eyes were bright, and her manner was just as alert and forceful as it must have been back when she was in charge of Army nurses during the Vietnam War. Age hadn't weakened her mind or personality, and she knew exactly what she wanted when it came to her birthday party. It had to be loud, fun, and full of good dance music, and at some point during the festivities, she wanted the DJ to play her favorite song.

Neither Debris nor Detritus mentioned the other

notable thing about Miz Maggie, as she told them to call her, but it was obvious to those who could see beyond the mortal veil.

Somewhere in her past, Captain Henderson had been loved by something divine, as evidenced by the streaks of purest white in her aura. It explained why Lisa had wanted to take this job. Earning the goodwill of other divine creatures, even those not in your own pantheon, was always a smart tactic.

"I think we can do that," Debris continued, twirling his sunglasses around by one earpiece as he ran through possibilities. "There's a new club that's just about to open down on Clematis. I think I can call in some favors and get them to host us as a pre-opening party—"

"Okay, Miz Maggie, I got your lunch—" A handsome Latino orderly with a tray backed into the room, turning and blinking when he saw Debris and Detritus. "Aw, I'm sorry, I didn't know you had guests. I'll bring this back later."

"Don't you move, Arturo," Maggie ordered, waving him in. "Boys, this is Arturo Rojas, one of the best damn orderlies I've ever had the pleasure of working with. Arturo, this is Detritus and Debris. They're with It's Divine Events."

Arturo's eyes widened even more. "Oh, wow. You guys did the Chris Payne and Selena Alvarado wedding!"

Detritus batted his eyelashes. "Not to mention the best man."

Maggie gave her orderly a fond look. "So they know

their stuff?"

Arturo nodded like a bobblehead doll. "They throw some of the best damn parties in south Florida," he said, enthused. "Damn, Miz Maggie, I had no idea you knew them."

"Well, I just met them," Maggie said. "And it's a good thing you're here. Boys, Arturo's boyfriend Reese is the DJ I want for my party."

To the gods' surprise, the orderly reacted as if the little old lady had punched him. "Uh, Miz Maggie, I don't know about that," he mumbled. "I mean, Reese is good, but—a party? You know what he's like."

She waved off the objection. "Sweetheart, you know I love Reese's stuff," she said. "It's time the rest of the world heard it, too. You just leave all the details to me and these nice boys here. Now put that tray down and scoot."

With another concerned look at Debris and Detritus, the orderly did as he was told. Once he was gone, Detritus leaned forward and said, "So, what's the catch?"

Miz Maggie's eyes twinkled. "I knew you boys were smart."

* * *

Catch One was Miss Delilah Montgomery, the manager of Shady Oaks Retirement Home. Or as Maggie referred to her, "Der Commandant." Miss Montgomery ran the retirement home on rails and according to her own strict views on propriety.

Maggie said that she had approached Miss Montgomery with the idea of holding the party in the home's entertainment room. Der Commandant had refused on the grounds that dancing, alcohol, dance music, late night dilly-dallying, or anything that raised a resident's blood pressure were not appropriate activities for those "in the sunset years of their lives." And by God, Delilah Montgomery was *not* going to let a bus full of her residents out of her sight for an evening of mayhem and debauchery.

The gods shared a knowing look. "Someone certainly needs to get laid," Debris murmured.

"Don't look at me," Detritus muttered back. "Finger-wagging nursing home administrators are not allowed on my 1200 thread count sheets."

The issue of Der Commandant was put to the side for a moment in order to deal with Catch Two, aka Reese Dilly, Arturo's boyfriend and putative DJ. The problem became more apparent when the gods headed over to the warehouse where Reese worked, making ceramic tchotchkes for Florida tourists. The owner, a swarthy individual by the name of Vlad who clearly wanted to return to the porn mag he'd been perusing, glared at them when they asked for Reese. "He's busy," Vlad grunted. "You can talk to him after he gets off work."

Detritus gave Vlad a disarming grin. "I bet you get all the honeys with that attitude, you big bear, you. But seriously, we need to talk to him now." The god pulled out a black leather wallet that contained a realistic FBI ID card he'd willed into existence. "If you don't mind."

Vlad straightened in his chair and squeaked, which was a disconcerting sound coming from a swarthy individual.

"Um, he's in the pouring room. Just go straight on back."

"Thank so much!" Detritus caroled. Within moments, he and his twin were in a grubby room where a tall, handsome man in a lumbersexual beard and some of the worst clothing choices either of them had ever seen since the 70s was busy pouring plaster into a set of forms.

Detritus introduced himself and explained their mission, then paused. "Just out of curiosity, sweetie, where on Earth did you get those clothes?"

The DJ looked down at his impromptu tank top made from a faded Brady Bunch t-shirt that had been attacked with what looked like pinking shears. The cutoff shorts in an improbable black and red calico floral, liberally spattered with dried plaster, didn't help. "St. Vincent's," he said. "Look, I can't afford designer clothes like you guys. And I *like* thrift shop stuff."

"That's fine, hon, but there's a difference between popping tags and shopping exclusively from the Goodwill sale area," Debris said, prowling around the DJ and analyzing the goods. "Even Macklemore couldn't make this outfit work."

"Tim Gunn himself couldn't make that outfit work," Detritus said with a thoughtful tongue pop. "Well, you know what that means."

His brother grinned. "Oh, yes I do."

The twins clapped in unison. "Shopping trip!"

Reese stared at them in dismay. "But I can't afford—I mean, I'm working—"

"Less talking, more walking," Detritus said, plucking the

bucket of plaster out of Reese's hands and shepherding him towards the door. "Don't worry, your boss isn't going to bitch."

"Much," Debris said merrily, handing the bucket off to Vlad, who had picked that moment to appear. "Darling, finish up Reese's plaster thingies, won't you? We'll bring him back in a few hours. Maybe."

Vlad didn't so much beetle his brow as armadillo it. "I don't know who the hell you think you are," he growled, "but you ain't Feds, and I'll be damned if—"

Detritus sighed. What he was about to do was a major no-no, but he didn't have time to be delicate. "You don't mind if Reese takes the rest of the day off, do you?" he purred, extruding some divine mojo and wrapping it around Vlad like an invisible blanket. "Especially since he's clearly one of your best workers." He eyed the hunky DJ. "In fact, you were thinking of giving him a raise."

He squeezed the mojo, and Vlad blinked. "I was? Oh, yeah, I was," the man said, much more amiable now. "Okay, buddy, take the day off."

"Fabulous, thank you!" Detritus sang, grabbing a mystified Reese's arm and guiding him out with a beaming Debris bringing up the rear.

Behind them, Vlad stared dreamily into his bucket of rapidly hardening plaster.

* * *

"I had no idea those shops even existed," Reese said five hours later, peering over the stuffed shopping bags in his arms.

"Consignment stores are a godsend to the fashion forward but financially frail," Debris said. "Now, can we hear some of these mixes of yours?"

The tall, bearded man blushed. "Uh, are you sure? I mean, Arturo likes it, but he's my boyfriend, so—"

"We need to hear it first if you're going to be DJing at Miz Maggie's party," Debris said firmly, guiding him back towards the sleek BMW M2 coupe the gods had borrowed for the afternoon. They stuffed the bags into the miniscule trunk and got in. "The sound system in this beast takes memory sticks, so if you have anything digital on you, hand it over."

With some effort, Reese produced a neon green flash drive from his jeans pocket. While he tried to get comfortable in the tiny back seat, Debris popped the drive into the car's sound system and selected a track at random.

The twin gods immediately understood why Maggie wanted Reese to play at her party. His music was a glorious combination of modern house with luscious 70's funk and glam rock hooks, anchored with deep R&B bass lines. There were even hints of disco here and there, luring the listener to get down and boogie.

"Honey, we can book you for multo parties with this kind of sound," Debris enthused. "And not just in Florida, either. New York will love it, and Ibiza will go positively insane. You'll be able to tell Vlad to go stick his head in a bucket of plaster within three months, mark my words."

The DJ squirmed uncomfortably. "Um, does that mean I'd have to play live? Like, in front of people?"

Detritus, now behind the wheel of the coupe, glanced in the rearview mirror. "That's kind of the idea, pumpkin. Is that a problem?"

Reese grimaced. "Yeah, that's . . . not so good."

"How 'not so good'?"

"I don't play in public. Like, ever. I don't mind putting mixes on memory sticks or CDs for other people, but I get scared in crowds." Broad shoulders sagged. "I thought Arturo told you. Do I have to take all that stuff back now?"

Debris shot his brother an exasperated look. Apparently new clothes weren't going to solve Catch Two after all.

* * *

After dropping a still-apologizing Reese off at his apartment, the gods decided to take another crack at Catch One. Detritus was hoping that Der Commandant would turn out to be a brassy, blowzy matron who was a hard-ass because she enjoyed throwing her weight around with her elderly charges. That would make mojoing her much easier, not to mention more enjoyable.

As it turned out, Fate needed a laugh as much as anyone else.

Delilah Montgomery was indeed somewhere in her late forties, but stick-thin and dressed in a prim beige twinset with a darker brown skirt that hit just below her knee, support hose, no-nonsense horn rims that millennials would call "authentic," and sturdy Dr. Scholl's shoes. Detritus suspected that if he pushed up her left sleeve, he would find a folded Kleenex tucked under the band of her watch. Her mouse-brown hair had been scraped back in a prim bun, and her eyes were magnified by her glasses into two pools of washed-out blue. All she needed was a wimple and a wedding ring, and she could walk straight into any nunnery in the country.

"I do my best to keep all of the residents as healthy and content as possible, considering their ages and medical conditions," she informed them with a huff after they'd flashed yet another governmental ID, this time from the Florida Department of Elder Affairs. "Their sunset years should be ones of peaceful contemplation. To that end, Shady Oaks provides balanced meals, wellness checks, and regular trips to the doctor and dentist. It's important to keep their minds stimulated as well, so we have weekly luncheons, a monthly outing to museums and other age-appropriate attractions, and holiday celebrations at the end of the year. My staff is vetted and has to pass drug screens, and all of my records are in order. You're welcome to check them if you like."

Balanced meals, luncheons, and museum visits. Detritus shuddered. "That's not necessary, Mrs. Montgomery—"

"Miss." She blinked, rabbit-like. "I'm not married. I consider taking care of the elderly to be my life's work."

Detritus glanced at his brother, but the other god was peering in interest at the bookcases in the office. "And I'm sure you do a splendid job," the god said, trying to sound professional. Or if not professional, then at least not like he was mentally rolling his eyes and gagging. "That being said, we had received word of a resident who wanted to throw an eightieth birthday party for herself. She said that you turned down her request."

Miss Montgomery's lips tightened. "That would be Miss Henderson. I appreciate her service to our country, but I'm afraid her plans for this—event—were completely inappropriate for the other residents. Dance music would greatly increase the risk of falls, heart attacks, and strokes, and drinking alcohol is contraindicated with many if not most of the medications the residents take. I offered to hold a party in the common room and play some nice orchestral music on our sound system, but—" The woman grimaced. "Well, what she said to me isn't something a lady is supposed to know, much less say out loud."

You go, Miz Maggie. Detritus could just imagine what the former Army nurse had said to her prim and proper custodian. There was no help for it; he'd have to use more divine mojo. "I appreciate your concerns, Miss Montgomery," he said, extending his power around the woman, "but considering Miss Henderson's age, plus her service, as you mentioned, I was wondering if there was some way we could see our way clear to a compromise?"

Miss Montgomery's eyes widened, and Detritus got ready for her to capitulate. He almost fell off the chair when she said, "Absolutely not. I have a duty to my residents, and I won't shirk that duty simply because Margaret Henderson wants to dance herself into a broken hip."

It was Detritus's turn to blink. "I—are you sure? Don't you want to, I don't know, think about it or something?"

"I have. There will be no orgiastic birthday party for

Miss Henderson." She leaned forward, glaring at him. "And I'm more than a bit offended that you would come in here and try to change my mind, Mr. Detritus."

The neckline of her shell blouse gaped just a bit with her movement, and a delicate gold cross swung into view. Detritus smothered a groan when he realized why his mojo wasn't working. Delilah Montgomery had to be a genuinely devout Christian. Divine mojo only worked on those who didn't really believe in any gods at all, such as Vlad and a large proportion of Western Civilization, or on those who believed in their particular pantheon. And since it was obvious that Miss Montgomery wasn't a secret worshipper of Zeus, Greek god mojo wasn't going to work. He would have to fall back on his charm, the gods help him.

"Well, if that's your decision, then that's your decision," Debris said cheerfully, surprising Detritus. "Thank you for your time, Miss Montgomery. We'll let you get back to work."

"Wha—" Detritus found himself physically lifted out of his chair and guided out of the nursing home by his brother. Once they were shielded by a pair of palm trees on the sidewalk, he turned on Debris. "What. The. *Tartarus*? I know she's a stick-in-the-mud, but I could have talked her into it if you hadn't interrupted."

"Oh, balls. I saw her cross, too. She's a wannabe nun who thinks it's her job to keep old people quiet and medicated until they pop their clogs," Debris said patiently. "That being said, did you notice what was on her bookshelves?"

"Uh, no," Detritus said, throwing up his hands. "Kinda busy trying to do a job for our client?"

The handsome god shook his head in mock disapproval. "I love you, brother mine, but you really need to learn how to multi-task. Her bookshelves are loaded with romance novels. I saw everything from *Sweet Savage Love* to *The Siren*. Miss Montgomery is clearly a smoldering stick figure of repressed sexual desire. If we find an appropriate outlet for that, she'll be too busy enjoying herself to notice her inmates going on a field trip."

"Oh, no." Detritus shuddered. "I like Miz Maggie, but I am *not* throwing myself on that grenade for her."

"Like she'd have you. Besides, I wasn't talking about you, doofus." Debris pulled out a sleek iPhone and tapped in a number, holding it to his ear. "Hi, Cupid? It's Debris. Oh, fabulous as usual. Look, could you send one of your cherubs to my location? We're working with It's Divine on a project, and we have a frustrated virgin named Delilah Montgomery who really needs a big Hollywood-style romance right now." He listened for a moment. "Great! Yes, see you at the Saturnalia party. Kisses!"

He cut the call, smirking at his brother. "Handled."

Detritus rolled his eyes. "Whatever. So, what are we going to do about our crowd-shy DJ?"

Debris' smirk grew even more annoying. "I have an idea. But we need to stop at a mirror outlet first."

* * *

Reese's thick eyebrows approached his hairline. "Wow. That's, uh . . . "

"I think the word you're looking for is brilliant," Debris said smugly. In the corner, a phone-perusing Detritus made a rude noise. "Ignore my brother—he's a twatwaffle when he's hungry."

"I know what you can go eat," Detritus muttered.

Unfazed, Debris walked around the panels of tall one-way mirrors that had been set up around Reese's turntables with the reflective sides turned inwards. "People can see you, but you can't see them," he explained. "All you can see is your own handsome face as you work. If anyone asks, you can say it's an isolation chamber that allows you to work with the music without being distracted by outside interference. Not only is it technically true, but it makes you sound like an *artiste*."

Arturo wandered in, still in his orderly whites. "Gotta say, babe, it looks kinda cool. Give it a try?"

The lumbersexual shrugged and slid through a gap in the mirrors, donning his earphones as Debris picked up a waiting mirror and slid it into the gap. Soon, more of that amazing music was pounding through the apartment. Arturo started dancing, and Debris did an impromptu little Hustle around his annoyed twin in celebration.

The music stopped and Reese slid off his headphones. "I think this is gonna work," he called, enthusiastic now. "So where am I playing?"

"Tonight, it's a place called Club Hosanna," Debris informed him. "Tomorrow, sweetie, it's the world."

* * *

After two quick calls to a moving company to transport

Reese's equipment and isolation booth to the club and a bus company to supply a minibus for Miz Maggie's friends, the gods headed back to the nursing home, confident that they would find Der Commandant in the arms of her new cherub-arranged inamorato and the home's residents free to boogie. "Now we just have to tell Miz Maggie to round up the usual suspects and have them meet us outside tonight," Debris said as they materialized in front of Shady Oaks. "Then we whisk them off to the club, and Bob's your . . . "

He trailed off as he spotted a giggling septugenarian tottering across the lawn, followed by an octogenarian with a Zimmer frame and a lusty grin. On the corner of the building, an orderly and what appeared to be one of the home's cooks were in a passionate embrace, tearing at each other's clothes while they enthusiastically swapped spit. The fact that the orderly was a hair over five feet tall and the cook was not only taller than him but old enough to be his mother didn't seem to bother either of them. From inside the home, more sighs and moans were drifting out to the sidewalk.

Debris said a very bad word in ancient Greek. "What did that cherub *do*?"

As if summoned, a pink cloud puffed into existence next to them, and a boggled-looking cherub limped out of it, golden bow dragging on the ground. "Oh. Uh, hi?"

"Hi, yourself," Debris said in a dangerous tone, looming over the shorter demigod. "What's going on here?"

The cherub gave the nursing home a hopeless glance.

"The boss said I was supposed to come here and give—" he fished a sticky note out of his quiver and peered at it "—a Delilah Montgomery a big romance. I found a good match for her with a local neighbor—nice guy, young widower, kinda goofy but sweet—and shot them. Or tried to, anyway."

Detritus smothered a laugh as Debris planted furious fists on his hips. "What do you mean, *anyway*?"

"They kept missing!" the cherub wailed. "I swear to Zeus, that lady moves like the dickens! I'd aim for her, and whoosh, she'd jink off and the arrow would hit someone else. I must've hit at least eight people by accident. Do you have any idea what the boss is going to do to me?"

"Send you to work for Tinder?" Detritus snarked.

Debris stared daggers at his brother. "So, you didn't fix her up with the neighbor?" he demanded.

"No," the cherub moaned. "Which sucks, because they really would make a great couple. But I can't get her to fall in love with him if I can't hit her with an arrow!"

Detritus glanced at his Rolex. They had three hours to get everyone rounded up and over to the club. "All right, junior. You go on standby. The A-Team will take it from here."

The dejected cherub slunk back into his cloud while Debris folded his arms in divine irritation. "And who, pray tell, is the A-Team?"

"Us, silly." Detritus popped his tongue. "Well, us with some help. The arrows are probably sliding off her for the same reason my mojo didn't work, which gives a big middle finger up to love conquering all. So we call in the big guns in her pantheon." He pulled out his iPhone and scrolled through the Favorites list, stopping when he got to the Ms. He double-tapped a name, grinning when he heard an urbane voice answer.

"Yeah, hi, it's Detritus," he said cheerily. "I'm fine, thanks for asking. Yes, I have *seen* the show. That Brit actor they have playing you is absolutely adorable, isn't he?" He winked at his waiting brother. "Anyway, we're in south Florida right now, and we've got kind of a sticky situation here with a believer in your pantheon. Very prim, very proper, and very much in our way. I was wondering, 'Seducer' is still one of your titles, right?"

* * *

Two hours later, the gods hung back behind the now-familiar set of palm trees as a tall, blond man dressed in a black suit so minimalist it was stunning and holding a matching Bible escorted a smitten Miss Montgomery off the nursing home premises. "I'm so glad you had the time to talk to me. You have no idea how it gladdens my heart to speak to good Christians about our missionary work in rural communities," the man said in warm tones. "So few people take an interest in what happens to souls these days."

He glanced over at the hidden gods. A passerby might have been startled by the red flash in his eyes. *You two owe me big-time for this. I'm not really big on good deeds.*

Name your price, Detritus sent back. *Just take her out and show her a nice time. And leave her soul right where you found it, mister.*

Oh, please. That's so fourteenth century. And I want my throne room redecorated.

Done.

Fine. White teeth gleaming in a charming smile that was just a shade wolfish, the Morningstar escorted the nursing home supervisor away from her vocation.

Debris and Detritus grinned at each other. "Showtime."

* * *

After separating the assorted cherub-struck couples (one particularly determined pair required a hose), persuading everyone to get cleaned up and dressed in their nicest attire, and juggling a last-minute cadre of orderlies and cooks who decided that in the absence of Miss Montgomery, they wanted to go dancing at a club, too, everyone from the Shady Oaks Nursing Home had been successfully delivered to Club Hosanna. The bouncer was somewhat taken aback by the shuffling line of senior citizens queuing up at the door, but a quick word with the manager and a quicker tip of a Benjamin had him smiling and ushering the folks into the building. Reese and his isolation booth had already been set up at the DJ space, and he was playing some slower tracks that felt like a musical welcome.

Miz Maggie, with her gleaming silver hair freshly set and wearing a silky black pantsuit that sparkled in the club's dancing spotlights, held onto Debris and Detritus's arms as they showed her around. "Oh, this is exactly what I wanted," she breathed, watching as a few tentative couples hit the floor to Reese's slowed-down mix. "I can't thank you enough, boys. You worked wonders here."

"It's what we do," Debris said modestly, summoning a flummoxed bartender who came over with three flutes of champagne. He handed them around, raising his to the old woman. "Happy birthday, Miz Maggie, and may you get everything you wished for tonight."

An odd expression crossed her face, a cross between regret and hope. "Did you tell Reese about that one song I wanted?"

"Yup, and he has it cued up. It's ready to go whenever you want."

"Not just yet. But . . . good." A corner of her mouth curled up as her mood changed, and she drained her champagne. "Well, then. How about you two tall, handsome men take a lady out for a spin on the dance floor?"

* * *

The night turned into one of the oddest but most enjoyable parties either of the gods had attended in a long time. The doorman had started selectively letting younger partiers into the club; to say they were a bit taken aback by the senior attendees was an understatement. But the occasional side eye and grumble disappeared when trays of free shots began making the rounds of the club. "Courtesy of the birthday girl," every waiter said, nodding back at Miz Maggie, who was now ensconced in the best booth in the house. A gaggle of cute guys that spanned an age gap from barely legal to barely breathing were also wedged into the red leather banquette with her, competing with each other to make her laugh. She was clearly having the time of her life.

Reese edged up the music tempo, but enough of the more mobile Shady Oaks residents kept up the pace on the dance floor, while others camped out in booths or showed eager young south Floridians how to do dances like the Bump and Bus Stop. Debris and Detritus were careful to keep circling around the club and keep an eye on things, defusing any potential hotspots or disagreements and keeping the vibe bright.

By the time the management wheeled out a huge, magnificent birthday cake covered in sparkler candles and everyone in the club sang "Happy Birthday" to Miz Maggie, the gods were busy congratulating themselves on a job well done. It wasn't until the cake had been blown out and pieces distributed to the laughing, happy attendees that Debris noticed Maggie raise a hand to her chest, a look of discomfort on her face.

She took a few steps away from the cake then grimaced and collapsed. Debris darted through the crowds to her side, beaten only by Arturo, who was already kneeling next to her, turning her over. "Miz Maggie, what's wrong?" the orderly shouted over the music.

She tried to smile but shook her head. Her hand curled into a fist, pressing harder against her chest in a clear sign of cardiac distress. "Someone call 911," Arturo bellowed. "We need an ambulance!"

Debris was abruptly aware of Detritus appearing at his side. "Oh, no," the other god said sadly. "I was afraid of that. Can we do something?"

Debris shook his head. Mortals had such short little lives, and if it was Maggie's time, then there wasn't anything they could do about it. But there was something niggling at him, something hovering on the edge of his awareness—

—something with wings—

"Excuse me." A tall, dark-haired man in old-fashioned solid green fatigues nudged them to one side, bending down and scooping Miz Maggie into his arms. "Not yet, Mags," he said with a smile. "You still owe me a dance."

"Dude, she's not dancing!" Arturo said, scrambling to his feet. "She needs to get to a hospital!"

"No," the man said, his tone kind but firm. "She owes me a dance, and I intend to collect."

The old woman blinked, focusing on the man. One trembling hand rose, coming to rest on his cheek. "It took you long enough," she said, her voice wobbly.

"I'm sorry. I had to wait until—well, you know."

And suddenly, Debris understood everything. He turned and scrambled through the crowd to Reese's DJ booth, yanking open the mirror "door." When Reese slid off his headphones he shouted, "I need you to play the song now!"

"But—"

"Now!" Debris screamed.

Reese cringed but did as instructed. The throbbing tones of house music abruptly ended, replaced by the lovely soaring sound of an old-school studio orchestra that segued into the smooth tones of Billy Preston.

The dark-haired man in the fatigues carried Miz Maggie out onto the floor. He eased her onto her feet, keeping his arms around her until she could stand on her own. The rhythm of the music caught them, and the two slowly moved into the classic steps of a waltz. As the spangled lights of the disco ball passed over the couple, the years fell away from the Army nurse, figuratively at first and then literally. Grey hair turned blond, wrinkles smoothed away, and tentative movement regained strength and surety as Miz Maggie and her suitor twirled around the dance floor. By the middle of the song, the old lady had been replaced by a vibrant woman in her mid-30s, dressed in Army fatigues that matched her paramour's. The two gazed at each other as if nothing else existed in the world.

The entire atmosphere of the club had changed as well, becoming an unabashed haven of joy. Arturo slipped past Debris into the isolation booth, sliding behind Reese and wrapping his arms around the other man. Resting his chin on Reese's shoulder, they watched Miz Maggie twirl around the dance floor in the arms of her lover.

Near the end of the song, shadowy wings erupted from the back of Miz Maggie's suitor, wrapping both of them in feathers of obsidian and jet. When the music ended, the lights went out for a second, but both humans and gods could feel the magic rolling through the building, fulfilling a decades-old promise.

When the light came back on again, the couple was gone.

As the crowd started chattering excitedly, Detritus

joined his brother. "Called it," he said smugly. "Angel of death. They're *so* dramatic."

"Oh, shut up," Debris chided, bumping Detritus's shoulder with his own. "Just be happy for them."

"I am. Think her body will show up in her bed tomorrow?"

"Most likely. Shouldn't surprise anyone—she was eighty, after all. And if anyone makes a fuss, we can try some mojo—" He felt his phone buzz in his jacket. Pulling it out, he read the text on the screen and chortled. "Oh, dear. It's Luce. Remember the neighbor that incompetent cherub was trying to hit? He saw Luce out with Delilah and threw a punch at him. Apparently, Der Commandant's arid little heart grew three sizes at the thought of two men fighting over her, and she and the goofy neighbor are eloping to Vegas. Luce says we need to redecorate his bedroom as well, to cover 'wear and tear.'"

"Meh. Whatever." Detritus reached out and pulled a pair of perfect margaritas out of the air, handing one to his twin. "Here's to another successful job, brother mine."

Debris clinked his salted rim against Detritus's. "Gods, we're good."

* * *

About the Story

Five Facts About This Story:

1. I was invited to contribute to this antho because I write erotic romance about Greek Gods as Nicola

Cameron. Seriously. 2. In my head, Debris and Detritus are played respectively by a de-dragged Courtney Act and Willam Belli from RuPaul's Drag Race. 3. It took me almost a year to finish it because I could *not* find a good plot handle until two weeks before the deadline. Yay pressure! 4. Lisa the Nereid has a much larger role in my/Nicola's fantasy romance novel Deep Water (Olympic Cove 3). 5. Miz Maggie's last name is a nod to Florence Henderson, who died shortly before I finished the piece.

MELANIE FLETCHER

BY ANY OTHER NAME
WEYODI

DETRITUS LOVED PARTIES AS a rule. He loved the abandoned plastic serving ware. He loved the dented red plastic party cups scattered like poppies blooming on the lawn. The half-eaten appetizers and dried-out cake. He loved the irreparably stained party clothes never to be worn again, and all the little wadded up napkins—oh, how his heart was touched by each and every crumpled darling! The empty cans and bottles tugged at him like the sight of a child tottering along the edge of a great precipice, and each one snatched from the hands of a potential recycler and thrown into the garbage was a tiny victory for him and did him good deep down. Yes, Detritus loved parties. Still, he had to admit he'd enjoy this particular party more if the guest list had been a bit more exclusive.

It seemed as though half the gods in the history of the world were here tonight, but weren't they always? Shortening the guest list invariably led to a divine battle, so it was generally not done. Not unless someone was incredibly bored.

255

All the same, he could have done without Jesus. Detritus liked him, of course—you couldn't help but like Jesus—but he did seem to bring out the worst in some people: Detritus's twin brother, Debris, for instance. As far as Detritus could tell, Debris was incapable of restraining himself when it came to poking at Jesus in hopes Jesus'd have one of his rare but impressive tantrums. Compared to other gods, Jesus was the very model of self-control, which was why the prospect of driving him into a violent rage appealed to Debris so much.

"Christmas? Christmas? Don't talk to me about Christmas!" Jesus said, shaking his woolly head. Maybe it was because he'd been human once, a long time ago, but Jesus stubbornly clung to the looks he'd been born with: short, curly black hair, brown skin, and on the far side of short; a painfully average lower class Judean of the time. Detritus chalked it up to some sort of reverse vanity.

"What's wrong with Christmas?" Detritus couldn't help but chime in with his brother on this one. Christmas was a personal favorite, for obvious reasons.

"It's not even on my birthday, for one thing," Jesus said, glaring and reaching for his wine glass for the first time all night and turning it straight to water.

"So?" Debris insisted. "If I had a holiday, if we—" he jerked his thumb in Detritus's general direction "—had a holiday in our honor, I'd count myself lucky no matter what day it was on."

"It's not what I told them to do. It's like my followers weren't even listening to a word I said." It looked as though

Debris' prodding had backfired, and Jesus was getting morose instead of stirred up.

"Come on," Detritus said, feeling bad for Jesus as he so often did. "Christmas is a wonderful holiday; think of all the wrapping paper."

"And the packaging," Debris said brightly.

"Gifts broken and discarded the next day," Detritus went on, perhaps getting a bit carried away in the moment.

Jesus looked at them over the top of his wine glass. Try as Detritus and his brother might, they could not get Jesus to appreciate the spirit of his own holiday. It was an uncomfortable fact that the fortunes of gods were no more stable than those of mortal men. Poor Jesus always found actual followers to be rather thin on the ground. Most of what purported to be his temples were, the way Detritus heard it, fronts for Mammon. Not that anyone called him Mammon anymore. Most gods changed their names the same way they changed their looks, to keep step with the times. Detritus and Debris were exceptions to the name thing, probably because trash was eternal.

Detritus held up three fingers, trying to think of any gods other than Debris and himself who had kept their original names. He was concentrating on that when a large hand slapped him hard on the back and spilled wine cooler all over his shirt.

Speak of the Devil and he appears, Detritus thought. Well, not literally. Detritus had never met Lucifer or Satan or whatever, and he didn't know anyone who had. Personally, Detritus had written him off as one of those imaginary gods, since as far as Detritus knew. Satan didn't have any real worshipers, not the kind who believed enough to breathe life into a god.

No, this was Mammon, or as Detritus knew him in the old days, Plutus, or, as he preferred to be known these days, Buck.

Detritus liked Buck, he was more or less required to. Buck had been largely responsible for the way Detritus's and Debris' fortunes had risen over the last hundred years. Buck and Kindle together. Kindle, who used to be— who? Vulcan? At least Detritus supposed he used to be Vulcan. Looks changed, names changed, and Detritus had never spent enough time with Vulcan in the old days to be completely sure. But Buck and Kindle, who had been fueling a mad technological frenzy in modern mortals, along with Ephemera, the goddess of trends, had plucked Detritus and Debris out of relative obscurity and elevated them to the top of the trash heap of divinities. He and his brother used to be happy with a simple midden. Now they had whole swirling continents of trash floating in the middle of the ocean; they had rubbish piles on land bigger than the grandest ancient cities with a full complement of inhabitants who were born, lived, and died in service to Detritus and Debris. They had worshippers who transformed their own homes into altars to refuse. Back in the old days, the best they could hope for was a baby thrown on a rubbish heap to take into their ragged retinue, but now they were important gods, living the high life.

Ephemera! That was the third god he'd been trying to

think of! It was a bit ironic for a goddess of passing trends, but Ephemera'd kept the name she'd always had. Detritus, Debris, and Ephemera, he counted on his fingers—that was right.

"Don't strain anything!" Buck laughed, his free hand tight around Gaia's arm.

Oh no. Gaia. Nothing could move a party from uninspiring to uncomfortable faster than having your mom show up.

"Gaia!" Jesus jumped to his feet and offered The Mother, the world, the goddess of Earth incarnate, his chair. She didn't appear impressed, but then she never did. All Jesus got for his trouble was a beautiful sneer.

Detritus worked hard not to stare; her silk dress was torn at the shoulder and her pink bra showed through like a dirty Band-Aid. Despite it all, she was eternally the most beautiful of all goddesses, which made it worse. He had no idea how anyone could look so exquisite with a black eye and a purple bruise turning yellow on the edges of her cheek.

Detritus liked Buck. He didn't have a choice. Even if he was a demanding jackass with no taste and less compassion, Buck was generous, funny, always and inevitably a good time. Detritus needed Buck. Without Buck he was nothing.

Detritus couldn't look at either Buck or Gaia, so he stared hard at the ice in his plastic cup.

"Your children have no idea," Jesus said, earnestly.

Detritus could practically hear Gaia's blank stare.

"I think Gaia would be happy if the kids left her alone for a minute, maybe went outside and played," Debris said.

Detritus noticed his brother had forced his mouth into a hopeful smile.

"Yeah, preferably on a busy street," Gaia said and snorted at her own joke. She'd always been a bitch, but now it seemed as if she was saving up for something really horrible. Detritus wondered why she came to these things. He tried not to notice the crescent moons Buck's nails were digging into Gaia's arm. Maybe Buck didn't give her a choice.

Detritus was an instant away from darting his eyes desperately around the room, searching for an out, when he realized Debris had beaten him to it.

"Ephemera!" Debris called out dramatically, camping it up. All it took was creasing the face into a smile, knocking over his bowl of peanuts, and he was off in pursuit of Ephemera.

When Detritus and his twin caught *up* with Ephemera, her hair was pink and her paper dress was emblazoned with the face of Kim Kardashian, FIVE times larger than life.

"Heyy eyyyy eyyy!" Ephemera called, all smiles, waving both hands at eye level. "Are you guys having fun? If you aren't, get busy! Eat, drink, and be—you know—fun! Because it's all gonna be over some day!"

Debris rolled his eyes. "Don't even get started," he said. "I am not in the mood for all this, whatever kinda apocalypso dance all these squares are up to."

"I wish square dancing would come back!" Ephemera said. She linked arms with Detritus and his brother and began spinning them both in opposite directions.

"Yeeha!" Debris called, and used his free arm to not-very-accidentally knock over a table full of drinks onto a couch full of guests before he circled back around to hug Ephemera's waist.

"Ride 'em cowpokes!" Detritus called, laughing at the sound of breaking glass as he came to embrace her from the other side.

"So far out that it's in again! So even cooler than bowling!" Ephemera said. "I love you boys," she said dreamily and leaned her head on Debris' shoulder. "Even more than I love Kindle, 'cause, you know, you and me, we're peanut butter and jelly, ham and eggs, sick and tired! If you liked girls, I'd marry both of you! But don't tell Kindle, 'cause it would break his heart, especially after, well, you know who."

"And we love you, too" Detritus said. His eyes drifted to where the goddess once known as Aphrodite stood wringing red wine out of her blouse with a look on her face that would curdle cream. No matter what name she went by, she had one principal attribute: she was a bitch.

"Oh, I almost forgot," Ephemera said, slipping off her shoes, "Kindle wants to talk to you. Asked me to mention it when I saw you. I'm seeing you now! So—"

"Which one of us?" Debris asked.

"You. Or you. Or both of you, I guess." Ephemera flexed her left foot, showing off golden nail polish.

"Err?" Detritus said. "Could you be a little more vague, sweetie?"

"I don't know! If you both go, then he'll see the right

one either way, right?" Ephemera flexed her foot again. "Like my toes?"

"When did he want to see us?" Debris asked.

Ephemera shrugged. "You know, I don't think I like this polish either."

Debris looked at Detritus and Detritus looked at Debris.

"Who around here has interesting shoes?" Ephemera asked, scanning the room.

Detritus wondered if he ought to stop her when Debris reached over and tugged his shirt sleeve. At the far end of the room, Kindle stood in a doorway. He jerked his head, a clear sign to follow.

Without looking at his brother, Detritus relaxed his hold on Ephemera and watched her skip away. Then he wove through the crowd toward Kindle in the other room.

He could never figure out how Debris made it to Kindle before he did, but there his brother was, with his hair playfully tousled and an artful stain on his cuff.

Kindle leaned against the fireplace mantle just as artfully in his black turtleneck and his high-tech computer spectacles. Detritus could never remember what they were called, and he likely wouldn't, either, until they were tossed on the trash heap of abandoned technology.

Kindle smiled a smile so smooth Detritus could have spread it on a slice of toast. "Good to see you guys. It's been so long since we had a talk, you know, a real heart-to-heart."

Detritus tried to recall if he'd ever had a heart-to-heart with Kindle. Even the orgy that led to dear little Planned

Obsolescence had been arranged by Ephemera and Buck. Detritus would say that Kindle was practically a stranger, except that no one was really a stranger after you'd fondled their genitals, even if it was just the once. Still, they weren't on the same level as Kindle, and they knew it. As the god of Modern Technology, Kindle was big. He was what mortals slaved for, what they lusted after and dreamed of, what they schooled their children in, and what they sacrificed their lives to. Without him, there would be no swirling islands of trash in the seas. Other gods virtually touched their foreheads to the ground when he entered the room, and even Buck had to acknowledge his superiority.

Debris looked as confused as Detritus felt as Kindle plowed on.

"I've done right by you guys, haven't I?" Kindle asked brightly. So brightly, in fact, that Detritus had the fleeting urge to hold onto his wallet. He didn't even carry a wallet. "I mean, we're all friends here, right?"

It would be sheer hubris to call Kindle a friend. Treasured acquaintance, then.

Kindle's eyes sparkled emerald green and sapphire blue and amethyst, and in their black heart was the most beautiful fire.

Detritus jerked himself away from the mesmerizing flame and answered the best he could. "Um, sure," he said and glanced at his brother. Debris' mouth was hanging ever so slightly open, and his head tilted slowly, as if listening to music only he could hear. For his brother's own good, Detritus brought his heel down hard on Debris' foot.

"Did someone say something?" Debris asked, shaking his head. "Why does my foot hurt?"

"I need the two of you—" Kindle began.

But Detritus cut him off right away. "No, no, no, no, no, sorry, not possible," he said. He knew the only way to do this was to not be looking into those eyes, so he turned to face the opposite wall. He didn't really know where this whole business was heading, but he knew, he could feel, that Kindle was nervous and needy, and if someone as big and powerful as Kindle was worried, then Detritus and his brother Debris wanted no part of it. Unfortunately Detritus hadn't thought any further than that, and he was now floundering.

Debris came to the rescue. "We have plans. We're heading to Japan. They have the most amazing packaging. Have you ever seen the way a soda comes out of a vending machine in Japan? An ordinary soda in an ordinary vending machine?"

"It's a thing of beauty," Detritus agreed, in no small part because it was truly amazing.

"First a bottle, then that's shrink wrapped, and that's inside a protective bubble," Debris waxed eloquent, sculpting the layers in the air with his elegant hands.

"And it's all plastic!" Detritus couldn't help but interject. In his enthusiasm, he turned around. That was his big mistake. Those eyes, they got him again.

"First, boys, what I need you to do is sit down and stop being so anxious," Kindle said, and Detritus knew, just knew, Debris, too, had fallen under Kindle's spell. "There's all the time in the world for your little excursion, but first I need you to do something for me. One. Tiny. Favor."

Detritus sat down in one of two peacock tail chairs he hadn't even noticed were there before.

"Good. Now, I need you to take a little break and collect a handful of mortals for me. Three hundred should suffice. There may be more than that, but by my calculations, three hundred is the minimum. Use your own discretion on bringing more. The important part is you can't let anyone know, not Buck, not War, and certainly not your mother," Kindle said. "And on the off chance you do get caught, I had nothing to do with it. Not a thing. Hear me?"

Detritus puzzled at that. It was odd of Kindle, not claiming Gaia as his parent, and she had to be, hadn't she? Still, he couldn't look away from the flame.

"But what for?" Debris' whine sounded like that of a frightened child, BUT Detritus was impressed that he could speak at all.

"For my gratitude, of course," Kindle replied. He lowered his head and whipped off his glasses, making a great show of cleaning the lenses on the edge of his turtleneck as he released the brothers from his gaze. For the tiniest split second, a measure of time no larger than a dust mote, Kindle seemed ancient even beyond Detritus's ability to reckon.

An hour later, Detritus stood on the balcony with his brother, sharing grain alcohol straight from the bottle.

"Do we want to know what we'll get if we don't earn Kindle's gratitude?" Detritus wiped his lips and passed the bottle.

"No," said Debris, "we do not."

Detritus could not bring himself to disagree.

* * *

Debris was surprised to discover Kindle's little favor was actually easier in practice than it had been in theory. It was almost, as Kindle put it in the midst of his highly detailed instructions, "A little nothing errand." Add to that the pleasant scenery exploding into something even more pleasant all around them, and it was almost the sort of thing they would have done on their own for fun. Almost.

The only part they wouldn't have thought of on their own was loading the transport trucks full of mortals and delivering them to Birmingham.

War zones had always been funny places. Lots of mess, lots of meddling gods and monkeyshines. It had always been possible for anyone, god or mortal, to get away with close to anything there. The entire business was yawningly uneventful. So dull, in fact, that Debris found himself bored enough to speak to one of the mortals.

The old man had been elected by the others to sit in the front of the transport truck when the back was full. He had a weathered, craggy face and a two piece suit to match; the tatty label read Sans-a-belt. Debris liked him right away.

"So," Debris asked, "why do you carry around that fire with you?" He remembered when all the mortals used to do that, with their sacred torches of emerald, and sapphire, and amethyst, back in the days before disposable lighters.

"Because it is a gift," the old man said in his language.

"A gift from God,"

"Which god?" Debris asked, forgetting, for a moment, to keep his eyes on the road.

"In the beginning of creation, the blind Creator God brought forth a special angel more brilliant and beautiful than all the rest, the Peacock Angel. But this Most Beautiful Angel was jealous, and when the creator brought forth mankind, the Peacock Angel flew into a rage and railed against his Maker and his Maker's newest creation.

"The Creator God cast the rebel into the fiery beyond for sixty thousand years. And in that time, the Creator grew tired and sickened of his creation. They were a miserable, stupid people. When it rained, they were wet, and when it was hot, they baked. They ate animals raw who were hardly less dignified than themselves. These beings had no order and knew no progress.

"All the while the Peacock Angel cried out from the void at his punishment. He cried and he wept until it seemed his tears would extinguish the flames that burned in the chasm of fire."

"Is that so?" Debris asked, surprised. He'd never heard this story before, and he thought he knew them all.

"In his almighty pity, the Creator recalled the Peacock Angel from his punishment and set his fallen angel over this world as ruler. When he did this, the Peacock Angel gifted to mankind the last flame of the fiery depth, that they might better themselves. The fire kept them warm in the winter and cooked their meats and breads. It brought the sun indoors in the darkest nighttime. The fire civilized them, yes, but it also had the power to burn and destroy." The old man whistled through broken teeth.

"Kinda like the god himself," Debris blurted.

"You know him," the old man said.

Debris nodded, lost in his own thoughts. "We're acquainted."

* * *

Given everything his brother had told him, Detritus felt it was perfectly reasonable to be anxious about handing off the mortals to Kindle under the statue of Vulcan in the middle of Birmingham. Still, there he was, alongside his brother, smiling his happiest smile at Kindle. He was no fool.

"Thanks for the favor," Kindle said, fairly shining in the early morning light "I won't forget this."

"Are they going to be taken care of?" Debris asked.

Kindle threw back his head and laughed. Nothing sinister, just a real, full body, genuine laugh. His voice grew quiet like a gathering storm. "These mortals will be going to work on my latest project in a new state-of-the-art facility. A facility which, I might add, happens to be earthquake, fire, tornado, and flood proof. Their urine, feces, even their very breath will be recycled to maintain their safety and health, regardless of the goings-on outside. An internal greenhouse will supply food and regulate building temperature. Boys, these are going to be the safest, most looked-after, mortals on earth."

Nasty. On every level, recycling was nasty, not that Detritus was going to say that to Kindle's face. Still, he caught a flicker of his brother's expression that assured him Debris felt exactly the same way. They were both smart enough not to think it too loudly in Kindle's presence.

Detritus wondered if, safe or not, these mortals were ever going to see the sky again. He searched the mortals' eyes for a hint of fear or worry, but all he saw mirrored back was the laughing soul of Lucifer and holy fire, emerald green, sapphire blue, and amethyst.

* * *

It wasn't too long after—time is difficult to parse when you're a god—that Debris saw Buck and Gaia again. It was another boring party, but what else has one to do when one is a god?

"Heeyy eyyyy eeeyyy!" Debris gave them Ephemera's new greeting; it was all the rage. He wished he'd painted his nails. Buck, at least, would have appreciated the effort.

Buck laughed and waved back. He was always up for a good time.

Gaia, gorgeous as ever, scowled, gorgeously of course, adjusting the sling on her arm.

"Gaia, darling, do you have to be a wet blanket 24/7?" Buck asked.

The goddess pulled up her bra strap with her one good hand. "One of these days, and you won't see it coming, I'm gonna shake off all these mortals like a bad cold. And without anyone to worship you, every last one of you fuckers is going to dry up and blow away, dead as last week's news."

"Yeah, right," Buck said. He smacked Gaia's bottom so

hard her buttocks jiggled.

"You know I hate your guts, right?" Gaia said. There was a tiny bit of blood obvious in the corner of her mouth, in spite of her lipstick.

"You can't hate me, Gaia, I'm your darling baby boy." Buck leaned forward and pinched her nipple.

The look of loathing on her face was colder than death.

Across the huge hall, Debris saw Kindle with his arm around Ephemera. He seemed to be whistling to himself.

* * *

About the Story

When I was asked to submit a story for the anthology, it was suggested that I might use the characters within a tribal context, since I am an enrolled member of the Comanche tribe, but the gap between European cosmology and the old Comanche religion as I understand it made the very prospect mind-boggling. So mind-boggling, in fact, that it led me to think about the very nature of the sacred in a modern context; what we say we hold sacred as opposed to what we as a society demonstrably worship. Add to that a tidbit about packaging in modern Japan and the story began to take shape in my head, one where the shifting sands of human values hide the nature of our gods and their identities even from one another.

Is an ancient god changed when they take on a new name and new attributes or merely obscured? And what is the end result of human behavior on the gods and on us humans ourselves?

WEYODI

Realms

BETH TELIHO

IT WAS THE KIND OF storm where the sky is sickly green, and the air is charged with so much electricity your scalp tingles with each bolt of lightning. Rain surges from the black sky in thick sheets, saturating the earth in seconds, and you wince and duck instinctively with each violent clap of thunder.

Yeah. That's the kind of storm we had the morning I got my fucking brain cooked while peering into the chest cavity of a man. Don't worry. He was already dead. I'm a medical examiner, not a killer.

I think.

Despite my wife's protests, I braved the storm and drove to work that morning. Most people would wait out severe weather of that magnitude. Most people don't have cadavers rotting on a metal slab and next of kin awaiting answers and death certificates.

As I entered the lab, my assistant, Gary, looked up from a tray of sterilized instruments he was preparing. "Mornin', Debris. Helluva storm. Gonna have our hands full today.

One wreck after another out there," he said with a shake of his head.

Yes, my name is Debris. Blame it on my mother. She had a thing for Greek mythology.

I nodded in Gary's direction, too cold and wet for conversation, and set my umbrella against the wall before squishing around the corner where the lockers are located, just outside the restroom door. I keep a fresh set of clothes and shoes there—body fluids happen despite the best of preventative efforts—and switched them for my wet clothes. I donned my lab coat, hairnet, mask, face shield, and latex gloves before moving to the examination area and shifting my focus to the dead body.

I scanned the information sheet belonging to the deceased: *38-year-old unidentified male, entered hospital 4:56AM with significant blood loss, flat-lined at 5:12AM, unable to revive, pronounced dead at 5:25AM. IIP*

Gary had already completed the preliminary procedures. He'd photographed, X-rayed, and fingerprinted the body. The clothes and physical characteristics were meticulously recorded. Any evidence detected on the body or clothing, such as fibers and residue, were collected, and samples of hair and nails were taken. Since the death was tagged IIP (investigation in process), an ultraviolet wand would've been swept to collect any further evidence undetectable by the naked eye. The clothing was removed, bagged, and the body was weighed and cleaned. Finally, a block was placed under the cadaver's back to lift the chest in preparation for internal examination.

I noted in my handheld voice recorder that the body was that of a white male with short, black hair. Stocky physique. A large tattoo of a cross bearing Jesus Christ spanned his entire upper torso, ironically following the path of the Y I would soon incise. Above the cross and below his clavicle was a Bible verse: *1 Peter 4:17*

My eyes scanned his body for what I assumed was a bullet wound, as so often is the case with bleed outs, when I noticed the wide gashes on the inside of each wrist. *Suicide*, I thought.

"What's the verse?" I asked Gary, who I knew would've looked it up.

Gary glanced up from his microscope and, replacing his round, wire glasses, read from the notebook on the table next to him. "For it is time for judgment to begin at the household of God; and if it begins with us, what will be the outcome for those who do not obey the gospel of God?"

The tray of instruments was at the end of the table, so I pulled it nearer, removed the scalpel, and placed the tip of the blade at the right shoulder, preparing for the Y incision that would open the chest.

Lightning blazed from the darkness on the other side of our sole, narrow window like an enormous camera flash. I squinted and blinked, blobs of light dancing in my vision, and I played the game. You know the game? After lightning, you count: one-Mississippi, two-Mississippi, until you hear thunder. Each second equals a mile; that's how you know how far away the storm is. I made it to first "issip" before thunder assaulted the air like a goddam atom bomb, leaving instruments quaking in their metal beds.

"Fuck's sake, that was a bad one," Gary mumbled. "Feels like the heavens are pissed off or somethin'."

"It's right over us," I said as I pierced the lifeless, greying flesh and sliced downward. At the precise moment I reached the bottom of the sternum, all the hair on my arms stood on end.

It's funny what the brain remembers. Even now, I can still feel the sensation of being struck by lightning so vividly it makes me break out in the shakes. Like a million bees stinging you at once, but worse because it moves through you like a tsunami of pain. Violent. Relentless. And I remember a deafening clap, combined with the sizzling sound of my flesh and hair burning.

And then nothing.

I awoke in a hospital bed three days later with a throbbing headache and raging hard-on. Remnants of an unsettling dream clung to me with wicked tendrils: I was folded in a dark closet, peering through the cracked door, barely breathing while I watched a woman undress in her bedroom. She removed her blouse, bra, and skirt before donning sweats and a t-shirt, and then gracefully twirled her long brown hair into a bun while sauntering out of the room.

Every night since then, the dream revisits. It's shockingly evocative. I'm stalking the same woman. I select the dark clothing I will wear when I break into her house. With ninja-like agility, I sneak through her fence into her backyard and surgically cut the screen of her dining room window with a razor blade. I hide in tiny closets and confined spaces in silence for hours upon hours, tolerating muscle cramps and unfathomable positions. I watch her. And I wait.

When I wake, I can still smell the scent of her body lotion.

* * *

The first time I saw her nearly a month ago, I was instantly smitten. Her nametag reads: *Birmingham Public Library: Christa*. She's tall and thin with legs like a dancer. Her long, chestnut hair parts just to the left of center and sweeps over her brow. Her eyes are an incredible, luminous brown that glows like wet henna. The most adorable cluster of barely visible freckles sprinkle across her nose, and her sweet, pink lips shape into a cute little pout when she's concentrating. Her voice is ethereal and angelic, and her skin, *oh God*, her skin. Pale. Virginal. Holy.

Even her name, Christa, so close to that of my Lord and Savior. She's perfection. *My little lamb.* If she only knew how much I loved her. But she doesn't because I'm a coward. I'm terrified to talk to her and can't seem to find a way to strike up a conversation. But today's my lucky day. She's working the front desk. I *will* talk to Christa today.

My palms sweat as I hand her a book of Psalms to check out, my library card, and *History of Christianity* to return.

She scans my card into the computer and my account pulls up, and there it is in illuminated white type, my name: Detritus Reynolds. Christa leans forward in her chair, eyes squinting at the screen. It's a look I am intimately familiar with.

My hands shake and I shove them deep into my pockets, nervous and excited to finally have a reason speak to her. "Detritus. It—it's . . . uh . . . My mom was a Greek mythology nut," I say, explaining my name like I've done countless times, but this time I'm stammering like a frigging idiot.

Her expression is impassive. She says nothing.

"Detritus and Debris. They were um . . . brothers," I continue, trying to save this sinking ship. "Fraternal twins, actually. Sons to the God of Lightning and Goddess of Retribution." I'm rambling but can't stop.

Still, her only response is a blank stare.

I fidget and glance around, embarrassed. "One brother was evil, the other a saint. Their mother knew they couldn't exist simultaneously without one canceling the other out, so . . . " *Someone shut me up.* "To her husband's dismay, she sent them to live out their lives in different dimensions, never to know the other brother existed." I shrug, sheepish and weak and I want to kick my own ass.

"That's fascinating, Mr. Reynolds," she says, "but you can't check anything out until you pay your fine. *History of Christianity* is a week late."

That's fascinating? Was that as patronizing as it sounded? My face gets hot. "Yeah, I was out of town. Sorry about that."

"It happens," she says, in an ambiguous tone. Could be benign. Could be bitchy.

I decide that in my anxious state, I must be hearing her wrong. I give her the benefit of doubt and try again. "You can call me Detri. All my friends do," I say, adding a warm and trustworthy smile.

She tilts her head toward me and presses her lips together in an expression that is either adorable or infuriating. I can't read this chick.

"I'm afraid I can't, Mr. Reynolds. We're not friends." Her words are cold. Wooden. With a flick of her wrist, she hands my library card back. "How will you be paying your fine today?"

I narrow my eyes, confused and offended by her flippant response. More than that.

I'm humiliated.

That's when I know what I must to do.

Cleansings, I call them. I balance the scales and rid the Universe of negativity. It's more than a vocation. It's a spiritual calling. One that takes insight. Thought. And careful planning.

I will covertly immerse myself into her world and observe her every move.

I will know everything there is to know about Christa. For death is an intimate moment, and as her savior, it's imperative I know her as intimately in life as when I deliver her to the House of Our Lord.

* * *

I limp into the lab on just two hours of sleep in the past four days. My right thigh hurts like a son-of-a-bitch. I don't recall doing anything to hurt it. No bruise or swelling to account for the pain.

"You okay, Debris?" Gary asks, concern pinching his

brows. "You didn't have to come in. I can handle this one. Go home and get some rest. You look like shit."

I wave him away. As Chief Medical Examiner, I typically don't have to come in on Sundays. But if I stay at home, I'll sleep. If I sleep, I'll dream. No more sleep. If I have to dream of hunting that woman one more time, I'll lose it.

I shouldn't kid myself. That ship has already sailed.

"What do we have today?" I ask Gary, while glancing over the chart of our newest cadaver: *33-year-old female. Dead on arrival. Stab wound to the chest. IIP*

He nods his head toward the body on the metal table; its back is arched over a block, ready for internal examination. "Just this one. I've got 'er prepped and ready for ya. Expect the press today. Rumor has it the Palm Sunday Killer got her."

"Is that right?" I mumble, only half-aware of what he's saying as I round the corner toward the lockers. I retrieve my autopsy garb and put it on, like I've done hundreds of times before, and then hobble into the main area toward the body. The instant I notice her long, chestnut hair, a déjà vu feeling comes over me, sending a chill up my spine. I take a few more steps, heart thundering in my chest, until her face comes into view. I grip the side of the metal table, certain I will lose my balance, breath coming in short gasps.

"Debris?" Gary says with concern.

I can't answer him. I can't speak. I can't breathe.

Although I've never laid eyes on her before in my life, I know everything about her. I know that she's reading the Harry Potter series for the third time. I know her secret indulgence is reality television. Through the sterile, antiseptic smell of the morgue, I can still detect a wisp of coconut that I know is from her shampoo. Before looking at her feet, I know her toenails are painted lavender. I know she takes her coffee with cream, no sugar. And I know her name is Christa.

My little lamb, I think, just before collapsing onto the cold tile.

* * *

My chest tightens. The blood is already coagulating on the knife. I typically work faster, but tonight there was a distraction—to put it mildly—and I'm fucking pissed. I hunch over the bathroom sink, scrubbing the knife, picking at the gelatinous, red nubs as the hot water sets them free.

I stop to admire the artwork in the sink, and I can't help but smile. The contrast of the virginal white sink splashed with sensual curves of bold, powerful red makes for a stunning abstract piece. Like an eclipse, the luminosity combined with the dichotomy of colors is at the same time difficult to look at and impossible to look away. Sometimes I take photos, but I don't have that luxury tonight. I need to work fast.

I resume clean-up, rinsing tonight's art down the drain. My mind returns to what happened and I begin to dissect it. I believe in learning from my mistakes.

I didn't know about the dog.

My leg throbs where the fucker got me, but I'll inspect the damage later. I hate the sight of my own blood. Amused at the irony, I cackle so loud it echoes off the bathroom walls.

The dog was never here before. I would've known. I would've seen him, watched her let him outside, or at the very least noticed dog bowls. It must have been a recent acquisition, definitely after Thursday, since that was the last night I was here. I'm absolutely certain there was no dog in the house that night.

He would have sniffed me out in the closet.

I have been over my strategy hundreds of times in the past few weeks: how I would enter her house, how I would listen to the rhythm of her slumbered breath, which knife I would use to exterminate her. Every second going by torturously slow as I awaited the chosen day for cleansings. Palm Sunday.

The damn dog nearly ruined the whole thing. I press a hand against my throbbing thigh and limp back into her bedroom, where blood still oozes from her gaping chest wound, dripping off a saturated sheet corner onto the furry heap lying dead on the floor beneath her.

* * *

I lift my lids enough to see the sun is rising and grit my teeth in anger that I've slept. *What the hell is wrong with my leg?* I rub my thigh that continues to ache like the devil. Foggy remnants of the dream haunt the corners of my mind, but I push them away with a shudder and pull myself out of bed, careful not to wake my wife.

Despite efforts to ignore them, pieces of the dream filter through my mind with sickening velocity. And that's when it hits me.

"No. That's impossible," I say in a panicked whisper as I realize the dog bite I dreamed is the reason for my pain. Christ-have-mercy-on-my-soul, what is happening? How can I wake with symptoms of injuries sustained in a dream?

I can't take it anymore. With each inhale I smell her blood, thick and coppery in my nose. I hear the juicy squish of the knife plunging into her chest. And feel the satisfaction and elation her death provides me.

I've tried everything to avoid sleep: caffeine, energy drinks, sugar, walking the streets all hours of the night, and most recently, amphetamines like Black Mollies and Benzies. But eventually I collapse, only to wake with the stench of violent death hovering around me like a hellish aura.

I enter the bathroom and take a leak. When I bend to the sink to wash my hands, I gasp and stumble backward.

There's blood under my fingernails.

The Taoist master Chuang Tzu once dreamed he was a butterfly fluttering around a group of flowers. In the dream, he had no awareness of his individuality as a person. He was only a butterfly. He awoke and found himself lying there, a person once again. He then thought to himself, "Was I before a man who dreams about being a butterfly, or am I now a butterfly who dreams about being a man?"

Perhaps Chuang Tzu made an error assuming he was one or the other.

Perhaps he was both.

* * *

After checking the laundry room and under the kitchen

sink, I finally locate garbage bags in the garage and bring them back with me into the bedroom. I take one and tear along the seams to open it flat, lay it on the floor, and roll the dog's large body onto it. It's a German Shepherd, male. Makes me wonder if she got him specifically to be a guard dog. Like maybe her intuition was trying to warn her she was in danger.

This pleases me.

I fold one side of the bag over its body and am about to wrap him burrito style when something flashes, catching my eye. A tag on his collar reflects the moonlight streaming through the top arch of her window. Curious, I take it in my hand and tilt it toward the light. Shock knocks me on my ass. The tag reads: *Detritus.*

I reel through details of our last conversation. Had I misread her tone? Did I confuse flirtatious words with patronizing ones? Was it possible she wasn't snubbing me?

She named

Her dog

Detritus.

I think back to a conversation I overheard a week or so ago, while nestled in the corner of her closet. She was lying on her bed talking to a friend on the phone. She mentioned a man she liked but was too shy to talk to. She said he was mysterious, and odd, but in a cute way. I was wounded by this revelation. My envy so vicious, I bit a large chunk out of the inside of my cheek and had to use one of her scarves to soak up all the blood.

Could she have been talking about me? Could Christa

have *liked me?* Had she been waiting all this time for me to make the first move?

I hear myself giggling, which turns into guffaws, and then I'm bursting into hysterics that echo in the dark, laughing back at me. *I'm a fool.*

I get on my knees and lift my eyes to the heavens. "I'm sorry, for I have erred," I say. I take my knife from its sheath and stand to hover over Christa's lifeless body, her mouth hanging open in a frozen face of terror. I dip my fingers in the pool of blood at her chest and smear it across my face like a warrior. A warrior who must now pay the ultimate price for his mistake.

My own screams ring in my ears as I stand over my little lamb's body and slice open my wrists.

* * *

"Mr. Reynolds," I hear a man shout from a million miles away. "Detritus, wake up."

My shoulders are being jostled hard. I open my eyes, startled and fighting back until I realize it's Freddy, the "high suicide risk" attendant assigned to me at the maximum security nut house. I exhale and relax against the sheets, my vision blurred.

"Same dream?" Freddy asks, retuning to his post—a stool five feet from my bed.

I close my eyes and nod, swallowing thick saliva down my throat. "Water."

Freddy takes a plastic cup and fills it at the sink. "You wantcher meds early?" he asks, holding the cup to my mouth.

I drink, letting the cool water glide down my throat before answering him. "No. No. They make me sleep. I don't want to want to sleep anymore. I can't."

I don't remember being admitted. My last memory is of standing over Christa's body, cutting my wrists, which are still bandaged in thick layers of gauze. Turns out one of her neighbors heard me screaming and called 911. I was saved, which is the opposite of what I deserve. Or maybe it's the precise cruel irony I asked for when I . . . I . . .

Vomit crawls up my throat. I swallow it down—along with the memory of murdering my soul mate. Yes, murder. Not a cleansing. Murder. For she was An Innocent.

But the prison nuthouse isn't my punishment, nor are these straps holding my arms to the side of the bed. The dreams are. Every night since I regained consciousness, I relive the morning of a violent storm, where I'm a coroner who gets struck by lightning while splaying open the chest of a dead man. A dead man I recognize even through his pallid death mask.

It's me. And clutched in my rigid, bloody hand is a dog collar.

* * *

About the Story

Knowing how much the odd and supernatural influence my writing, it shouldn't surprise anyone to learn that I was irrevocably fascinated and inspired when, years ago, I first learned of Chuang Tzu's musings on dreaming and existence. When I was given Debris and Detritus as a writing prompt, I knew they were the perfect characters to tackle this concept. However, in keeping with the delicious thrill of unanswerable, tangled logic, I chose to leave it up to the reader to discern if only one of the characters truly exists and the other is a mere delusion, or if they simultaneously exist in alternate universes and become entangled in a strange twist of fate. What do you think? Are you Team Debris? Team Detritus? Team both? Visit bethteliho.me and share your thoughts. Or perhaps I will find them out on my own . . . when I visit your dreams . . .

BETH TELIHO

"Let's Put on a Show!"
Patricia Burroughs (aka Pooks)

Okay, the actual words were "This could be an anthology!" but they were spoken with every bit as much energy, enthusiasm, and horrifying naiveté as Judy and Mickey ever portrayed.

I had no clue.

I had no clue what I was doing, and even though I knew I was the last person who should ever be put in charge of organizing something like this, I didn't realize *how freaking much* I was the last person who should ever be put in charge of organizing something like this.

I had no clue what was involved in putting together an anthology, getting writers, wrangling stories, and the rest of the process.

I had no clue how these wonderful writers I hand-picked and sometimes begged, bribed, and bullied into participating would deliver fabulous story after fabulous story, and in such an array of styles, worlds, and approaches that my original concept was confirmed.

Yes.

Yes, it *is* amazing to see how different writers interpret the concept, Rhonda Eudaly's words, "Debris & Detritus, The Lesser Greek Gods."

But if I was the Mickey and Judy in this endeavor, we all had the huge benefit of Busby Berkeley (aka Toni McGee Causey) walking onto the set and saying, "Oh, is this what you wanted on the cover? I like that. Will you please let me play with it? You don't have to use it if you don't like it."

Stop right now. Look at that cover again.

Let me play with it.

That is what she calls playing.

You don't have to use it if you don't like it.

In what universe would anybody not *have* to use that cover? Heck no, I don't like it. I love it.

Of course we had to use that cover. It is every bit the high-kicking, spiraling up a wedding cake, Busby Berkeley cover of all anthology covers.

Thanks for coming along for the ride. I hope you enjoyed the show.

POOKS

About the Authors

Max Adams has worked with Columbia Pictures, Hollywood Pictures, Touchstone Pictures, Universal Pictures, Walt Disney Studios, and Tri-Star Pictures on myriad projects "in development." And is now lobbying her congressman for a "return of fire" medal (something sparkly would be nice). Her produced film projects include *Excess Baggage, The Ladykillers,* and *One for the Money.* Her non-filmic writing credits include journalism, short fiction, essays, theatre, humor, and radio. Max is the author of *The New Screenwriter's Survival Guide*—and has an almost criminal love of shoes.

MJ Butler has been writing, directing and producing Internet shows for over a decade. His show *The Lonely Astronaut* beat out Tim Burton and Kelsey Grammer for "Best Comedic Web Series" and "Strangest Grouping of Nominees" at the U.S. Comedy Arts Festival in Aspen. Conversely, Garry Trudeau beat him out at the 2008 Harvey Awards for "Best Syndicated Strip or Panel" and was heard to cackle maniacally. *Entertainment Weekly* wrote Butler's show "*The Real Whatever* . . . may be closer to reality than The Real World—and it's loads funnier." Those and his other videos can be found at TwistedMojo.com.

In his spare time, he enjoys writing about himself in the third person.

Toni McGee Causey writes dark mystery-suspense as T.M. Causey. Her first full-length novel in this genre is *The Saints of the Lost and Found.*

As Toni McGee Causey, she is the author of the critically acclaimed and nationally bestselling "Bobbie Faye" novels—an action/caper series set in south Louisiana. She is also a contributor to the USA Today Bestselling anthology *Love is Murder* as well as the *Killer Year* and the *Do You Know What It Means to Miss New Orleans* anthologies.

She and her husband, Carl, thrive in the French Quarter, where they're not the craziest ones on the block. Sometimes, they're not even second craziest. Together they are remodeling a beautiful historic property right in the heart of the Quarter. Details about this project are featured on her blog.

Want more news, contests, prizes? Check out her Facebook author page—and for exclusive free short stories/gifts, sign up for her newsletter. Your email will never be shared, traded, or sold.

Rhonda Eudaly lives in Arlington, Texas, where she's ventured into several industries and occupations for a wide variety of experience. She's married with dogs and a rapidly growing Minion© army. Her two passions are writing and music, which is evident in her increasing hoard of writing instruments.

Rhonda has a well-rounded publication history in fiction, non-fiction and script writing. Check out her website for her latest publications and downloads.

Mark Finn is an author, an editor, an actor, and a pop culture critic. He is a nationally recognized authority on the life and works of Robert E.Howard (his biography of REH was nominated for a World Fantasy Award). In addition to fiction writing and the occasional comic book script, Finn is a contributing editor to *Skelos: The Journal of Weird Fiction and Dark Fantasy*, and one of the four hosts of *The Gentlemen Nerds* podcast. He lives above an old movie theater in North Texas with his long-suffering wife, far too many books, and an affable pit bull named Sonya.

Melanie Fletcher is an expatriate Chicagoan who currently lives in North Dallas with her husband the Bodacious Brit™ and their five fabulous furbags: JJ, Jessica, Jeremy, Jemma, and Jasmine. When not herding cats, she turns into Writer Girl and has membership cards from SFWA and RWA to prove it. Her speculative fiction spans over two decades and ranges from the humorous to the dark. When not writing SF, she also writes specfic romance as Nicola Cameron and is currently finishing up the first book in a new SF romance series, *Intersection* (Pacifica Rising 1). She is continually fascinated by handsome older men who take off their clothes in the name of art and enjoys celebrating them in her stories.

Jeanne Lyet Gassman holds an MFA in Writing from Vermont College of Fine Arts and resides in Arizona. Her debut novel, *Blood of a Stone* (Tuscany Press), received a 2015 Independent Publisher Book Award (bronze) in the national category of religious fiction and was a finalist for the New Mexico-Arizona Book Awards and the 2015 Independent Author Network Book of the Year Award. Her short work has been nominated for Best Small Fictions and the Pushcart Prize. Additional awards include fellowships from Ragdale and the Arizona Commission on the Arts. Jeanne's short stories and creative nonfiction have appeared in *Queen Mob's Tea House, Hippocampus Magazine, Altarwork, Hermeneutic Chaos Literary Journal, Literary Mama, Red Savina Review, Switchback, Barrelhouse,* and *The Museum of Americana,* among many others. Visit Jeanne at her website.

Antioch Grey is an English author and lawyer who lives in London with her collection of shoes. She has no cats because she doesn't trust them not to be plotting against her and would rather keep a pet blond. In her spare time, she drafts elaborate plans for formal poison gardens. Other interests include chocolate and classical statuary, but not at the same time because there's nothing worse than chocolate smears on statues. Connect with Antioch Gray at her Facebook page.

More stories by Antioch Grey appear in *Immanence,*

Thoroughly Modern Monsters, and Teeth Long and Sharp.

Claire M. Johnson attended the California Culinary Academy in 1983 and worked as a pastry chef in San Francisco and Oakland for several years. Set in the restaurant world, Ms. Johnson's first novel, *Beat Until Stiff*, was nominated for the 2003 Agatha Award for Best First Novel and was a Book Sense pick. Her second book in this series, *Roux Morgue*, received a starred review from *Publishers Weekly*.

Recently, Ms. Johnson decided to jump with both feet into the world of dedicated Janeites. Using the mystery writing world as a backdrop, *Pen and Prejudice* is a modern pastiche of the Jane Austen classic, *Pride and Prejudice*, but instead of our witty, playful heroine and attractive but arrogant suitor willfully misunderstanding each other while attending balls and dinner parties in the nineteenth century, they metaphorically duke it out in the twentieth at mystery writing conferences. Ms. Johnson currently works as a Technical Editor. In her spare time, she bakes pies.

Michelle Muenzler, known at local science fiction and fantasy conventions as "The Cookie Lady," writes fiction both dark and strange to counterbalance the sweetness of her baking. Her short fiction and poetry can be read in numerous science fiction and fantasy magazines (full list and links), and she takes immense joy in crinkling words like little foil puppets. Michelle is an SFWA member and represented by Howard Morhaim of the Howard Morhaim

Literary Agency.

If you wish to lure her out of hiding, you can friend her on Facebook or chase her down at a local SF/F convention, where she will ply you with hundreds of home-baked cookies while gleefully describing the latest horror she's written. She supposes you could also contact her through her webpage, but she finds electronic cookies far less tasty than real ones.

Robin D. Owens RITA® Award Winning author Robin D. Owens has been writing longer than she cares to recall and has published twenty-eight books, five novellas, and three short stories (including "HeartStones").

She credits the "telepathic cat with attitude" in selling her first book, *HeartMate*, published by Berkley, December 2001.

She loves writing fantasy with romance or romance with fantasy, and particularly likes adding quirky characters for comic relief and leaving little threads dangling from book to book to see if readers pick up on them (usually, yes! Reader intelligence is awesome!).

She also spends (too much) time on Facebook and will answer questions and interact with fans there.

Irene Radford has been writing stories ever since she figured out what a pencil was for. Editing grew out of her love of the craft of writing.

A member of an endangered species—a native Oregonian who lives in Oregon—she lives with her husband in Welches, Oregon where deer, bears, coyotes, hawks, owls, and woodpeckers feed regularly on their back deck.

A museum-trained historian, Irene has spent many hours prowling pioneer cemeteries, deepening her connections to the past. Raised in a military family, she grew up all over the US and learned early on that books are friends that don't get left behind with a move. Her interests and reading range from ancient history to spiritual meditations to space stations, and a whole lot in between.

Mostly Irene writes fantasy and historical fantasy, including the best-selling Dragon Nimbus Series and the masterwork Merlin's Descendants series. In other lifetimes, she writes urban fantasy as P.R. Frost or Phyllis Ames and space opera as C.F. Bentley. Lately she ventured into Steampunk as Julia Verne St. John.

If you wish information on the latest releases from Ms. Radford under any of her pen names, you can subscribe to her newsletter. (Promises of no spam, merely occasional updates and personal news.)

ChandaElaine Spurlock, after working as a personal assistant, executive assistant, and landman's assistant, decided to assist herself by becoming a ghostwriter—which is a totally real job. Under various names (which she can't tell you), she has written blogs, articles, flash fiction, short stories, and novellas in every genre from homeopathy to Amish romance to horror. Usually for Someone who (she still can't tell you) watched their deadline scream by without so much as batting an eye . . . until a nice young editor stepped out of the shadows, politely cleared his throat, and said to Someone, "We'd like our advance money back."

A short-arse who wears denim and tweed without regard to fashion or sense, she sometimes lives in Texas.

This is the first story published under her real name.

Seriously.

Beth Teliho is an award-winning author and artist who lives in Texas with her husband, two adventurous sons, and a veritable menagerie of pets. Restless in the mundane, she writes about the abnormal, paranormal, and otherwise fantastical because that's what quickens her heartbeat. She loves spicy food and margaritas more than just about anything and aspires to one day live in a tree house with a cat. Or ten.

Ms. Teliho's debut novel, *Order of Seven,* won the Independent Publishers of New England Book Award for Young Adult and Book of the Year and was a Readers' Favorite International Book Award for Fiction - Supernatural

She will love you forever if you take the time to write a review on Amazon and/or Goodreads!

All ways to connect with Beth Teliho are found on her website.

Weyodi doesn't like to brag, but she once knocked Ernest Hemingway unconscious in a bare-knuckle fistfight. She has also been banned from the state of Indiana. Over the years, she has developed a finely honed ability to trigger a burglar alarm with a fast food taco thrown at high speed from a moving vehicle.

She writes primarily poetry and speculative fiction. Her prose often revolves around our species' primary motivations: sex, food and power. Indigenous people figure prominently in her work, but few if any are mystical sages or tragic noble savages. She has written screenplays for independent film and for documentary and three volumes of poetry, two of which are out of print. She has an erotic feminist steampunk romp called *Monster Bride* currently available on Amazon. In 2017, her trilogy The Glicksberg Chronicles: *Stealing the Morning Star*, *The Burning Lie*, and *Bees Made Honey in the Rich Man's Skull* will be released in addition to the comic book *The Life and Times of Pocomodo* and the short story "One Erotic Misadventure Furnished in Early Hominid." She is currently at work on a sequel to *Monster Bride* tentatively titled *Polycorpus Among the Serpentine*.

About the Editor
Patricia (Pooks) Burroughs

Pooks (a.k.a. Patricia Burroughs) is an award-winning novelist, screenwriter, and a fifth-generation Texan. (You get to guess which of the above she considers the highest honor.)

She loves Pratchett, Aaronovitch, Dunnett, and Heyer and never wants to tell the same kind of story twice, thus her scattershooting approach to her career and this anthology.

A lifelong Anglophile, she cherishes her trips to the British Isles researching The Fury Triad, the epic YA romantic fantasy that has taken over her life and heart. She and her high school sweetheart husband (a.k.a. The Resident Storm Chaser) are living happily ever after in Dallas.

She would love you to sign up for her newsletter or visit her on social media, or even (gasp!) buy her books.

About the Cover

Toni McGee Causey

Every once in a while, someone I adore is in need of a cover and describes what they're trying to find or hire to be done, and they're frustrated because it's missing the mark. And for a small percentage of those times, an idea, clear as the sun, pops into my head.

Pooks had a seriously difficult challenge for this cover: find a way to convey the Greek God type of connection for the stories without anchoring the cover in any particular era or genre, so that every story felt included. When we were talking about what she'd love to have, she kept referencing works by several artists that seemed to have a theme: Art Deco/iconic imagery.

Immediately, I could "see" the column, the golden colors bleeding down over a landscape, almost like the river Styx, and then dropping sharply off the cliff, falling into pieces, indicating the "debris" and "detritus" and the powers running amok. In my mind's eye, there were textures, indicating (subtly) the layers and textures of the different stories, and the (very subtle) "Amok" littering the clouds, raining down. I do a lot of photography, but I also like to play with Photoshop for design ideas, and this was a perfect fun-for-me challenge. Happily, Pooks was brave enough to let me have a run at it and trusted me enough with those first drafts (before she could fully see the effects I was going to create) to believe that it might turn out okay.

Sometimes, things turn out better than you hope, and you have a ball doing it. That was the case here. I hope you like it.

About Story Spring Publishing

We hope you've enjoyed *Debris & Detritus: The Lesser Greek Gods Running Amok*. Anthologies are always fun to publish; each story is a miniature novel in and of itself, with different voices, needs, and tones. We've thoroughly enjoyed working on this anthology and can't wait for the next one!

A quick note about our editing decisions: One of the things we value and respect most is authorial voice. While we look to *The Chicago Manual of Style (16th Edition)* for our basic editorial standard, different stories and authors sometimes require variation. Our British authors, for example, use commas very differently from our American authors. We strive to honor the essential "Britishness" of their stories while ensuring that the text is accessible to all readers. Some stories are told in a formal style, while others are conversational, with the kinds of sentence flexibility used in everyday speech. As a result, each story has its own style sheet, and we work to ensure internal consistency of style and voice.

Story Spring Publishing is an indie publisher based in central Illinois. We publish both fiction and nonfiction books across a variety of genres and topics. Our novels and fiction anthologies feature diverse, well-developed characters and worlds, while our nonfiction books feature interesting, innovative ideas about fascinating topics. Each of us at Story Spring is committed to our mission of providing an enjoyable, high-quality reading experience, regardless of whether the reader is holding a book or reading a screen.

Made in the USA
Middletown, DE
29 September 2020